frostfire

AMANDA HOCKING lives in Minnesota, had never sold a book before April 2010 and has now sold over a million. She is now 'the most spectacular example of an author striking gold through ebooks' (*Observer*). Amanda is a self-confessed 'Obsessive Tweeter. John Hughes mourner. Batman devotee. Muppets activist. Unicorn enthusiast.' Please see more at

www.worldofamandahocking.com

frostfire

Amanda Hocking

TOR

First published 2015 by St Martin's Press

First published in the UK 2015 by Tor
an imprint of Pan Macmillan
20 New Wharf Road, London N1 9RR
Associated companies throughout the world
www.panmacmillan.com

ISBN 978-1-4472-5664-9

5 7 9 8 6 4

A CIP catalogue record for this book is available from the British Library.

Printed and bound by CPI Group (UK) Ltd, Croydon, CR0 4YY

Visit **www.panmacmillan.com** to read more about all our books
and to buy them. You will also find features, author interviews and
news of any author events, and you can sign up for e-newsletters
so that you're always first to hear about our new releases.

frostfire

four years ago

As dawn began to approach, the celebration finally wound to a close. Even though I had been working for over twelve hours, I felt wide awake and even a little buzzed, like I'd gotten a contact high from the energy around me, not to mention the thrill of completing my first real assignment as a tracker.

Since my graduation was still several months away, I hadn't been given any major detail or heady responsibility. My duties for the night involved standing at attention during the formalities, and surveying the rooms for signs of trouble the rest of the night, which mostly meant directing the increasingly inebriated party guests to the bathroom.

But still, I had been here, working alongside other trackers and even the more elite Högdragen—the guards charged with protecting the Kanin kingdom. That's why at the end of the night, despite the growing ache in my bare feet, I was a little saddened to be relieved of my duties.

King Evert and Queen Mina had opened the doors to all the Kanin in our capital of Doldastam, and there were over ten thousand of us living here. With that many people streaming in through the doors for an impromptu party, the royal couple needed all the hands they could get, including trackers-in-training.

We'd just gotten word a few days before that another tribe, the Trylle, had defeated our shared enemy, the Vittra. For the past few months, our King and Queen had been quietly preparing the Kanin. If the Vittra had taken out the Trylle, we would have been the next logical target, since we were wealthier and more powerful than the Trylle. We were too strong and plentiful for the Vittra to go after first, but once they conquered the Trylle and turned their army to Vittra, they would be strong enough to go after us.

But when the Trylle did away with the Vittra King and his entire army, they did away with our impending war as well. So naturally our good King Evert found reason to celebrate, which was how I'd ended up working a party until the early hours of the morning.

By now the King and Queen had retired to their chambers for the evening, and nearly all of the guests had gone home. A handful of trackers and Högdragen stayed on to oversee the party until everyone had departed, while the cleaning crew had begun the unenviable task of taking care of the mess.

Since so few people were left, I was relieved of my duty and sent home for the night. I felt a bit like Cinderella then, her lovely coach turning back into a pumpkin, as I walked slowly into the front hall. Though I had been wearing the trackers' formal uniform—a tailored, frosty white suit, all crisp and new since this was the first time I'd worn it—instead of a gown given to me by a fairy godmother, at the end of the night my uniform would be put away, and I wouldn't perform any more duties until after I graduated.

Once I did graduate, I'd be given a silver sash to hold my sword, but until then they didn't quite trust me with a weapon, not that I'd really needed one for a celebration like this anyway.

As I made my way toward the front door, unbuttoning my jacket and letting it fall loose, I let out a heavy sigh. Many of the kerosene lamps had gone out, leaving the large entrance glowing dimly. The white banners that decorated the high stone walls of the palace had begun to sag, and silver confetti carpeted the cool floor.

The creak of a heavy door closing gave me pause, because it sounded like the door to my father's office. I glanced down the narrow corridor off the main hall, and sure enough, I saw my dad emerging from his office. His black hair—which he normally kept smoothed back—had become slightly disheveled, and his tie was loosened, with the top buttons of his shirt undone.

"What are you doing?" I asked in surprise. "I thought you went home hours ago."

"I had some paperwork I needed to finish up." He gestured to the office behind him as he walked slowly toward me, suppressing a yawn as he did.

My dad worked as a Chancellor for the kingdom. I knew

that Dad took his job very seriously, and he often worked late nights, but I'd never known him to work quite this late before.

"Paperwork?" I raised an eyebrow. "While a party was going on?"

"We needed to send a letter to the Trylle." Dad gave a half shrug, which did little to convince me that that was really why he was still working. "They're poised to oversee two kingdoms now, and it's in our best interest to align with them."

"And you needed to do that right now?" I pressed.

"It could've waited until the morning," Dad admitted, and his mouth turned to a sheepish smile as he shoved his hands in his pockets. "I wanted to see how your night went. It is your first big night on the job."

"It went well," I said, then paused when a wave of doubt hit me. I tried to replay the night in my head, searching for any mistakes I might've made. "I think."

"I'm sure you did wonderful," Dad assured me, and his grin broadened, stretching into one of pride and affection. "Every time I looked over, I saw you standing at attention. You looked so grown up and so . . . . official."

"Thank you."

"My little girl is all grown up," he said wistfully and reached to tousle my blond waves.

"Dad." I ducked away from his hand, but I couldn't help but smile at him. "Can you at least wait until we're out of the palace to get all mushy?"

He opened his mouth, probably to point out that we were alone, but then we both heard the sound of footsteps coming down the corridor. Instinctively, I stood up straighter and put my shoulders back. I was about to start buttoning my jacket back up, but then I saw Konstantin Black walking right toward my dad and me, and for a second I forgot to breathe.

We allowed movies and music from the human world, but the true rock stars of our society were the Högdragen. They had been ordinary Kanin who worked their way up to powerful positions of respect and authority, and none had done it quite so quickly or with as much flare as Konstantin Black. Still in his twenties, he was already the Queen's personal guard—the youngest in recorded history to have such a position.

His black velvet uniform, embellished with silver thread and jewels, was the most luxurious of all the Högdragen uniforms, and even though it was standard for Kanin in his position, his somehow seemed even more divine. His silver sash caught the dim light from the lanterns and managed to glint a little. Even the diamond-encrusted bell handle of his sword sparkled.

He strode confidently over to us, and I tried to remain as blank and composed as I could, as I had been taught. But it was impossible to keep my stomach from doing flips inside me. For years I had been admiring him from afar—for his abilities, his strength, his composure, and, if I'm being honest, in more recent years for how handsome he was—and this was already the most personal encounter I'd had with him.

We'd been in the same room before, but always separated by a sea of people, since his duties kept him close to the Queen, and mine kept me far from her or the King. He'd brushed past me in halls. I'd seen him from the crowd as he'd demonstrated his skill in fencing games during the summer. But I'd never seen him really look at me before, or notice my attentive gaze among all the other adoring faces.

Now here he was, smiling as he stopped in front of us, and it had the same overwhelming effect as looking down from a great height.

I'd gotten so used to gazing at him from a distance, it was hard not to stare. The way his lips curved up slightly more on the left side as he smiled, or the shadow of stubble that had grown darker on the smooth line of his chin as the night progressed, or the way his black hair was slick and straight until it began to curl at the nape of his neck, where it stopped just above his collar.

"Chancellor, I wasn't expecting to see you here at this hour," Konstantin said to my dad.

"I was seeing my daughter home." Dad motioned in my direction, and Konstantin looked down at me. He wasn't much taller than I was, but he seemed to tower over me, with his gray eyes like smoke resting warmly on my face.

"It was your first night working something like this, wasn't it?" Konstantin asked.

I nodded. "Yes," I said, relieved that my voice stayed even and normal.

"You did very well." He smiled at me, causing my heart to flutter. "I'll put in a good word to your Rektor."

"Thank you very much, but that's not necessary," I told him firmly.

Konstantin laughed, the sound filling up the front hall and echoing through it. "Modesty is a noble thing, but it won't get you a coveted spot on the Högdragen. Take help whenever it's offered if you want to make it in this world."

I'd always insisted that I only looked up to him as a guard, as someone I wanted to emulate. But now, with the mere sound of his laughter sending pleasurable shivers through me, I couldn't deny that I'd been harboring a crush on him for so long it had begun to turn into something that felt dangerously like love.

"That's very sound advice, Konstantin," my dad said, pulling me from my thoughts, and pulling Konstantin's gaze from me.

"You sound surprised that I have good ideas, Chancellor," Konstantin said with a wry smirk.

Dad returned the smirk in kind and adjusted his loosened tie. "I think it's just the night wearing on me."

"Sorry, I should be letting you get on your way," Konstantin said apologetically, and my heart sank when I realized this brief exchange would soon end, leaving me feeling even more like Cinderella than ever before.

"Thank you." My dad nodded and stepped back toward the door, then Konstantin held out his hand.

"Actually, Chancellor, if I could keep you just a few minutes longer I might save you some trouble in the morning."

"What do you mean?" Dad asked.

"The Queen just went to her chambers, but before she did, she let me know that she wanted you to sign a document first thing in the morning to be sent out to the Trylle." Konstantin gestured to the grand windows above the door, which were starting to show the first hints of dawn. "And with morning so close, if you wanted to sign it now, you would have a few hours longer to sleep in."

"A document?" Dad shook his head. The bags under his eyes revealed how truly tired he was, and his dark eyes were confused. "I was drafting a letter for the Trylle. What was she working on?"

"I'm not entirely sure, sir. I believe she left it in her office, if you'd like to have a look at it," Konstantin said.

"I suppose I should." Dad nodded wearily, then turned to me. "You can go on, Bryn. I'll be home soon."

"No, it's all right," I replied quickly. "I can wait for you."

Dad shrugged in a way that said I could suit myself, and then he started down the corridor toward the Queen's office.

Konstantin went after him, but he turned back to me as he did. "Don't worry. We won't be too long, white rabbit," he promised me.

I turned away, hoping my cheeks wouldn't burn at Konstantin's use of a nickname. It was one I'd heard a few times in my life, but it never really stuck. *White* because of my fair complexion, and *rabbit* because that was the symbol of the Kanin.

As soon as they were out of sight, I put my hand on my stomach and let out a shaky breath. Having my first taste of official duty left me feeling intoxicated and light-headed, but that last exchange with Konstantin made me weak. I'd never been that interested in boys, preferring to focus on my training, but now I finally understood what my friends meant when they were going on about being in love.

But all too quickly the adrenaline from talking with Konstantin began to fade away, and for the first time all night I realized how tired I really was. I hadn't slept much the night before because I'd been so excited to work at the party, and corralling drunk Kanin townspeople was more work than it sounded.

Dad hadn't been gone with Konstantin for long, but my feet were beginning to throb and I needed to get home and get to bed. I knew where the Queen's office was, so I thought it would be best to go down and let Dad know that I was heading out. Plus it would give me a chance to say something more to Konstantin.

The office wasn't far from the front hall, and I'd almost made it there when I heard a surprised yell, a man crying out, *"No!"* I froze at first, trying to register it, then it was quickly followed by an agonized scream.

If my head wasn't swimming from the night, I would've noticed sooner. And a second too late—maybe even a split second too long—I realized that it was my father screaming.

I ran to the Queen's office and threw open the door.

When I've later tried to remember that moment, I can't see the rest of the room. It's all a haze and a blur, but the one thing that's focused—and it is in perfect, startling clarity—is Konstantin standing over my dad. His sword is drawn, and the blade is dark crimson with blood, as my dad lies bleeding on the floor.

Konstantin looked up at me. His handsome face, usually bright and confident, was chillingly blank. He almost appeared dead, except for his gray eyes—dark and frightfully alert.

"I'm sorry," Konstantin said simply. "I am bound to something much higher than this kingdom, and I must complete my mission."

"Bryn, get out of here!" Dad yelled as Konstantin raised his sword again.

Weaponless, I did the only thing I could do—I charged at Konstantin. As I ran at him, he pivoted, turning his sword on me. I felt the thin blade sliding sharply through my shoulder, but I barely registered the pain. The only thing that mattered was stopping Konstantin from killing my dad.

I knocked him to the floor, and I managed to punch once before he threw me off him. And then I heard other voices behind me. Other members of the Högdragen had been alerted by the yelling.

In a flash, Konstantin was on his feet and diving out the window behind the Queen's desk. Glass shattered, and the cold and snow billowed into the room. The other guards ran after Konstantin, but I went back to my dad, kneeling beside him.

His shirt was stained red, and I pressed my hand to the wound on his chest, trying to stop the bleeding. Dad put his hand over mine, and his dark eyes were filled with worry.

"I'm sorry I didn't get here sooner," I told him as I tried to blink back my tears.

"No, Bryn, you saved my life." He reached up, touching my cheek with a bloody hand. "You did amazing tonight."

I stayed with my dad, pressing my hand hard against his chest, doing everything in my power to hold the life in him, until the medical staff came and pulled me off. They whisked him away, promising that he would be just fine, and thankfully, they ended up being right.

But after they'd gone, I stayed behind, alone in the office. My crisp white uniform was now stained red with my dad's blood, mixing with my own from my shoulder wound. I stared out the broken window.

It was snowing so hard that it had already covered up Konstantin's tracks. Whatever I had been stupid enough to think I'd felt for Konstantin was gone. He had been my hero, but none of that mattered now. He'd tried to kill my dad, and now I would stop at nothing until he was brought to justice.

ambushed

April 8, 2014

Three years of tracker school—including extensive combat training, courses on social etiquette, and peer integration— and none of it ever changed the fact that I really hated human high school. Every time I started a new school to get close to a new charge, I found myself rethinking my career choice.

Back before I chose to go to tracker school, rather than finishing out Kanin high school to become a farmer or a teacher or maybe a horse trainer, I remember watching the trackers come and go from missions. They all seemed so worldly and powerful. They earned the respect and admiration of everybody in Doldastam.

I imagined the kinds of adventures they must be having, traveling the world. Most of them stayed in North America, but sometimes I'd hear stories of a tracker going off to England or Italy, and some even went as far as Japan.

The prospect of traveling and protecting my people sounded

exciting and noble. Then I had graduated, and I spent the next four years actually doing the job. If only I had known how much of my "missions" as a tracker involved wearing itchy school uniforms and trying to keep up on slang so I could fit in with spoiled rich kids, I might've reconsidered.

It was during lunch on my fifth day in Chicago, as I followed Linus off the high school campus, when I realized they were watching him, too. I wasn't exactly sure who "they" were, but I'd spotted the car—a black sedan with tinted windows—parked nearby several times since yesterday morning, and that was too much for coincidence.

As I trailed behind Linus and two of his friends, deliberately staying far enough behind so he wouldn't see me, I wondered if the mystery men in the sedan had noticed me yet. If they were staking out Linus, then they had to have seen me, since I'd been interacting with him. But that didn't mean they knew who I was. At least not yet.

Tracking was usually simple when done correctly. The first step was surveillance. I found the target—in this case Linus Berling—and for the first day or two I did nothing but watch him. The goal was to figure out who he was and what he liked, so it would be easier to earn his trust.

The second step was infiltrating his life, which was why I was wearing a ridiculous prep school uniform with a blue plaid skirt and a cardigan that felt too warm.

With a combination of bribery, charm, and a bit of Kanin skill, I'd gotten as many classes with Linus as I could, and started bumping into him "accidentally." We'd talk a little, I'd bring up his interests, laugh at his jokes, and ingratiate myself to him.

This would lead to step three. Once I had the target's trust, I'd drop the bombshell on them about who they really were, and hope like hell that they'd believe me. Usually they already had inclinations that they were different, and if I'd done my job right, everything would fall into place.

Then it was just a matter of getting them back home, preferably with trust fund in hand.

Now there was this issue with the black sedan, bogging things down right at the beginning of the second step, and I had to figure out what to do.

Linus and his friends from school had gone into a restaurant, but I didn't follow them. I stayed outside, watching through the front window as they sat down at a table. In his dark blue blazer, Linus's shoulders appeared broad, but he was actually tall and lean. After watching him fall half a dozen times during gym class, I knew he'd be no good in a fight.

The restaurant was crowded, and his friends were talking and laughing with him. Whoever was following him in the dark sedan, they were trying to be inconspicuous, which meant that they wouldn't want to create a scene in a place like this. For now, Linus was safe.

I walked away, going around the restaurant and cutting through the alley. When I came back to the street, the sedan was parked a few feet from me, but I stayed in the alley, peering around the corner. I did my best to blend in, and once again, I found myself wishing that I had more Kanin blood in me.

Even this close, the tint on the windows of the car was still too dark for me to see through. I needed more information, so I decided to call Ridley Dresden.

He was the Rektor, so he might have a better idea of what was going on. The Rektor was in charge of trackers, organizing placements, assigning changelings, and basically just keeping us all in order. Because of his position, Ridley was privy to more information than I was, and he might be able to shed some light on the sedan.

Before I called, I decided to use the video option on my phone. It seemed like a smarter choice, because then I could actually show Ridley the car instead of just describing it to him.

But when Ridley finally answered—shirtless, with his brown curls even more untamed than normal—I realized that maybe I should've sent him a text first, letting him know that I'd be video-chatting with him.

"Bryn?" he asked, and behind him I saw movement as someone got up, wrapping themselves in a dark comforter. "Is everything okay?"

"Yes. And no," I said, keeping my voice low so people walking by on the street wouldn't hear. "Sorry if I'm disturbing you."

"No, it's okay." He sat up straighter, and the rabbit amulet he wore on a leather strap around his neck slid across his bare chest. I heard a girl's voice in the background, but I couldn't understand her. "One second." He held his hand over the phone, covering both the camera and the mic, but I could still hear him promising to call her later. "Sorry. I'm back."

"Aren't you supposed to be working right now?" I asked, raising a disapproving eyebrow.

"I'm on a lunch break. It's called a nooner," Ridley said, meeting my gaze with a devilish gleam in his eye.

The year I graduated from the tracker program was the year Ridley became the Rektor. I hadn't really known him before that, but his reputation had preceded him. Everyone regarded him as one of the finest trackers, but though he was only twenty-four, he'd been forced to retire three years ago. He was still youthful looking, especially for a guy in his mid-twenties, but thanks in part to his persistent stubble, he couldn't pass for a teenager any longer.

But that was the only bit of his reputation that I'd heard about. He had a long history of being a serial dater, and this wasn't the first time I'd accidentally caught him in a compromising situation.

But over the years he'd proved himself to be an excellent Rektor and a loyal friend. So I tried not to fault him too much for his escapades.

"But anyway, what's going on with you?" Ridley asked. The glint in his dark eyes was quickly replaced by concern.

"Do you know anything about someone else following Linus Berling?" I asked.

His brow furrowed. "What do you mean?"

"Is there any reason for someone else to be tracking him?" I clarified. "Anyone else from Doldastam, or another Kanin tracker? Maybe even from another tribe?"

"Why would anyone else be following him?" Ridley shook

his head. "You're his tracker. You're the only one that should be on him. Did you see someone?"

"Not exactly." I chewed the inside of my cheek and looked up from the phone at the dark sedan, which hadn't moved. "I haven't seen any*one*, but this car has been following him." I turned the phone around to show it to Ridley.

"Which one?" Ridley asked, and I tilted the phone to show him more directly.

"The black one with the windows tinted. Do you recognize it?"

Ridley was quiet for a moment, considering. "No, I can't say that I do."

"I was afraid of that." I leaned back against the brick wall and turned the phone back around to me. Ridley had leaned forward, like he'd been inspecting the image of the car closely.

"You haven't seen anyone get in or out of it yet?" Ridley asked.

"No." I shook my head.

"It could just be a human thing," Ridley suggested, but he didn't sound like he believed it.

"I don't think so." I sighed. "I'm gonna go check it out."

"Okay." Ridley pressed his lips into a thin line and nodded once, reluctant to agree that I should put myself in a possibly dangerous situation. "Just don't do anything stupid, Bryn."

"I never do," I assured him with a smile, but that just caused him to roll his eyes.

"I mean it," he insisted. "Investigate, but do not interact with them until you figure out who we're dealing with. In the meantime, I'll see if I can run the plates or find out anything on that car. I'll check in with you later today, okay?"

"Okay. And I'll let you know if I find anything out."

"Stay safe, Bryn," Ridley said, and before he could say anything else, I ended the call.

According to the clock on the phone, I only had twenty minutes left of lunch and then afternoon class began. My options were limited, but I knew I didn't want to wait outside all day, hoping the passengers would make a move so I could see them. If somebody was after Linus, I needed to find out who it was before something bad happened.

So I walked out of the alley and straight to the car. Ridley might consider what I was doing stupid, but it was my best option. Out of the past twelve changelings I'd tracked, I'd brought twelve of them back home. I wasn't about to let Linus be the first one I lost.

I grabbed the handle of the back door, half expecting it to be locked, but it opened, so I got in. Two men were sitting in front, and they both turned around to look at me as I slid across the seat.

"What the hell?" the driver snarled.

When I saw who it was—his steel-gray eyes meeting mine—my heart clenched, and all the air went out of my lungs. For that moment everything felt frozen as he glared at me, then the rage and horror surged through me in a nauseating mixture.

I recovered as quickly as I could, holding back my anger, and smiled at him. Somehow in an even voice, I said his name. "Konstantin Black."

vengeance

His eyes narrowed, and his lip twitched ever so slightly. "Do I know you?"

"Not exactly," I admitted, not surprised that he didn't remember me.

The only time I'd spoken to him had been one of the most important and traumatic nights of my life, but that night he'd clearly had his mind on something else. Before that, I had only been one adoring fan out of thousands that he'd met in his tenure at Doldastam.

Konstantin had changed some in the four years since I'd last seen him—four long years since he'd attacked my father and disappeared into the night. His eyes seemed harder, and there were lines etched in the once-smooth skin around them. He'd grown a beard, and his hair was a bit longer and wilder than I remembered him wearing it.

But he was still unmistakably him. I'd spent years nursing a schoolgirl crush on him, picturing that face in my daydreams, and then I'd spent years plotting my revenge against him, picturing that face in my nightmares.

Now here it was, his eyes mere inches from my own, and he had no idea who I was.

"You're a tracker," Konstantin realized, and the corner of his mouth curved up into a smirk. I remembered the way that smirk had once filled me with butterflies, but now it only made me want to punch it off his face.

"So you do know her? Or not?" his companion asked.

"No, I don't know her, Bent," Konstantin told him, and I glanced over at his partner in crime.

His friend—Bent, apparently—I didn't recognize, but by his features I guessed he was Omte. His skin was smooth, and he appeared to be tall, but he had the same lopsided square head and beady eyes of a hobgoblin. Not to mention he didn't seem that bright.

"You're a wanted man, Konstantin. What are you doing here?" I asked, instead of hitting him or spitting in his face. Despite my wish for vengeance, I needed to find out what he wanted with Linus Berling and what he was doing here.

"Same thing as you, I would guess," Konstantin admitted.

Pressing my hands on the black leather of the seat to keep from slapping him, I asked, "What do you want with Linus? You don't have a tribe to take him back to. What's the point of even tracking him?"

"We were just waiting for a chance to grab him, and then

we're—" Bent began, but then Konstantin shot him a glare and he fell silent.

"Kidnapping? Really?" I shook my head. "Are you planning to hold him for ransom?"

Konstantin pressed a button in the center console, and the doors clicked as they locked. "Things are far more complicated than they seem."

I licked my lips, and, going against my better instincts, I offered him an olive branch. "How about I make a deal with you? I won't kill you if you let Linus leave with me." Then I paused, recalling the last thing Konstantin had ever said to me: *I am bound to something much higher than this kingdom, and I must complete my mission.*

Konstantin tilted his head then, eyeing me as if he were seeing me for the first time. "Do I know *you*?"

Bent had apparently grown tired of me, and he turned around in the seat with a dopey, crooked smile plastered across his face. "Whatever. I'm taking care of her."

"Bent, maybe—" Konstantin began, but Bent was already in motion.

He leaned over the front seat, reaching for me. His hands were disproportionally large, like massive bear paws, but he was slow, and I easily ducked out of the way.

I grabbed a clump of his dark curly hair, and then I yanked his head to the side, slamming it into the back passenger window. I let go of him and leaned back quickly, then I kicked his head, crashing it into the window again. The glass was shatterproof, and it instantly turned into a crackled sheet as blood streamed down the side of Bent's head.

Konstantin reached over the seat for me—going after me for the first time—but I slid past him. Bent was now slumped unconscious on the backseat, and I climbed over him. Konstantin grabbed my leg as I pushed through the crumbled glass of the window, but thankfully I'd been wearing knee-high socks, so I wriggled out of his grasp. He was left with a sock and a shoe in his hand as I dove out.

I fell onto the sidewalk, scraping my knee on the cement, but I was up in a flash. Konstantin got out of the car, but I wanted to get to Linus before he went back to the school, so that I could take him far away from Konstantin.

He grabbed my arm, and I whirled on him and punched him hard in the stomach. It felt so good that I had to punch him again, harder this time. It wasn't quite the same as running him through with a sword, but it would do for now.

As he doubled over in pain, I said into his ear, "That was for my father. You should've taken the deal."

His grip tightened on my arm as realization dawned on him, and his eyes widened in surprise. "You're the Chancellor's daughter."

"Bryn Aven," I told him, still whispering in his ear. "Remember my name. Because I'm going to be the one that kills you." Then I kneed him in the crotch. He let go, and I stepped back.

"This man is a child molester!" I shouted, and pointed to Konstantin. "He tried to touch me, and he's staking out the school for more kids to molest!"

I was nineteen, but the uniform made me look younger. The sidewalks were crowded over lunch hour, and people had stopped to watch since I'd broken out of the car window. My knee was bleeding, and my clothes looked disheveled from fighting.

As people circled closer to Konstantin and several of them pulled out their cell phones to call the police, I slid back in the crowd. For a moment I stayed around, protected by a small sea of people, and I watched him.

He was looking right back at me, his eyes locked on mine. I'd expected to see anger or arrogance, but he wore neither of those. Instead, he almost seemed to look at me with remorse, and for a split second I felt my hatred of him softening, but I refused to let it.

In the investigation following Konstantin's attempt on my dad's life, nobody had ever been able to figure out his motive. By all accounts, Konstantin had been a good and loyal servant of the kingdom since he'd become a tracker over a decade ago. He'd never had any disagreements with my father, or the King or Queen.

But in the years following that, I'd decided that it didn't matter what his motive was. No reason would ever be good enough for what he had done, and even if he was filled with regret and someday begged me to forgive him, I never would.

The crowd was overtaking him, so I turned and ran down the block. People called after me, and I ran faster.

Since I was only wearing one shoe, it felt awkward, so when I reached the restaurant, I stopped and pulled it and my remaining sock off. The cold cement felt better on my feet than socks did anyway.

When I looked through the window, I saw that Linus was just finishing up, and I pushed down all of the emotions that seeing Konstantin Black had brought up. I had a mission at hand, and it required my full attention.

I didn't know how things would go with Linus. I'd only been talking with him for three days. In an ideal situation, I'd make a connection for two or three weeks, sometimes even a month, before I took a changeling back to Doldastam.

"Linus!" I shouted as I opened the door. A waitress tried to stop me, but I pushed past her and hurried over to his table.

"Bryn?" He stared up at me with confused brown eyes. "What are you doing here?"

"Do you trust me?" I asked, a little out of breath from running all the way here.

"What?" Linus looked over at his friend, who laughed nervously, and then back at me. "You're bleeding. Were you in an accident?"

"Okay, seriously. We don't have time for this." I glanced back at the door. Then I looked down at him. "Come with me if you want to live."

Both his friends burst out laughing at that, but Linus swallowed hard. The sleeves of his blazer had been pushed to his elbows, and I saw the subtle shift of his skin tone. It didn't completely change, but the olive color began to take on a bluish hue.

That was good. It meant Linus was scared, which meant he believed me.

"Miss, I'm gonna have to ask you to leave," a waitress was saying to me.

"Linus, we have to go. *Now.*"

He nodded. "Okay."

One of his friends asked incredulously, "Linus, are you seriously going with this crazy chick?"

He stood up, ignoring his friend, but he'd only taken a step away from the table when he tripped over his shoelace. I caught his arm before he fell, and he offered me an embarrassed grimace.

"You are so lucky I'm here," I muttered as I took his arm and led him out of the restaurant.

"What's going on?" Linus asked.

When we got outside, I looked back down the street. There was still a small crowd of people milling around where I'd escaped from Konstantin and Bent, but the black sedan was gone. They were on the move.

"I'll explain later. But right now we just have to get out of Chicago as fast as we can."

The car I'd rented was in the school parking lot, but there was a chance that Konstantin knew its make. And even if he didn't, he could still be waiting in the parking lot.

"Where are we going?" Linus asked as I hailed a cab.

"To get a car, and then home." I held the door to the orange cab open for him.

"But my home is here in Chicago." He looked puzzled as he slid into the car.

I smiled at him. "No, your *real* home."

THREE

changeling

Doldastam," Linus repeated, the same way he'd been repeating it over the past day and a half. Every time he said it, he'd put the emphasis on a different syllable, trying so hard to match my pronunciation.

I'd rented a new car, and the drive from Chicago to the train station in Canada was over twenty hours, and we'd only stopped for gas and bathroom breaks.

Before we'd left Chicago, we'd swung by my hotel, and I'd changed into a much more comfortable pair of jeans and a T-shirt. But I hadn't had any clothes for him, and I didn't want to risk going back to his apartment. In Winnipeg, we'd stopped so I could pick up an appropriate winter jacket and hat for Linus, and I'd finally gotten him a change of clothes so he could get out of his uniform.

I didn't know if Konstantin and Bent were working alone or with others, and I wouldn't feel safe until we were back behind the walls of Doldastam. Really, it didn't matter if they were working with others. Seeing Konstantin Black was enough to unnerve me.

As confident as I'd tried to sound with him and as well as I'd fought him, I'd thrown up as soon as we got to my hotel. Coming face-to-face with the man from my nightmares had that effect on me.

But when I was around Linus, I did my best to keep my feelings in check and seem as normal as possible. I needed to be vigilant to keep him safe, which meant staying calm. So I sat rigidly next to him, staring out the window, and not letting my panic show on my face.

"Did I say it right?" Linus asked, and I could feel him looking at me, waiting for an answer.

"Yep. You said it great," I assured him with a forced smile.

"It's pretty out here." Linus motioned to the window, at the snow and tree-lined landscape of Manitoba as we sped through it.

"Yeah, it is," I agreed.

"This is where I was born?" Linus asked.

"Well, not out *here*, exactly. We're still a ways away from Doldastam, but yeah, you were born out here."

"I'm a changeling." No matter how many times he said this, Linus still managed to sound mystified every time. "I'm Kanin, and you're Kanin."

"Right," I said, because that was easier than correcting him. I was Kanin—sort of. He already had enough to digest without me breaking into my life story.

If he'd known more about what it meant to be Kanin, he'd be able to tell that I wasn't really one just by looking at me.

Linus had dark brown hair, cropped short and gelled smooth to tame the unruly curls, and eyes that matched. I, on the other hand, had easily managed blond waves that landed just below my shoulders, and my eyes were the color of the blue sky out the window. Even his skin was several shades darker than mine.

On his cheeks he had a subtle spotting of freckles. They weren't typical of the Kanin, but they seemed to suit him. Linus had an openness to his face, an innocent inability to hide any of his emotions, and his expression shifted from awe to pained confusion every few minutes.

He furrowed his brow. "I'm a troll."

The long drive up had given me plenty of time to explain all the big points to him, but he still couldn't completely process it. It usually took much longer, and that's why I often spent so long with the changelings before revealing the truth. It was much easier to understand when you had time to digest it instead of your whole sense of reality instantly being dashed away.

"I always knew I was different." He stared down at the floor, the crease in his brow deepening. "Even before my skin started changing color. But when that happened, I guess I just thought I was like an X-Men or something."

"Sorry, we're not superheroes. But being Kanin can still be awesome," I tried to reassure him.

He turned to look at me, relief relaxing some of his apprehension. "Yeah? How so?"

"Well, you're a Berling."

"I'm a what?"

"Sorry. Berling. That's your last name."

"No, my name is—"

"No, that's your host family's last name," I said, cutting him off. The sooner he started severing mental and emotional ties with his host family, the easier it would be for him to accept who he was. "Your parents are Dylan and Eva Berling. You are a Berling."

"Oh. Right." He nodded, like he should know better, and then looked down at his lap. "Will I ever see my host family again?"

"Maybe," I lied, then passed the buck so I wouldn't have to be the one to break it to him that he'd never again see the people he'd spent the past eighteen years believing were his mom and dad. "You'll talk about it with your real family."

"So what's so great about being a Berling?" Linus asked.

"Well, for starters, you're royalty."

"I'm royalty?" He grinned at that. Being royalty always sounded so much better than it actually was.

"Yeah." I nodded and returned his smile. "Your father is a Markis, and your mother is a Marksinna—which are basically Kanin words for Duke and Duchess."

"So am I a Markis?"

"Yep. You have a big house. Not quite as nice as the palace, but close. You'll have servants and horses and cars. Your dad is best friends with the King. You'll go to lavish parties, date the prettiest girls, and really, just live happily ever after."

"You're saying that I just woke up in a fairy tale?" Linus asked.

I laughed a little. "Kind of, yeah."

"Holy crap." He leaned his head back against the seat. "Are you a Marksinna?"

I shook my head. "No. I'm a tracker. Which is almost as far away from being a Marksinna as being human."

"So we're . . ." He paused and licked his lips. "Not human?"

"No. It's like a lion and tiger," I said, using my go-to analogy to explain the difference to changelings. "They're both cats, and they have similar traits, but they're not the same. A lion isn't a tiger. A Kanin isn't a human."

"We're still, like, the same species, then?" Linus asked, sounding relieved.

"Yep. The fact that humans and trolls are so similar is how we're able to have changelings. We have to pass for human."

"Okay." He settled back in his seat, and that seemed to placate him for a few minutes, then he asked, "I get that I'm a changeling. But *why* am I a changeling?"

"What do you mean?"

"Why didn't my real parents just raise me themselves?" Linus asked.

I took a deep breath. So far, Linus hadn't asked that, and I'd been hoping he wouldn't until we got back to Doldastam. It always sounded much better coming from the parents than it did from a tracker, especially if the changelings had follow-up questions like, *Didn't you love me?* or *How could you abandon your baby like that?* Which were fair questions.

But since he'd asked, I figured I ought to tell him something.

"It started a long time ago, when humans had more advanced medical care and schools than we did," I explained. "Our infant mortality rate was terrible. Babies weren't surviving, and when they did, they weren't thriving. We needed to do something, but we didn't want to give up our ways completely and join the human race.

"We decided to use changelings," I went on. "We'd take a human baby, leave a Kanin baby in its place, and then we'd drop the human baby at an orphanage."

Other tribes brought that human baby back to the village, believing it gave them a bargaining chip with their host families if the changeling decided not to return. But that rarely happened, and we thought the insurance policy—raising a human child with intimate knowledge of our society—cost more than it was worth, so we left the human babies among other humans.

"Our babies would grow up healthy and strong, and when they were old enough, they'd come back home," I said.

"So you guys still have crappy hospitals and schools?" Linus asked.

"They're not the best," I admitted. "But that's not all of it."

"What's the rest?"

I sighed but didn't answer right away. The truth was, the main reason we still practiced changelings was money.

The Kanin lived in small compounds, as far removed from human civilization as we could manage. To maintain our lifestyle, to live closer to the land and avoid the scramble of the humans' lives with their daily commutes and their credit card debt, their pandering politicians and their wars, we refused to live among them.

We could be self-sustaining without living with the humans, but truth be told, we did love our luxuries. The only reason we ever came in contact with humans was because we wanted their trinkets. Kanin, like all trolls, have an almost insatiable lust for jewels.

Even Linus, who otherwise seemed to be an average teenage boy, had on a large class ring with a gaudy ruby, a silver thumb ring, a leather bracelet, and a chain bracelet. The only human man I'd ever seen adorn himself with as much jewelry and accessories as a troll was Johnny Depp, and based on his looks, I'd grown to suspect that he might actually be Trylle.

That's where changelings came in. We'd place the Kanin babies with some of the wealthiest families we could find. Not quite royalty or celebrity status, but enough to be sure they'd leave hefty trust funds for their children.

When they were old enough to be collected, trackers like myself would go retrieve them. We'd earn their trust, explain to them who they were, then get them to access and drain their bank accounts. They'd return to the Kanin community, infusing our society with a much-needed surge in funds.

So in the end, what it all came down to was tradition and greed, and when I looked over at the hopeful expression on Linus's face, I just didn't have it in me to tell him. Our world still had so much beauty and greatness, and I wanted Linus to see that before showing him its darkest flaw.

"Your parents will explain it to you when you get back," I said instead.

Linus fell silent after that, but I didn't even bother trying to sleep. When the train pulled into the station, I slipped my heavy winter boots back on. I hated wearing them, but it was better than losing my toes to frostbite. I bundled up in my jacket and hat, then instructed Linus to do the same.

I grabbed my oversized backpack and slung it over my shoulders. One good thing about being a tracker was that I'd been trained to pack concisely. On a trip I expected to last three or four weeks, I managed to get everything I needed into one bag.

As soon as we stepped off the train and the icy wind hit us, Linus gasped.

"How is it so cold here?" Linus pulled a scarf up over his face. "It's April. Shouldn't it be all spring and flowers?"

"Flowers don't come for another couple months," I told him as I led him away from the train platform to where I had left the silver Land Rover LR4 parked.

Fortunately, it hadn't snowed since I'd been gone. Sometimes when I came back, the SUV was buried underneath snow. I tossed my bag in the back, then hopped in the driver's seat. Linus got in quickly, shivering as I started the SUV.

"I don't know how much I'll enjoy living here," Linus said between chattering teeth.

"You get used to it." I pointed to the digital temperature monitor in the dash. "It's just below freezing today. That's actually pretty warm for this time of year."

Once the vehicle had warmed up enough, I put it in drive and pulled out on the road, heading south along the Hudson Bay. It was almost an hour to Doldastam from the train station, but Linus didn't say much. He was too focused on watching the scenery. Everything was still covered in snow, and most of it was unsullied, so it all appeared pure and white.

"Why are the trees like that?" Linus asked, pointing at the only vegetation that grew in the winter.

Tall evergreens dotted the landscape, and all of them were tilted slightly toward the east, with all their branches growing out on only one side. To people who hadn't seen it before, it did look a bit strange.

"It's called the Krummholz effect," I explained. "The strong wind comes from the northwest, making it hard for branches and trees to grow against it, so they all end up bending away from it."

As we got closer to Doldastam, the foliage grew thicker. The road narrowed, becoming a thin path that was barely wide enough for the Land Rover. If another car came toward us, we'd have to squeeze off the road between the trees.

The trees around the road seemed to be reaching for us, bent and hunched over, their long branches extending out toward the path. They had long viny branches, like weeping willows, but they were darker green and thicker than any willow I'd seen. These were actually hybrids, grown only by the Kanin people. They were made to help conceal the road to the kingdom, so humans would be less likely to stumble across us.

But no other car came. The empty road was normal. Other than trackers, no one really left the city.

The wall wasn't visible until we were almost upon Doldastam, thanks to all the trees hiding it. It was twenty feet tall, built out of stone by Kanin over two centuries ago, but it held up stunningly well.

The wrought-iron gate in front of the road was open, and I waved at the guard who manned the gate as we drove past. The guard recognized me, so he smiled and waved me on.

Linus leaned forward, staring up through the windshield. Small cottages lined the narrow roads as we weaved our way through town, hidden among bushes as much as they could be, but Linus wasn't paying attention to them.

It was the large palace looming over everything at the other end of town that had caught his attention. The gray stone made it look like a castle, though it lacked any towers. It was a massive rectangle, covered in glittering windows.

I drove through the center of town, and when I reached the south side of Doldastam, where the palace towered above us, I slowed down so Linus could get a better look. But then I kept going, stopping two houses away, in front of a slightly smaller but still majestic stone house. This one had a pitched roof, so it resembled a mansion much more than it did a castle.

"This is it?" Linus asked, but he didn't look any less impressed by his smaller home than he did by the castle.

"Yep. This is where you live."

"Wow." He shook his head, sounding completely awed. "This really is like a fairy tale."

stable

It was dark by the time I pulled the Land Rover into the garage, narrowly parking it between another SUV and a full-sized Hummer. I clicked the button, closing the garage door behind me.

Technically it was a garage, but in reality it was a massive brick fortress that housed dozens of vehicles and all kinds of tracker supplies. To the left of the garage were the classrooms and the gym where trackers trained, along with the Rektor's office.

I hadn't bothered to put on my jacket or boots after I had gotten Linus settled in at the Berlings' house, because I knew I was coming right here. The garage was heated, as were most things in Doldastam. Even the floor was heated, so when I stepped out of the SUV, the concrete felt warm on my bare feet.

I'd just gone around to the side of the car to get my bag out of the back when I heard the side door close. The Rektor's office connected to the garage, and I looked over to see Ridley Dresden walking in.

"Need a hand?" he asked.

"Nah, I think I got it. But thanks." I slung my bag over my shoulder and went over to the storage closets.

He wore a vest and a tie, with his sleeves rolled up above his elbow. But like me, he was barefoot. His dark hair was kept short, but it still curled a little. In that way, his hair fit him perfectly. Try as he might to be straitlaced, there was just a part of him that wouldn't completely be tamed.

I dropped my bag on the floor in front of the shelves and crouched down to rummage through it. I'd pulled out a couple fake passports—both for me and for Linus—when Ridley reached me.

"You don't look that bad," he said with his hands shoved in his pockets.

I looked up at him, smirking. "And here I didn't think you liked blondes."

As far as I knew, his last couple girlfriends had been brunettes, but that really wasn't saying much when it came to the Kanin. Like all trolls, the Kanin had certain physical characteristics. Dark curly hair; brown or gray eyes; olive skin; shorter in stature and petite; and often physically attractive. In that regard, the Kanin appeared similar to the Trylle, the Vittra, and, other than the attractive part, even the Omte.

It was only the Skojare who stood out, with fair skin, blond hair, and blue eyes. And it was the Skojare blood that betrayed my true nature. In Doldastam, over 99 percent of the population had brown hair. And I didn't.

"Come on. Everyone likes blondes," Ridley countered with a grin.

I laughed darkly. Outside of the walls surrounding Doldastam the world may have shared that opinion, as Ridley would know from his tracking days. But here, my appearance had never been anything but a detriment.

"I was referring to your run-in," Ridley said.

I stood up and gave him a sharp look. "I can handle myself in a fight."

"I know." He'd grown serious, and he looked down at me with a level of concern that was unusual for him. "But I know how hard dealing with Konstantin Black had to be."

I turned away from him, unwilling to let him see how badly it had shaken me up. "Thanks, but you know you don't have to worry about me."

"I can't help it," Ridley said, then waited a beat before adding, "It's my job."

I pulled open a cabinet drawer and flitted through the files, looking for the one with my name on it, and dropped the passports inside of it.

"It must've taken all your restraint not to kill him," Ridley went on when I didn't say anything.

"On the subject of your job, have you figured out why they were after Linus?" I bent over and dug through my bag, refusing to talk about it. I wouldn't even say Konstantin's name aloud.

"No. So far we've come up empty. I've scheduled a phone call with the Queen of Omte first thing in the morning, and I have a meeting at ten in the morning tomorrow with the King,

Queen, and the Chancellor." He paused. "I'd like you to be there too."

"I'm no good at meetings." That wasn't a lie, exactly, but it also wasn't the reason I didn't want to go to the meeting.

As the Chancellor, my dad would be at the meeting, and I didn't want to talk about letting his attempted murderer get away. I knew he would never hold it against me, but that didn't make me feel any less guilty.

I grabbed stacks of American and Canadian cash out of my bag. Ridley pulled his keys out of his pocket and unlocked the safe at the end of the cabinets. My own set of keys were buried somewhere in my bag, and it was a bit quicker to let him unlock it.

"You know more about this than we do," Ridley reasoned. "For the sake of Linus and the other changelings, we need you at this meeting."

"I'll be there," I said reluctantly. I crouched back down over my bag and dug out what was left of my tracker supplies—a knife, a cell phone, a mileage log, and a few other odds and ends—and began putting them in the cabinets.

"What are you doing out here, anyway?" I asked. "Aren't you off for the night?" His job was much more of a nine-to-five gig than mine.

"I saw you pull in." He leaned back against an SUV parked next to me and watched me. "I wanted to see that everything went okay."

"Other than the dustup, everything was fine." I shrugged. "I got Linus back, and he's getting settled in with his parents. I did a quicker intro than I normally do, but Linus seems to be taking this all really well, and I needed to get out and get some sleep."

His dark eyes lingered on me. "When was the last time you slept?"

"What day is it?"

He arched an eyebrow. "Wednesday."

"Then . . ." I paused, thinking. "Monday."

"Bryn." Ridley stepped over to me. "Let me do this. Go get some sleep."

"I'm almost done, and if I don't log it myself, then my jerk of a boss will have my head," I teased, and he sighed.

"Well, whatever. I'm helping you even if you don't want me to." He grabbed the logbook and started filling it out.

With his help, everything was put away and accounted for within a matter of minutes, leaving only my clothing and laptop in my bag. I started to pull on my heavy winter boots and jacket, and Ridley told me to wait there for a second. He came back wearing his charcoal-gray peacoat and slick black boots.

"I'll walk you home," he said.

"You sure?"

He nodded. "I'm done for the night, and you don't live that far anyhow."

That was an understatement. My place was a two-minute walk from the garage. Ridley lived farther than that, but honestly, most people in Doldastam did.

The night had grown even colder, and Ridley popped up the collar of his jacket and shoved his hands in his pockets as he walked. I was smart enough to wear a hat, so I didn't mind it so much. The snow crunched beneath our boots as we slowly walked down the cobblestone road toward my loft.

I turned to him and couldn't help but admire him in the moonlight—tall and strong with the beginnings of a light scruff. Ridley's looks could be a distraction if I allowed them to be. Fortunately, I was a master at reining in useless, dangerous feelings like attraction, and I looked away from him.

"I'm not gonna be in trouble, am I?" I asked.

Ridley looked over at me like I was insane. "Why would you be in trouble?"

"Because I'm not sure that the Berlings will be able to get Linus's money now. He's a few days shy of eighteen, and there's no telling what'll happen to his trust fund."

"You got him home safely. That's the most important thing," he said. "Everything after that is icing."

"So you think I did the right thing by taking him home early?"

"Absolutely." Ridley stopped walking, so I did too, and he looked down at me. Our path was lit by lanterns and the moonlight, and I could see the sincerity in his chestnut eyes. "You have great instincts, Bryn. If you thought that Linus was in real danger, then he was. And who knows what Konstantin Black would've done with him?"

"I know." I sighed. "I mean, I do. But what if his parents don't feel the same way?"

"The Berlings aren't like that, and if they are . . ." He shrugged. "Screw 'em. You protected their son, and that's all that should matter."

I smiled. "Thanks."

"No problem." He smiled back at me, then motioned to the barn just up the road. "Now go up and get some sleep, and don't forget about the meeting in the morning."

"See you tomorrow, Ridley."

"Good night."

I turned and jogged toward the barn, but he stayed where he was in the street, waiting until I'd made it inside safely. The lower level of the barn was a stable, but the stairway along the side of the building led up to a small loft apartment, and that was where I lived.

It was chilly inside, since I'd turned down the heat because I'd planned on being in Chicago for a month or more. Before I took my coat off, I threw a couple logs in the wood-burning stove and got it going. I had a furnace, of course, but the natural heat always seemed to feel better.

I could hear the Tralla horses downstairs, their large hooves stomping on the concrete of the barn, and their neighing and rustling as they settled in for the night. The Tralla horses were huge workhorses the Kanin had brought over from Scandinavia centuries ago, and they stood even larger than Clydesdales, with broad shoulders, long manes, and thick tufts of fur around their hooves.

The horses in the stable all belonged to the King and Queen, and, like most Tralla horses, they were only used for show, pulling a carriage through town if the Queen was making a visit or marching in a parade.

They could be ridden, and I did ride one horse—Bloom—as

often as I had the chance. Bloom was a younger steed with silvery gray fur. Even as tired as I was, I wanted to go down to say hello to him, maybe brush his fur while he nuzzled against me, searching my pockets for hidden carrots or apples.

But I knew I had to be up for the meeting, so I figured I'd better postpone my reunion with Bloom until the next day.

Instead, I settled in and put the rest of my things away. My apartment was small, taking up only a quarter of the loft space. A wall separated my place from the room where the hay bales and some horse equipment were stored.

But I didn't need that much space. I had my bed, a worn couch, a wardrobe, a couple shelves overflowing with books, and a chair and a desk where I put my laptop. Those were the only things I really needed.

While I waited for the loft to warm up, I changed into my pajamas. I'd decided that it was about as warm as it would get when I heard footsteps thudding up the steps. Based on the speed and intensity—like a herd of small but anxious elephants—I guessed that it either had to be a major emergency or it was Ember Holmes.

"Bryn!" Ember exclaimed as she threw the door open, and then she ran over and threw her arms around me, squeezing me painfully tight. "I'm so glad you're okay!"

"Thanks," I managed to squeak out as she hugged me.

Then as abruptly as she'd grabbed me, she let go. She'd barely even stepped back when she swatted me hard on the arm.

"Ow." I rubbed my arm and scowled at her. "What the hell?"

"Why didn't you call and tell me you were coming home?"

Ember demanded, staring up at me with piercing dark eyes and her hands on her hips. "I had to hear about it from Ridley that you'd been attacked and were leaving early."

"Thanks, Ridley," I muttered.

"Why didn't you tell me what was going on?" Ember asked.

"I didn't want word getting out." I sat back on my bed. "I thought it'd be best to keep mum until we figured out what's going on."

"Well . . ." She didn't know how to argue with that, so she brushed her bangs out from her eyes. "You can still tell me. I'm your best friend."

Ember was lithe and petite, standing at least four inches shorter than me, and I wasn't that tall to begin with. But she was a good fighter, quick on her feet and determined. I respected that about her, but that wasn't what bonded us together.

Like me, she didn't quite fit into Kanin society. In her case, it was because she was actually Trylle. Her father had worked for the Trylle Queen before they'd moved here to Doldastam four years ago. They hadn't exactly been welcomed with open arms. Outsiders never were, but Ember and her parents had made their place here.

She did have the added struggle of being a lesbian in a society that wasn't exactly thrilled about that kind of thing. But since she was a tracker, and not a royal with an important bloodline—or even Kanin—she'd gotten a bit of a break and tended to slip under people's radar. Not that Ember would ever let anybody keep her down anyway.

"I know. I'm sorry," I said. "Next time I'll be sure to tell you."

"So what happened?" She sat down on the bed next to me.

I shook my head. "There's not much to tell."

"Ridley mentioned . . ." Ember paused, her tone softening with concern. "He said that Konstantin Black was involved."

I lowered my eyes and took a deep breath, but I could feel her eyes on me, searching for any signs of trauma or despair. When Ember had moved here, it had only been days after Konstantin had left. She may not have been here for the attack, but she definitely witnessed the aftermath.

His attack on my dad had left my nerves raw and I was struggling to control my anger at both Konstantin and myself. Myself for not being able to protect my dad better, and for having had such strong feelings for Konstantin.

Ember, along with my friend Tilda Moller, had been instrumental in helping me deal with it. But that didn't mean I wanted Ember or anyone else to have to deal with it now.

"It was Konstantin," I said finally.

Ember didn't say anything for a minute, waiting to see if I'd continue, and when I didn't, she cautiously asked, "Did you kill him?"

"No." The word felt heavy and terrible in my mouth, and an ache grew in the pit of my stomach like a forgotten ulcer flaring up.

"Good," she said, and I looked up at her in surprise. "You don't need that on your conscience."

I scoffed. "His death I could handle. It's his life that I don't need weighing on me."

"I don't know what happened, because I wasn't there, but I

know that you did the right thing." Ember put her hand on my shoulder, warm and reassuring. "You always do. You got the Berling boy home safe and sound, and you're here and you're alive. So I know you did everything right."

I smiled wanly at her. "Thank you."

"You look exhausted. But I'm sure you had a very long trip back." Ember'd only been a tracker for a little over a year, but already she understood how taxing the journey could be, even without a run-in with my nemesis. "I'll let you get some rest."

"You have no idea," I admitted with a dry laugh.

Ember stood up. "I really am glad you're back. And your timing is perfect."

"What do you mean?" I asked.

"My birthday's on Friday, and the big anniversary party's on Saturday. You're back just in time for all the fun," Ember said with a broad grin.

I tried not to grimace. "Right. Fun."

The birthday party would be fun, but the anniversary party I'd been hoping to avoid. It would mean guard duty at the palace all night long, which sounded like it would be right up my alley. But every party or ball I'd guarded had always turned out to be nothing but trouble.

sovereign

The footman who answered the door to the palace helped me take off my coat, even though I assured him it wasn't necessary, and he nearly pulled off my blazer with it as I tried to wriggle away. I'd kicked off my boots, and before I could collect them he was already bending over and picking them up.

If I hadn't been in such a hurry, I would've insisted on doing things myself. Just because I was in the palace didn't mean I needed a servant doing everything for me. But as it was, I'd barely had time to shower, and I didn't have time to dry my hair, so it had frozen on the way over from my apartment.

I mumbled apologies to the footman and thanked him for his trouble. He offered to lead me down the hall to where the meeting was being held, but I didn't need it. I knew the building like the back of my hand.

The opulence of the palace was nearly lost on me by now. Like the exterior, most of the walls inside were stone or brick.

Two massive wooden doors opened into the majestic front hall, but despite the openness, it felt dark and cavernous, thanks to the gray tones of the stone.

The only natural light filtered through stained-glass windows featuring famous battles and royalty long since gone. At the right times of the day, when the light came through the window depicting the Kanin's voyage across the sea, the hall would glow blue, and when it shone through the window immortalizing the Kanin's role in the Long Winter War, the hall would shine blood-red.

The rest of the palace was designed much the same way. Since the palace had been built right after the Kanin settled Doldastam, the key to keeping the cold out seemed to be building as many brick walls with as few windows as possible. Not to mention an abundance of fireplaces, which was another reason the stone was so necessary. Less chance of the building going up in flames.

Not much had been changed in the palace since it was built. At least not in the wing where business was conducted. The private quarters where the King and Queen lived were updated when each new monarch began his reign, so they were much more personal, with wallpaper and wood floors.

Most of the palace did seem dark and cold, but there were elegant flourishes and royal touches. Masterworks of art and antique Baroque furniture were carefully arranged throughout. The kerosene lamps that still lit the corridors were made of silver and adorned with jewels. The ceilings were astonishingly high, and were often broken up by skylights that the poor servants had to constantly clear of snow so they wouldn't come crashing in under the weight.

As I jogged down the corridor, constantly pulling up my black slacks—my nicest pair, though they were too large—I barely even noticed any of the majestic trappings around me. When I reached the meeting hall, I paused outside the door to catch my breath and rake my fingers through my thawing hair.

Then I took a deep breath and opened the doors, and it was just as I had feared. Everyone was already here, waiting. Around a square table that sat ten, there were five of us.

King Evert Strinne sat at the end of the table, next to the crackling fireplace and a massive portrait of himself. He wore a handsomely tailored black suit, but he'd forgone a tie and left the top few buttons undone.

His wife, Queen Mina Strinne, wore her crown, though her husband did not. It was really more of a tiara anyway, silver and encrusted with diamonds. Her long brown hair was pulled back in a loose bun that rested on the nape of her neck, and she smiled warmly at me when I came in. This was a rather casual meeting, but she still wore an ornate gown of white and silver.

The table was wide enough that the Queen could sit next to her husband at the head of it, though her chair was much smaller than his. The dark wood of the high back rose a full two feet above the King's head, while Mina's only came up to the top of her tiara.

Directly to the King's right was Ridley. With a stack of papers in front of him, he smiled grimly at me, and I knew that my tardiness had not gone unnoticed.

Then, sitting to the left of the Queen, with the gravest expression of anyone in the room, was the Chancellor, Iver Aven. My father. His wavy black hair was smoothed back, unintentionally highlighting the silver at his temples, and he wore a suit and tie, the way he did nearly every day. The ire in his toffee eyes was unmistakable, but I met his irritation as evenly as I could and held my head high.

"Bryn Aven." King Evert eyed me with a severe gaze and his perpetual smirk. "How nice of you to join us."

"I'm sorry, my lord," I said with genuine contrition and bowed. "I overslept."

The last few days had worn much harder on me than I had thought they would, and I'd slept straight through my alarm, which led to a frantic scramble to get here on time. Although the fact that I'd only been a few minutes late was really a credit to my determination.

"She just got back from the mission late last night, and she didn't have time to sleep while she was transporting the Berling boy," Ridley said, coming to my aid. "She needed to remain vigilant after his attempted kidnapping."

"We appreciate your diligence, Bryn," the King said, but I couldn't tell if it was approval or condescension in his voice.

I smiled politely. "Thank you, Your Majesty."

"Why don't you have a seat, Bryn?" the Queen suggested, and motioned to the table, the rings on her fingers glinting in the light.

"Thank you."

I took a seat at the end of the table across from the King, and deliberately left empty chairs between myself and my dad, and myself and Ridley. While I loved my dad, and I thought the King approved of him as Chancellor, I always tried to put distance between us at occasions like this.

I didn't want anyone to think that I was relying on my dad and his position in the King's court to get where I was, or that Ridley showed me any favoritism because he was my friend as well as the Rektor. I earned everything on my own merit.

"So. Back to what we were saying." The smirk finally fell away from Evert's face and he looked to Ridley. "How are we even sure this was an attempted kidnapping?"

"Well, we're not," Ridley admitted.

"Are we sure that they were even going after the Berling boy?" Mina asked, her smoky gray eyes surveying the room.

"They all but confessed it to me," I said, and everyone turned to look at me.

"You spoke to him?" Dad asked, and worry hardened his expression. "How did that happen?"

"I got in the car, and I asked him what he was doing," I said simply.

"You got in his car?" Dad asked, nearly shouting. Then he clenched his fist and forced a pained smile, doing his best to keep control of himself in front of the King and Queen. When he spoke again, his voice was tight. "What were you thinking?"

"I was thinking that I needed to do my job, and my job was protecting Linus Berling." I sat up straighter in my chair, defending myself. "I did what I needed to."

"Chancellor, my trackers are trained to handle themselves in all situations." Ridley bristled a little, as if my dad were calling into question his abilities as a Rektor.

"Well, what did they say?" Queen Mina asked, bringing us back on topic.

"They said they were following Linus and waiting for their chance to grab him," I said.

The King sighed and shook his head. "Dammit."

"Did they say why?" Mina pressed.

"No. They refused to say why. Then they tried to prevent me from leaving, and things became . . . violent," I said, choosing my words carefully, and from the corner of my eye I saw my dad flinch, though he did his best to hide it. "One of the men—the one called Bent—was injured. But Konstantin Black evaded serious damage before I got away."

Dad couldn't help himself and whispered harshly, "You shouldn't have gotten in the car."

Ridley cast my dad a look from across the table. "Sir, Bryn can handle herself in a fight."

"It was definitely Konstantin Black, then?" the Queen asked.

I nodded. "Yes."

"How can you be so sure?" King Evert looked at me skeptically. "Did you ever meet him?"

"Everybody in the kingdom knew who Konstantin Black was," Ridley interjected, attempting to spare me from explaining how I knew him so well.

"Only once," I said, speaking loudly but still clear and even. It was getting harder to keep a steady tone when the King was patronizing me about something I was certain of. "When

Konstantin stabbed my father. I'll remember his face until I die."

The King lowered his eyes, faltering only for a moment. "I'd forgotten you were there for his altercation with the Chancellor.

"What about this other man?" The King cleared his throat and continued, "The one called Bent. Do we know anything about him?"

"I've been doing some research and making a few calls." Ridley flipped through the papers in front of him and scanned his notes. "Bryn thought he might be Omte, and they can be reluctant to give any information. However, the Queen did confirm that a young man named Bent Stum was exiled from their community last year, but they wouldn't say why."

"So a wanted Kanin and an exiled criminal Omte joined forces to track down a changeling in Chicago? Why?" Dad shook his head. "And how did they find him?"

"I've been looking over all the paperwork on Berling's place-ment, and I can't see any sign of why it went wrong." Ridley shrugged helplessly. "The only people who should've known where he was were Linus's parents, and then Bryn."

"Did the Markis or Marksinna Berling tell anyone?" my dad asked.

"No." The King dismissed this instantly. "Dylan and Eva are too smart for that. They know better." Then he looked at me. "What about you, Bryn?"

"No, Your Majesty. I never tell anyone where I'm sent."

"You sure?" King Evert pressed. "You didn't mention it to any of your friends?"

"Bryn's one of our best, my lord," Ridley said. "If she says she didn't tell anybody, she didn't tell anybody."

"Well, somehow they found one of our highest-priority Markis changelings. If nobody told anyone, how the hell did they manage that?" King Evert snapped.

"I'm not sure, sire," Ridley admitted, but he met the King's annoyed glare.

"What about your files? You have it all written down, don't you?" the King asked.

"Yes, of course I do. But it's all locked away."

"Who has access to it?" King Evert asked.

"Myself and the Chancellor," Ridley said. "And, of course, you and the Queen would have access to anything you wanted."

My dad furrowed his brow as he considered this. "So, the people in this room."

"Obviously it was none of us, so it must be someone else," Queen Mina said.

The King looked over at Ridley. "What about you?"

Ridley shook his head. "I didn't tell anyone, Your Highness."

"Perhaps Konstantin Black was tracking the trackers," Queen Mina offered, and she turned to me. "Were you followed?"

"I don't believe so," I said. "Konstantin didn't know that Berling was being tracked at first, and I don't think he realized I was Kanin."

The King snorted. "Well . . ."

This time I didn't even try to keep the emotion from my voice, though it was a struggle not to yell. "I was born in Doldastam and raised here. I have pledged my fealty to this kingdom. I am as much a Kanin as any of you."

King Evert smirked, unmoved by my outburst. "I appreciate your service, Bryn, but you know that—"

"Evert, my King." Queen Mina reached over and touched his hand, and she looked up at him with deference. "If the girl has pledged her loyalty to you, then she is a Kanin, and by saving the young Markis Berling, she's proved it."

He looked at his wife, then shifted in his seat and nodded. "You're right, of course, my Queen. I apologize, Bryn."

"No apology is necessary, my lord," I said.

"Back to the matter at hand—what to do about Konstantin Black and Bent Stum?" my dad said. "Didn't the Trylle have a problem like this once? Their changelings were kidnapped by an enemy. What did they do?"

"They went to war," the King replied with a heavy sigh.

"We're not prepared for war," Queen Mina said quickly, as if anyone had actively proposed it. "The Trylle have a smaller population than us, but thanks to their heavier reliance on changelings they have many more trackers, and their army is at least twice that of ours."

"More than that, the Trylle knew who their enemy was," King Evert agreed. "They had that long-standing feud with the Vittra, so the Trylle knew exactly who to go after. Who would we even fight against?"

"Could the Omte be behind it?" Mina asked.

Ridley shook his head. "Doubtful. They're not smart enough

to have found the Berling changeling, and if the Omte Queen was aware of Bent Stum's activities, she would've denied his very existence."

"We don't even know if this is going to be a recurring problem," Dad pointed out. "The Berling boy may have been a one-time thing."

"He is the highest-ranking Markis in the entire Kanin now," Ridley said, thinking aloud. "Until the King and Queen have a child, Linus is actually next in line for the throne. We don't know what Black wanted with Linus, but it can't be good. He could have been planning an assassination."

"Or it could've been a plot for ransom. Both Konstantin and Bent have been exiled," Dad said. "Konstantin has been on the run for years. He has to be in desperate need of money."

The King nodded. "Until we learn otherwise, I think we should treat this as an isolated incident."

"But what if it's not?" I asked.

"It might not be," Evert agreed. "But what would you have us do? Bring all the changelings home right now? Send out all our trackers after Konstantin Black and Bent Stum, leaving Doldastam unguarded?"

"No, of course not, my King. But there should be a compromise," I argued. "Bring home our highest-ranking changelings, especially those over the age of twelve, and send a few trackers after Konstantin and Bent. I would gladly volunteer for that mission."

"Absolutely not," the King said, so swiftly that I was too

stunned to speak for a moment. He hadn't even considered what I'd suggested.

"But my lord—" I said when I found my words.

"We can't afford to bring in that many changelings, not this early," King Evert defended his veto.

"And can we afford to have our changelings kidnapped or slaughtered?" I shot back.

"Bryn," Dad said, trying to silence me.

"Tracker, I think you've forgotten your place," King Evert said, and I swallowed hard. "This is my kingdom, and my decision. Your invitation to this meeting was little more than a courtesy."

I lowered my eyes. "I'm sorry, my King. I'm only thinking of what's in the best interest of the kingdom."

"So are we, Bryn," Queen Mina said, much more gently than her husband had spoken to me. "Many of the highest-ranking Markis and Marksinna in the Kanin, not to mention the Kings and Queens from friendly tribes, will be descending on Doldastam this weekend. If there is a threat to our kingdom, then we will need all our guards here. And if this was targeted on Linus Berling in particular, then it's even more important that you, as his tracker, are here to keep him safe."

"The Queen is right, Bryn," Ridley said, but he sounded sympathetic to my position. "We don't know much right now, and our highest priority should be keeping the kingdom safe."

"Then it's settled," the Queen declared. "I will hear no more of this over the weekend. We have much to celebrate, and friends and dignitaries will be coming into town beginning to-morrow."

"You will stick with Linus Berling like he's your shadow," the King commanded me. "Help him acclimate and understand our community, the way you would with any other changeling, but you also need to be more vigilant, in case there is a price on his head."

I nodded. "Yes, my lord."

mistakes

The meeting appeared to be over, and the Queen was the first to make her exit. As soon as she rose from her place at the end of the table, the rest of us stood up. The backs of my legs smacked into my chair, and it creaked loudly against the floor.

"If you don't mind, I have much to attend to with guests arriving soon." She smiled at all of us as she gathered her dress, and she left the hall.

"I should be on my way, also," King Evert said. "Thank you for attending."

"My King," Dad said, stopping him before he left. "If I could have a word with you for a moment. It's about the new tax."

While the King and Queen were appointed to their roles by birth or marriage, the Chancellor was elected by the people so they could have a voice in the running of the government.

The King nodded. "Yes, of course, Chancellor. Let's walk

and talk." He and my dad left the room together, speaking in hushed tones.

"You always gotta make an entrance, don't you?" Ridley grinned at me as he gathered his papers together.

"I overslept, I swear. I didn't think I'd sleep for twelve hours straight." My pants had begun slipping down my waist again, and with the royalty gone, I was free to pull them back up without earning a scrutinizing look from the King.

"Well, you made it, so that's what counts."

I sighed and sat down, resting against the arm of the chair. "Maybe it would've been better if I hadn't come at all."

"You mean because the King got a little miffed there for a second?" Ridley asked as he walked over to me. "He'll get over it. And you weren't wrong."

"So you're saying I was right?" I asked with raised eyebrows.

"Not exactly." He leaned a hip against the table next to me, crossing his arms so his stack of papers was against his chest. "We need to protect here first, but once this anniversary party is over, then we should really implement your ideas. Even if Konstantin and Bent were only targeting Linus, we can't just let them get away with it."

"So you don't think this was a one-time thing?"

"Honestly?" He looked at me from behind his thick lashes and hesitated before saying, "No, I don't."

"Dammit. I was kinda hoping I was wrong." I ran a hand through my hair. "Anyway, thanks for having my back."

"I'll always have your back," Ridley said with a wry smile. "Or any part of your body."

I rolled my eyes and smiled despite myself. "Way to ruin a perfectly nice moment, Ridley."

"Sorry." He laughed. "I can't help myself sometimes."

"Mmm, I've noticed."

"Have you?"

He leaned back, appraising me, and there was something in his dark eyes, a kind of heat that made my heart beat out of time. It was something new, something I'd only begun to detect in the past few months. Most of the time when we were together it was the same as always, but more and more there was that look in his eyes, a smoldering that I had no idea how to react to.

I suddenly became aware of my very close proximity to him. My knee had brushed up against his leg, and if I wanted to, I could reach out and touch him, putting my hand on the warm skin of his arm, which was bare below where he'd pushed up his sleeves.

As soon as the thought popped into my head, I pushed it away.

The door to the hall swung open, and he lowered his eyes, breaking whatever moment we'd both been in.

"Good, Bryn, you're still here," Dad said as he came into the room.

Ridley looked up and gave me a crooked smile, then shook his head. "I don't even know what I'm talking about."

That's what he said, but it felt like a lie. Still, I'd become acutely aware that my dad was staring at us both, watching us look at each other, and the whole situation felt increasingly awkward.

"Anyway, I should get back to the office." He straightened up and stepped away from the table. "It was nice seeing you again, Chancellor."

"You too." Dad nodded at him, then turned his attention to me. "I wanted to talk to you."

"What did you want to talk to me about?" I asked after Ridley made his escape. "A lecture on how I shouldn't put myself in danger? Or maybe how I should retire and become a teacher like Mom?"

"That would be nice, yes, but actually I wanted to invite you over for dinner tonight."

"I don't know, Dad." I hurried to think up some kind of excuse, *any* excuse. "I'm supposed to be spending time helping Linus get situated."

"Bryn, you just got back in town after being attacked."

"I wouldn't call it an 'attack' per se."

"Your mother wants to see you. *I* want to see you. It's been weeks since you've been over to our house." Dad used a tone so close to pleading that it made my heart twist up with guilt. "Mom will make a nice supper. Just come over. It'll be good."

"Okay," I relented. "What time?"

"Six? Does that work for you?"

"Yep. That'll be great," I said and tried to look happy about it.

"Great." A relieved grin spread across his face. "I know I said some stuff in the meeting that made you mad, but it's just because I love you and I want you to be safe."

"I know, Dad."

And I did know that. Dad was just trying to express concern. But I wished he'd do it in a way that didn't undermine me in front of my superiors.

"Good," he said. "Is it okay if I hug you now, or does that break your no-hugs-at-work policy?"

That was a policy I'd instated when I was fifteen and Dad had ruffled my hair and called me his "adorable little girl" in front of the Högdragen, making them chuckle. It was already hard enough for me to earn their respect without moments like that.

I nodded, and he wrapped his arms around me. When he let me go, I smiled and said, "Don't go making a habit of it."

We both left the meeting hall after that. Dad had work to be done, and so did I. I knew I should go down to help Linus Berling. Even without the King's order to guard him, as his tracker I was supposed to be the one helping him adjust to his new life here in Doldastam.

But right at that moment I didn't think it would be the best idea. The meeting had left me in a sour mood. Things had not gone well with the King, and I really needed to burn off steam.

I could spend an hour at the gym, then go down and help Linus. It'd be better for him if I got in my daily training anyway. If someone was coming after him, I needed to be strong and sharp enough to fight them off.

The gym in the tracker school had a locker room attached to it, where I changed into my workout clothes. As I pulled on my tank top, I was acutely aware of the jagged scar on my shoulder—the gift Konstantin had given me the first time we'd fought.

That only helped fuel my anger, and I pulled my hair up into a ponytail and strode into the gym.

The younger recruits in tracker school were running laps around the side. A couple of older kids were practicing fencing at the other end. Swordplay probably wouldn't be that useful in the outside world, but the Kanin liked to keep things old school. We were a culture steeped in tradition, sometimes to a maddening degree.

A few other full-fledged trackers were doing general workouts, including Ember Holmes and Tilda Moller. Tilda was lifting weights, and Ember hovered over her, spotting for her.

While Ember was a couple years younger than me, Tilda and I were the same age. We were actually the only two girls in our graduating tracker class, and that hadn't been an easy feat for either of us.

Tilda and I had become friends in kindergarten, when we'd both been deemed outsiders—me for blond hair and fair skin, and her for her height. As a child, she had been unnaturally tall, towering over everyone in our class, though as we'd gotten older her height had become an asset, and she'd filled out with curves and muscles that made her almost Amazonian.

Growing up, we were subjected to all kinds of bullying—mostly by the royals but even by our own "peers." I was quick to anger, and Tilda helped ground me, reminding me that my temper wouldn't help the situation. She bore the taunts with poise and stoicism.

Most of the time, anyway. In our first year at tracker school, a boy had made a derisive comment about us girls not being able to handle the physical training, and Tilda had punched him, laying him out flat on his back. That was the last time anybody said anything like that around her.

Hanging down over the weight-lifting bench, Tilda's long hair shimmered a luscious dark chestnut. But the only thing about her I'd ever been jealous of was her skin. As she lifted the barbell, straining against the weight, the tanned color of her skin shifted, turning dark blue to match the color of the mats propped against the wall behind her.

Unlike Ember and me, Tilda was full-blooded Kanin. Not everyone could do what she did either, the chameleonlike ability to blend into her surroundings. As time went on, it was becoming a rarer and rarer occurrence, and if the bloodlines were diluted by anyone other than a pure Kanin, the offspring would be unable to do it at all.

And that's why my skin had the same pallor no matter how angry or frightened I might get. I was only half Kanin, so I had none of their traits or abilities.

"Hey, Bryn," Ember said brightly, and I wrapped my hands with boxing tape as I approached them. "How'd your meeting go?"

As Tilda rested the barbell back in its holder and sat up, her skin slowly shifted back to its normal color, and she wiped the sweat from her brow with the back of her arm. By the grave look in her eyes, I knew that Ember had filled her in about everything that had happened with Konstantin.

She didn't ask about it, though. We'd been friends so long that she didn't really need to say anything. She just gave me a look—her charcoal-gray eyes warm and concerned as they rested heavily on me—and I returned her gaze evenly, trying to assure her with a pained smile that I was handling everything with Konstantin better than I actually was.

Of course, Tilda probably knew I was holding back, but she accepted what I was willing to give and offered me a supportive smile. She would never press or pry, trusting me to come to her if I needed to.

I shrugged. "I'm here to blow off steam, if that answers your question."

Ember asked with a smirk, "That bad, huh?"

"The King hates me." I sighed and adjusted the tape on my hands as I walked over to the punching bag.

"I'm sure he doesn't hate you," Ember said.

Tilda took a long drink from her water bottle, accidentally spilling a few droplets on her baggy tank top, and Ember walked over to help me. She stood on the other side of the punching bag, holding it in place, so that when I hit it, it wouldn't sway away. I started punching, throwing all my frustration into the bag.

"I have to learn to keep my mouth shut if I'll ever stand a chance of being on the Högdragen," I said, and my words came out in short bursts between punches. "It's already gonna be hard enough without me pissing off the King."

"How did you piss him off?" Tilda asked as she came over to us. She put one hand on her hip as she watched me, letting her other fall to the side.

"I was just arguing with him. I was right, but it doesn't matter," I said, punching the bag harder. "If the King says the sky is purple and it rains diamonds, then it does. The King's word is law."

I don't know what made me angrier. The fact the King was wrong and refused to see it, or that I'd once again botched my own attempts at being one of the Högdragen. That was all I'd ever wanted for as long as I could remember, and if I wanted to be in the guard, I'd have to learn to follow orders without talking back.

But I didn't know how I was supposed to keep my mouth shut if I thought the King was doing things that might endanger the kingdom.

I started alternating between punching and kicking the bag, taking out all my anger at the King and at myself. I finally hit it hard enough that the bag swung back, knocking Ember to the floor.

"Sorry," I said, and held my hand out to her.

"No harm, no foul." Ember grinned as I helped her to her feet.

"You make it sound like we live in an Orwellian dystopia, and I know you don't think that," Tilda said, but there was an arch to her eyebrows, like maybe she didn't completely disagree with the idea.

She'd never openly speak ill of the kingdom—or of anything, really—but that didn't mean she approved of everything that happened here. Neither did I, but Tilda always managed to handle things with more grace and tact than I could muster.

"No, I don't." I rubbed the back of my neck. "But I won't ever get ahead if I keep arguing with everyone."

"Maybe you will," Tilda said. "You've argued and fought your way to where you are now. Nobody wanted you to be a tracker, but you insisted that you could do it, and now you're one of the best."

"Thanks." I smiled at her. "Speaking of which, I'm supposed to be shadowing Linus, so I need to fly through today's workout. You wanna spar?"

"I think I'll sit this one out, since the last time you gave me a fat lip," Tilda reminded me, pointing to her full lips.

They had been briefly swollen and purplish last month when I accidentally punched her right in the mouth, temporarily marring her otherwise beautiful face. She'd never been vain or complained of the bumps and bruises we'd both get during our practicing fights before, but if she didn't want to fight today, I wasn't going to push her.

"Ember, you wanna go?" I asked.

"Sure. But you have to promise not to hit me in the face." She motioned a circle around her face. "I don't want any visible marks for my birthday party."

I nodded. "Deal. Let's go."

estate

I'd moved out when I turned sixteen three years ago, and it still felt kinda strange going back to the house I'd grown up in. It always looked the same and smelled the same, but there were subtle differences that reminded me it wasn't my home anymore.

My mom and dad lived in a cottage near the town square, and as far as cottages in Doldastam went, theirs was fairly spacious. It wasn't as nice as the house my dad had grown up in, but that had been passed to the Eckwells after my grandparents had died, since Dad had given up his Markis title.

Mom had probably grown up in a nicer house too, though she didn't talk about it that much. In fact, she rarely ever mentioned Storvatten except to talk about the lake.

As soon as I opened the door, the scent of seawater hit me. We lived over a half hour away from Hudson Bay, so I have no idea how Mom did it, but the house always smelled like the ocean. Now it was mixed with salmon and citrus, the supper she was cooking in the oven.

"Hello?" I called, since no one was there to greet me at the door, and I began unwinding my scarf.

"Bryn?" Dad came out from the study at the back of the house, with his reading glasses pushed up on his head. "You're here early."

"Only fifteen minutes," I said, glancing over at the grand-father clock in the living room to be sure I was right. "Linus was sitting down for supper with his parents, so I thought it would be a good time to duck out. If I'm interrupting something, I can entertain myself while you finish up."

"No, I was just doing some paperwork, but it can wait." He waved in the direction of his study. "Take off your coat. Stay awhile."

"Where's Mom?" I asked as I took off my jacket and hung it on the coatrack by the door.

"She's in the bath," Dad said.

I should've known. Mom was always in the bath. It was be-cause she was Skojare. She needed the water.

Some of my fondest memories from being a small child were sitting in the bathroom with her. She'd be soaking in the claw-footed tub, and I'd sit on the floor. Sometimes she'd sing to me, other times I'd read her stories, or just play with my toys. A lot of time was spent in there.

Fortunately, Mom didn't have gills, the way some of the Skojare did. If she had, then I don't know how she would've sur-vived here, with the rivers and bay frozen over so often. The

Skojare didn't actually live in the water, but they needed to spend a lot of time in it, or they'd get sick.

When Mom stayed away from water too long, she'd get headaches. Her skin would become ashen, and her golden hair would lose its usual luster. She'd say, "I'm drying out," and then she'd go take a long soak in the tub.

I don't think that was the ideal course of action for her symptoms, but Mom made do.

"Supper smells good," I said as I walked into the kitchen.

"Yeah. Your mom put it in before she got in the tub," Dad said. "It should be ready soon, I think."

Upstairs, I heard the bathroom door open, followed by my mom shouting, "Bryn? Is that you?"

"Yeah, Mom. I got here a little early," I called up to her.

"Oh, gosh. I'll be right down."

"You don't need to rush on my account," I said, but I knew she would anyway.

A few seconds later, Mom came running down the stairs wearing a white robe. A clip held up her long wet hair.

"Bryn!" Mom beamed at me, and she ran over and embraced me tightly. "I'm so happy to see you!"

"Glad to see you too, Mom."

"How are you?" She let go of me and brushed my hair back from my face, so she could look at me fully. "Are you okay? They didn't hurt you, right?"

"Nope. I'm totally fine."

"Good." Her lips pressed into a thin line, and her aqua eyes were pained. "I worry so much when you're away."

"I know, but I'm okay. Honest."

"I love you." She leaned down and kissed my forehead. "Now I'll go get dressed. I just wanted to see you first."

Mom dashed back upstairs to her bedroom, and I sat down at the kitchen table. Even without makeup, and rapidly approaching forty, my mom still had to be the most stunning woman in Doldastam. She had the kind of beauty that launched a thousand wars.

Fortunately, that hadn't happened. Although there had definitely been repercussions from her union with my dad, and they'd both sacrificed their titles and riches to be together.

Their relationship had been quite the scandal. My mom had been born in Storvatten—the Skojare capital—and she was a high-ranking Marksinna. My dad had been Markis from a prominent family in Doldastam. When Mom was only sixteen, she'd been invited to a ball here in Doldastam, and though my dad was a few years older than her, they'd instantly fallen in love.

Dad had become involved in politics, and he didn't want to leave Doldastam because he had a career. So Mom defected from Storvatten, since they both agreed that they had a better chance to make a life here.

The fact that Dad was Chancellor, and had been for the past ten years, was a very big deal. Especially since his family had basically disowned him. But I'd always thought that the fact that my mom was so beautiful helped his case. Everyone understood why he'd give up his title and his riches to be with her.

I'd like to say that life had been easy for my mom and me,

that the Kanin people had been as forgiving of us as they had been for Dad. But they hadn't.

Other tribes like the Trylle were more understanding about intertribal marriages, especially if the marriage wasn't among high-ranking royals. They thought it helped unite the tribes. But the Kanin definitely did not feel that way. Any romance outside your own tribe could dilute the precious bloodlines, and that was an act against the kingdom itself and nearly on par with treason.

Perhaps that's why they were slightly easier on my mom than they were on me. Her bloodline was still pure. It may have been Skojare, but it was untainted. Mine was a mixture, a travesty against both the Kanin and the Skojare.

"So how are things going with Linus?" Dad walked over to the counter and poured himself a glass of red wine, then held out an empty glass toward me. "You want something to drink?"

"Sure." I sat down at the kitchen table, and Dad poured me a glass of wine before joining me. "Linus is adjusting well, and he's curious and easygoing, which makes the transition easier. He's trying really hard to learn all of our words and phrases. He's even tried mimicking our dialect."

When trackers went out into the world, we were taught to use whatever dialect was common in that area, which was actually incredibly difficult to master. But in Doldastam, we returned to the usual Kanin accent—slightly Canadian but with a bit of a Swedish flare to it, especially on Kanin words. Linus's Chicago accent wasn't too far off, but he still tried to imitate ours perfectly.

Dad took a drink, then looked toward the stairs, as if searching for my mother, and when he spoke, his voice was barely above a whisper. "I didn't tell her about Konstantin. She knows you were attacked, but not by *whom*."

Dad swirled the wine in his glass, staring down at it so he wouldn't have to look at me, then he took another drink. This time I joined him, taking a long drink myself.

"Thank you," I said finally, and he shook his head.

My parents had a very open relationship, and I'd rarely known them to keep secrets from each other. So my dad not telling my mom about Konstantin was actually a very big deal, but I understood exactly why he withheld that information, and I appreciated it.

Mom would lose her mind if she found out. After Konstantin had stabbed Dad, she'd begged and pleaded for us all to leave, to go live among the humans, but both Dad and I had wanted to stay, so finally she had relented. It was my dad's argument that we were safer here, with other guards and trackers to protect us from one crazed vigilante.

But if Mom knew that Konstantin was involved again, that he'd attacked another member of her family, that would be the final straw for her.

After changing into an oversized sweater and yoga pants, Mom came down the stairs, tousling her damp hair with her hand.

"What are we talking about?" Mom touched my shoulder as she walked by on her way to the oven.

"Just that Linus Berling is getting along well with his parents," I told her.

She opened the oven and peeked in at whatever was simmering in a casserole dish, then she glanced back at me. "They don't always?"

"Changelings and their parents?" I laughed darkly. "No, no, they usually don't."

At times they even seemed to hate each other, not that that was totally outlandish. These were wealthy people, living in a childless home, when suddenly an eighteen- to twenty-year-old stranger going through a major bout of culture shock was thrust into their lives.

Maternal and paternal instincts did kick in more often than not, and an unseen bond would pull them together. Eventually, most changelings and their parents came to love and understand each other.

But that was over time. Initially, there was often friction, and lots of it. Changelings were hurt and confused, and wanted to rebel against a society they didn't understand. The parents, meanwhile, struggled to raise someone who was more adult than child and mold them into an acceptable member of the Kanin hierarchy.

"The whole practice has always seemed barbaric to me." Mom closed the oven, apparently deciding supper wasn't quite done yet, and sat down at the table next to my dad. "Taking a child and leaving it with total strangers. I don't know how anyone can part with their child like that. There's no way I would've allowed that to happen to you."

The Skojare didn't have changelings—not any of them. They earned their money through more honest means. The general population worked as fishermen, and they had for centuries, originally trading their fish for jewels and gold. Now it was mostly a cash business, and the royalty maintained their wealth through exorbitant taxes on the people.

That's part of the reason why the Skojare population had dwindled down so low compared to the other troll tribes. The lifestyle wasn't as lavish or as kind to those who weren't direct royalty.

"The Changeling practice isn't as bad as it sounds," Dad said.

Mom shook her head, dismissing him. "You were never a changeling. You don't know."

"No, but my brother was," he said, and as soon as Mom shot him a look, I knew he regretted it.

My uncle Edmund was five years older than my dad. I'd only met him a handful of times when I was very young, because Edmund was kind of insane. Nobody was exactly sure what happened to him, but by the time I was in school, Edmund had left Doldastam and now traveled the subarctic like a nomad.

"Exactly, Iver," Mom said. "And where is he now?"

Dad cleared his throat, then took a sip of his wine. "That was a bad example."

Mom turned back to me. "So with the Berling boy back, are you here for a while?"

I nodded. "It looks that way."

"Well, good." She smiled warmly at me. "With all this nonsense going on, you don't need to be out there."

"That is exactly why I do need to be out there," I said, even though I knew I should just keep my mouth shut. This was supposed to be a nice visit, and we didn't need to get into this again. It was an old argument we'd repeated too many times, but I couldn't seem to stop myself. "I should be out there protecting the changelings."

"We shouldn't even have changelings. You shouldn't be out there risking your life for some archaic practice!" Mom insisted.

"Would you like a glass of wine, Runa?" Dad asked in a futile attempt to keep the conversation civil, but both my mom and I ignored him.

"But we do have changelings." I leaned forward, resting my arms on the table. "And as long as we do, someone needs to bring them home and keep them safe."

Mom shook her head. "By being a tracker, you're buying right into this awful system. You're enabling it."

"I'm not . . ." I trailed off and changed the direction of my argument. "I'm not saying it's perfect or it's right—"

"Good." She cut me off and leaned back in her seat. "Because it isn't."

"Mom, what else do you want our people to do? This is the way things have been done for thousands of years."

She laughed, like she couldn't believe I was saying it. "That doesn't make it okay, Bryn! Just because something has been done for a long time doesn't make it right. Every time a changeling is left with a human family, they are risking their children's lives to steal from strangers. It's sick."

"Runa, maybe now isn't the time to have this discussion." Dad reached out, putting his hand on her arm. She let him, but her eyes stayed on me, darkened with anger.

"I'm not condoning the stealing," I told her.

"But you are," Mom persisted. "By working for them, by helping them the way you do, you are tacitly agreeing with all of it."

"The Kanin have a way of life here. I'm not talking about the Markis or the trackers or the changelings. I am talking about the average Kanin person, the majority of the ten thousand people that live in Doldastam," I said, trying to appeal to her sense of reason and fair play.

"They don't have changelings," I reminded her. "They work for their money. They're teachers and bakers and farmers and shop owners. They raise families and live quietly and more peacefully and closer to nature. They're allowed to leave, yet time and time again they choose to stay. And it's a good thing too. You don't know what the world is like outside the city walls anymore. You haven't been anywhere except Storvatten and Doldastam."

Mom rolled her eyes at that, but she didn't say anything, letting me finish my speech.

"The life for the humans, outside in the real cities, it's not like this," I said. "The drugs, the violence, the excessive commercialism. Everything is a product, even people themselves. I know that things here are not perfect. We have our problems too, but the way we live as a whole, I wouldn't trade it for anything.

"And the way that we support this lifestyle is with the changelings," I went on. "I wish there was a different way, a better way, but as of right now, there's not. And if the Markis and Marksinna didn't get their money from the changelings, they wouldn't have anything to pay the teachers and bakers and farmers and shop owners. This town would shrivel up and die. The things I do make this possible.

"I am part of what keeps this all together, and that's why I became a tracker. That's why I do what I do." I leaned back in my chair, satisfied with my argument.

Mom folded her arms over her chest, and there was a mixture of sympathy and disappointment in her eyes. "The ends don't justify the means, Bryn."

"Maybe they do, maybe they don't." I shrugged. "But I love this town. I think you do too."

A smile twisted across her face. "You are mistaken again."

"Fine." I sighed. "But haven't you ever loved a place?"

"No, I've loved *people*. I love you, and I love your dad." She reached out, taking Dad's hand in her own. "Wherever the two of you are, I'll be happy. But that doesn't mean I love Doldastam, and it certainly doesn't mean that I love you risking your life to protect it. I tolerate it because I have no choice. You're an adult and this is the life you chose."

"It is. And it would be great if every time I visited didn't turn into a fight about it."

"Is it so wrong that I want something better for you?" Mom asked, almost desperately.

"Yes, yes, it is," I replied flatly.

"How is that wrong?" She threw her hands in the air. "Every mother just wants the best for her child."

I leaned forward again and slapped my hand on the table. "This is the best. Don't you get that?"

"You're selling yourself short, Bryn. You can have so much better." Mom tried to reach out and hold my hand, but I pulled away from her.

"I can't do this anymore." I pushed back my chair and stood up. "I knew coming over was a mistake."

"Bryn, no." Her face fell, her disapproval giving way to remorse. "I'm sorry. I promise I won't talk about work anymore. Don't go."

I looked away from her so I wouldn't get suckered in by guilt again, and ran my hand through my hair. "No, I have stuff I need to do anyway. I shouldn't have even agreed to this."

"Bryn," Dad said.

"No, I need to go." I turned to walk toward the door, and Mom stood up.

"Honey. Please," Mom begged. "Don't go. I love you."

"I love you too," I told her without looking at her. "I just . . . I'll talk to you later."

I yanked on my boots and grabbed my coat from the rack. My mom said my name again as I opened the door and stepped outside, but I didn't look back. As I walked down the dirt road my parents lived on, I breathed in deeply. The cold hurt my lungs and stung my cheeks, but I didn't mind. In fact, I didn't even put on my coat, preferring the chill. I just held my jacket to my chest and let the fresh air clear my head.

"Bryn!" Dad called after me just as I made it around the corner past the house.

An errant chicken crossed my path, and when I brushed past,

it squawked in annoyance. But I didn't slow down, not until I heard my dad's footsteps behind me.

"Wait," he said, puffing because he was out of breath from chasing after me.

I finally stopped and turned back to him. He was still adjusting his jacket, and he slowed to a walk as he approached me.

"Dad, I'm not going back in there."

"Your mom is heartbroken. She didn't mean to upset you."

I looked away, staring down at the chicken pecking at pebbles in the road. "I know. I just . . . I can't deal with it. I can't handle her criticisms tonight. That's all."

"She's not trying to criticize you," Dad said.

"I know. It's just . . . I work *so* hard." I finally looked up at him. "And it's like no matter what I do, it's never good enough."

"No, that's not true at all." Dad shook his head adamantly. "Your mom takes issue with some of the practices here. She gets on me about it too. But she knows how hard you work, and she's proud of you. We both are."

I swallowed hard. "Thank you. But I can't go back right now."

His shoulders slacked but he nodded. "I understand."

"Tell Mom I'll talk to her another day, okay?"

"I will," he said, and as I turned to walk away, he added, "Put your coat on."

history

B ooks were stacked from the floor all the way up to the ceil-ing thirty feet above us. Tall, precarious ladders enabled people to reach the books on the top shelves, but fortunately, I didn't need any books from up that high. Most of the ones people read were kept on the lower, more reachable shelves.

The height of the ceiling made it harder to heat the room, and since Linus and I were the first people here this morning, it had a definite chill to it. Disturbing dreams of Konstantin Black had filled my slumber last night, and I'd finally given up on sleep very early this morning, so I'd decided to get a jump start on acclimating Linus. He had quite a bit to learn before the anniversary party tomorrow night, where he'd be intro-duced to all sorts of royalty—both from the Kanin and from the other tribes.

I doubted anybody else would come to the library today, which would make it the perfect place for studying. The halls in the palace had been chaotic with the bustling of servants and guards as dignitaries from other tribes arrived.

Linus had very nearly gotten trampled by a maid carrying stacks of silken sheets, and I'd pulled him out of the way in the nick of time. The upcoming party had turned the normally sedate palace into bedlam.

The library was still a bastion of solitude, though. Even when everyone wasn't distracted by a hundred guests, it wasn't exactly a popular place to hang out. Several chairs and sofas filled the room, along with a couple tables, but I'd almost never seen anyone use them.

"It's okay that we're here, right?" Linus asked as I crouched in front of the fireplace and threw in another log.

"The library is open to the public," I told him and straightened up. "But as a Berling, you're allowed to move freely in the palace. The King is your dad's cousin and best friend. The door is always open for you."

"Cool." Linus shivered, and rubbed his arms through his thick sweater. "So is it winter here year-round?"

"No, it'll get warm soon. There's a real summer with flowers and birds."

"Good. I don't know if I could handle it being cold all the time."

I walked over to where he'd sat down at a table. "Does it really bother you that much?"

"What do you mean?"

"Most Kanin prefer the cold. Actually, most trolls in general do."

"So do all the tribes live up around here?"

"Not really." I went over to a shelf to start gathering books for him. "Almost all of us live in North America or Europe, but we like to keep distance between tribes. It's better that way."

"You guys don't get along?" Linus asked as I grabbed a couple of old texts from a shelf.

"I wouldn't say that, exactly, but we can get territorial. And most trolls are known for being grumpy, especially the Vittra and the Omte."

"What about the Kanin?"

"We're actually more peaceful than most of the other tribes."

After grabbing about a dozen books that seemed to weigh about half a ton, I carried them back to the table and plunked them down in front of Linus.

Apprehension flickered in his brown eyes when he looked up at me. "Do I really need to read all this?"

"The more you know about your heritage, the better," I said, and sat down in the chair across from him.

"Great." He picked up the first book off the stack and flipped through it absently. "I do like the cold."

"What?"

"The winters back in Chicago, they were always so much harder on my sisters. Er, host sisters," he corrected himself. "But the cold never really got to me."

"We withstand it much better."

Linus pushed the books to the side so it'd be easier for him to see me. "How come?"

"I don't know exactly." I shrugged. "We all came from Scandinavia, so that probably has something to do with it. We're genetically built for colder climates."

"You came from Scandinavia?" Linus leaned forward and rested his arms on the table.

"Well, not me personally. I was born here. But our people." I sifted through the books I'd brought over until I found a thin book bound in worn brown paper, then I handed it to him. "This kinda helps break it down."

"This?" He flipped through the first few pages, which showed illustrations of several different animals living in a forest, and he wrinkled his nose. "It's a story about rabbits and lions. It's like a fairy tale."

"It's a simplistic version of how we came to be," I said.

When he lifted his eyes to look at me, they were filled with bewilderment. "I don't get it."

"All the trolls were one tribe." I tapped the picture showing the rabbit sitting with the cougar, and the fox cuddling with a bird. "We all lived together in relative peace in Scandinavia. We bickered and backstabbed, but we didn't declare war on one another. Then the Crusades happened."

He turned the page, as if expecting to see a picture of a priest with a sword, but it was only more pictures of animals, so he looked back up at me. "Like the stuff with the Catholic Church in the Middle Ages?"

"Exactly. You've noticed that trolls have different abilities, like how you can change your skin."

"Yeah?"

"That's not the only thing we can do," I explained. "The

Trylle have psychokinesis, so they can move objects with their minds and see the future. The Skojare are very aquatic and are born with gills. The Vittra are supernaturally strong and give birth to hobgoblins. The Omte . . . well, the Omte don't have much of anything, except persuasion. And all trolls have that."

"Persuasion?"

"It's the ability to compel someone with your thoughts. Like, I'd think, *Dance,* and then you would dance," I tried to elaborate. "It's like mind control."

Linus's eyes widened and he leaned back in his chair, moving away from me. "Can you do that?"

"No. I actually can't do any of those things," I said with a heavy sigh, and he seemed to relax again. "But we're getting off track."

"Right. Trolls have magic powers," he said.

"And during the Crusades, those powers looked like witchcraft," I told him. "So humans started rounding us up, slaughtering us by the dozens, because they believed we'd made pacts with the devil."

It was actually the changelings that got hit the worst, but I didn't tell Linus that. I didn't want him to know the kind of risk our previous changelings had gone through, not yet anyway.

Babies that exhibited even the slightest hint of being nonhuman were murdered. They had all kinds of tests, like if a baby had an unruly lock of hair, or the mother experienced painful breast-feeding. Some were much worse, though, like throwing a baby in boiling water. If it wasn't cooked, it was a troll, they thought, but no matter—the baby was cooked and killed anyway.

Many innocent human babies were murdered during that time too. Babies with Down's syndrome or colic would be killed. If a child demonstrated any kind of abnormal behavior, it could be suspected of being a troll or evil, and it was killed.

It was a very dark time for humankind and trollkind alike.

"Had we made a deal with the devil?" Linus asked cautiously.

I shook my head. "No, of course not. We're no more satanic than rabbits or chameleons. Just because we're different than humans doesn't make us evil."

"So we were all one big happy family of trolls, until the Crusades happened. They drove us out of our homes, and I'm assuming that's what led us to migrate to North America," Linus filled in.

"Correct. Most of the troll population migrated here with early human settlers, mostly Vikings, and that's why so much of our culture is still based in our Scandinavian ancestry."

His brow scrunched up as he seemed to consider this for a moment, then he asked, "Okay, I get that, but if we're Scandinavian, how come so many of us have darker skin and brown hair? Not to sound racist here, but aren't people from Sweden blond and blue-eyed? You're the only one I've seen that looks like that."

"Our coloration has to do with how we lived," I explained. "Originally, we lived very close to nature. The Omte lived in trees, building their homes in trunks or high in the branches.

The Trylle, the Vittra, and the Kanin lived in the ground. The Kanin especially lived much the way rabbits do now, with burrows in the dirt and tunnels connecting them."

"What does that have to do with having brown hair?" he asked.

"It was about blending into our surroundings." I pointed to the picture again, pointing to where a rabbit was sitting in the long grass. "The Kanin lived in the dirt and grass, and those that matched the dirt and grass had a higher survival rate."

"What about you, then?"

"I'm half Skojare," I told him, and just like every other time I'd said it, the very words left a bitter taste in my mouth.

"Skojare? That's the aquatic one?"

I nodded. "They lived in the water or near it, and they are pale with blond hair and blue eyes."

"Make sense, I guess." He didn't sound completely convinced, but he continued anyway. "So what happened after we came to North America?"

"We'd already divided into groups. Those with certain skills and aptitudes tended to band together. But we hadn't officially broken off," I said. "Then when we came here, we all kind of spread out and started doing our own thing."

"That's when you became the Kanin and the Skojare, et cetera?"

"Sort of." I wagged my head. "We'd split off in different groups, but we hadn't officially named ourselves yet. Some tribes did better than others. The Trylle and the Kanin, in particular, flourished. I don't know if it was just that they were lucky in establishing their settlements or they worked smarter. But whatever the reason, they thrived, while others suffered. And that's really what the story is about."

"What?" Linus glanced down at the book, then back up at me. "I feel like you skipped a step there."

"Each animal in the story represents a different tribe." I tapped the picture of a cougar, his eyes red and fangs sharp. "The cougar is the Vittra, who were starving and suffering. So they began attacking and stealing from the other tribes, and soon the Omte, who are the birds, joined in. And it wasn't long until everyone was fighting everyone, and we'd completely broken off from each other."

"Which one are the Kanin?" Linus asked as he stared down at the page.

"We're the rabbits. That's literally what *kanin* translates into."

"Really?" Linus questioned in surprise. "Why rabbits? Shouldn't we be, like, chameleons or something?"

"Probably, but when the trolls named themselves, they didn't know what chameleons were. Not a lot of reptiles in northern Canada. So we went with rabbits because they burrowed deep, ran fast, and they did a good job of blending in with their surroundings."

Linus stared sadly at the books in front of him. "I don't think I'll ever be able to remember all this stuff, especially not with all the different tribes."

"Here." I grabbed a thick book from the bottom of the pile and flipped through its yellowing pages until I found the one I was looking for.

It had a symbol for each of the tribes, the actual emblems that we used on flags when we bothered to use flags—a white rabbit for the Kanin, a green flowering vine for the Trylle, a red cougar for the Vittra, a blue fish for the Skojare, and a brown-bearded vulture for the Omte.

Next to each emblem were a few short facts about each of the tribes. Not enough to make anyone an expert, but enough for now.

He grimaced and stared down at the page. "Great."

"It won't be that bad," I assured him.

As Linus studied the page in front of him, his brown hair fell across his forehead, and his lips moved as he silently read the pages. The freckles on his cheeks darkened the harder he concentrated—an unconscious reaction brought on by his Kanin abilities.

"Bryn Aven." A sharp voice pulled me from watching Linus, and I looked up to see Astrid Eckwell. "What on earth are you doing here?"

Her raven waves of hair cascaded down her back. The coral chiffon of her dress popped beautifully against the olive tone of her skin. In her arms she held a small rabbit. A smirk was already forming on her lips, and I knew that couldn't be a good sign.

"Working with Markis Linus Berling," I told her as I got to my feet. Linus glanced at both Astrid and myself, and then he got up. "You don't have to stand."

"What?" He looked uncertainly at me, like it was a trick. "But . . . you did."

"Of course she did," Astrid said as she walked over to us,

absently stroking the white rabbit. "She's the *help*, and I'm a Marksinna. She has to stand whenever anyone higher up than her enters the room, and that's everyone."

"As the Markis Berling, you only need to stand for the King and Queen," I said, but Linus still didn't seem to understand.

"Bryn, aren't you going to introduce us?" Astrid asked as she stared up at him with her wide dark eyes, but he kept looking past her, down at the rabbit in her arms.

"My apologies, Marksinna. Linus Berling, this is Astrid Eckwell." I motioned between the two of them.

"It's a pleasure to meet you," Linus said, and gave her a lop-sided smile.

"Likewise. Are you going to the anniversary party tomorrow?" Astrid asked.

"Um, yeah, I think so." He turned to me for confirmation, and I nodded once.

"He will be there with his parents."

Astrid looked at me with contempt in her eyes. "I suppose that means you'll be there too."

"Most likely I will be assisting Markis Berling and the Högdragen," I said, and I didn't sound any more thrilled about it than she did.

"You better dig something nice out of your closet." She cast a disparaging look over my outfit. "You can't go to the party wearing your ratty old jeans. That might fly for the trashy Skojare, but you know that won't do for the Kanin."

I kept my hands folded neatly behind my back and didn't look down. As a tracker, I had to dress appropriately for many different occasions, and I knew there was nothing wrong with my outfit. I might be wearing dark denim, but they were nice.

"Thank you for the tip, Marksinna, but I'm certain that you won't be speaking derogatorily of the Skojare anymore, as their King, Queen, and Prince have already arrived in the palace for tomorrow's anniversary party," I replied icily. "You wouldn't want them to hear you speaking negatively of them, since they are King Evert and Queen Mina's guests."

"I know they're here," Astrid snapped, and her nostrils flared. "That's why I'm dressed properly today, unlike you. What would the King of the Skojare say if he saw you running around like that?"

"Since he's a gentleman, I'm sure he would say hello," I said.

Taking a deep breath through her nose, Astrid pressed her lips into a thin, acrid smile. "You are just as impossible as you were in school. I can't believe they let you be a tracker."

When she spoke like that, it wasn't hard to remember back when we'd been kids in grade school together. I couldn't have been more than six or seven years old the first time Astrid pushed me down in the mud and sneered at me as she called me a *half-breed*.

For the past century or so, the Kanin had been trying to reduce their reliance on changelings. If there were multiple children in a family, only one would be left as a changeling. It wasn't uncommon for particularly wealthy families to go a whole generation without leaving one.

And in Astrid's case, both her parents had been changelings, so they were freshly infused with cash from their host families and didn't need their child to bring in more of an income.

So, unfortunately, that left me forced to deal with Astrid all through grade school. There were many times when I wanted nothing more than to punch her, but Tilda had always held me back, reminding me that violence against a Marksinna could damage my chance of being a tracker.

That hadn't stopped me from hurling a few insults at Astrid in my time, but that had been long ago, before I'd joined the tracker school. Now I was sworn to protect the Marksinna and Markis, which meant I wasn't even supposed to speak ill of them.

Astrid knew that, and it pleased her no end.

"Linus, if you ever need any real help, you can always ask me," she said, with her derisive gaze still fixed on me. "You mustn't be forced to rely on an inferior tutor like Bryn."

"Markis," Linus said.

Startled, she looked up at him. "What?"

"You called me Linus, but I'm your superior, right?" he asked as he stared back down at her. "That's why I didn't have to stand when you came in?"

"That's . . ." Her smile faltered. "That's correct."

"Then you should call me Markis," Linus told her evenly, and it was a struggle for me not to smile. "If I'm understanding correctly."

"You understand it right, Markis," I assured him.

"Yes, of course you are, Markis." Astrid gave him her best eat-shit grin. "Well, I should let you get back to your lessons.

I'm sure you have much to learn before tomorrow night's ball if you don't want to make a fool of yourself."

She turned on her heel, the length of her dress billowing out behind her. Once she was gone, I let out a deep breath, and Linus sat back down at the table.

"That chick seemed kinda like a jerk," he commented.

"She is," I agreed, and sat down across from him. "We went to grade school together, and she was always horrible."

"She wasn't a changeling?"

"No, she's been here every day for the past nineteen years."

"What was the deal with the rabbit?" Linus asked. He sounded so totally baffled by it that I had to laugh.

"Oh, it's kind of a tradition. They're Gotland rabbits, and legend has it we brought them over with us when we came from Sweden. Supposedly they helped us find where to build Doldastam and helped us survive the first cold winter."

"How did they help the Kanin survive?"

"Well, they ate them," I explained. "But not all of them, and now people raise them, and we'd never eat them because they're like a sacred mascot. Some of the Marksinna carry them around now, like rich American girls used to do with Chihuahuas. The Queen has a rabbit named Vita. You'll probably see it."

He laid his hands flat on the table and looked me in the eye. "Can I be totally candid with you?"

"Of course." I sat up straighter, preparing myself for any number of inflammatory statements he might make. "I'm your tracker. You can always speak freely with me."

"You guys are super-weird."

regret

I can't do this," I announced as I threw the office door open. It swung back harder than I meant for it to, and when the doorknob banged into the brick wall, Ridley grimaced.

"If by 'this' you mean knocking, then yes, that's very apparent," he said dryly.

I flopped in the chair across from his large oak desk. A widescreen monitor for his computer was tilted toward the edge of the desk. Being trolls, we craved all things shiny and new.

Our love of such things extended to the latest gadgets and fastest technology, but once we had them, it seemed that we usually preferred the old ways of doing things. The Kanin royalty collected computers and tablets the way others did baseball cards—storing them in boxes and closets and out of sight.

That's why the Rektor's office contained a high-speed computer, a massive printer, and all sorts of devices that would make his work so much easier, but it was rarely used. Stacks of paper covered the desk, since, inevitably, most things were done by hand.

A bulletin board on one side of the room was overflowing with flyers. Reminders for meetings and trainings, sign-up sheets for less glamorous jobs like cleaning out the garage, and missing persons posters for the rare changeling who ran away.

Behind Ridley's desk were two massive paintings of King Evert and Queen Mina. The rest of the wall was covered in smaller eight-by-tens of the latest changelings who had come back, as a reminder of why we did the job.

Outside the office, classes were in session, so I could hear the muted sounds of kids talking.

"I can't stay here," I told Ridley.

"Like in this office?" He scribbled something down on a piece of paper in front of him, then he looked at me. "Or can you be more specific?"

"I can't stay in Doldastam," I said. His shoulders slacked, and he set the pen down. "Linus is safe. He's fine. There are tons of people here to watch him. I have no reason to stay."

"That's true," he said sarcastically, then he snapped his fingers like something had just occurred to him. "Oh, wait. There is that one reason. The King *ordered* you to stay and personally watch Linus."

I rubbed my forehead, hating that he was right. "I need a break."

"A break?" Ridley asked in confused shock, and for a few seconds he appeared speechless. "You're a workaholic. What nonsense are you going on about?"

"I'm not asking to do nothing," I clarified. "I need a break from here. I just got done breaking in the last changeling, and that went fine, but I was stuck here for weeks and weeks. And then I just got to go out after Linus, and I had to turn around and come back."

He ran a hand along the dark stubble of his cheek. "What's going on?" he asked, and his tone softened. "What happened?"

"Nothing."

"Bryn." From across the desk, he gave me a look—one that said he knew me too well to let me bullshit him.

Instead of replying, I turned away from him. I twisted the silver band around my thumb and looked over at the bulletin board, eyeing the wanted posters.

Any fugitive who was still at large had their picture up, even if they'd escaped years ago. The incident with Viktor Dålig had to have happened fifteen years ago, but his picture was still prominently displayed at the top of the wanted section. The bright red font for "wanted" had faded to more of a dull pink, but his picture was still clear and visible. The heavy dark black beard, his cold eyes, even the scar that ran across his face from just above his left eye down to his right cheek.

There were two new posters that popped out on crisp white paper with fresh ink. An updated one for Konstantin Black, and a brand-new one for Bent Stum. Even in his picture, Konstantin seemed to be smirking at me, like he knew he'd gotten away with what he'd done.

But his eyes caught me. Even in black-and-white, they appeared livelier than when I had seen them in real life. It was the look he'd had when I'd last seen him standing in the crowd in Chicago, and the same look he'd had when I saw him standing over my father. And it was his eyes that had haunted my dreams last night, but I struggled to push that back, refusing to replay it in my head again, the way I had been all morning.

"Bryn," Ridley repeated, since I hadn't answered him.

Reluctantly I turned back to look at him. "I just ran into Astrid Eckwell in the library at the palace."

Ridley shrugged, like he didn't know why that would bother me. "Astrid's an idiot."

"Yeah, I know."

"You never let her get to you."

I inhaled deeply. "I usually don't."

"What'd she say this time that got under your skin?"

"Nothing, really. It was just the same old crap." I started bouncing my leg up and down, needing to do something to relieve my agitation. "And usually I'm over it. But this time it was really hard for me to not punch her in the face."

"Well, I commend you on not doing that. Because that would've been very bad."

"I know. I think I've just been cooped up here too long." I shifted in my chair. "This winter is taking forever to end. And the King is being ridiculous. I should be out in the field, and you know it, Ridley."

"Shh." He glanced toward the open door. "Lower your voice. You don't want the new cadets to hear."

"I don't care who hears," I said, nearly shouting.

Ridley went over to the door and peeked out in the hall, then closed the door. Instead of going back to his chair, he came over to me. He leaned on the desk right in front of me, so he was almost at eye level.

He wore a button-down shirt and vest, but he'd skipped a tie today, so I could see his necklace. It was a thin leather strap with an iron rabbit amulet—his present upon becoming Rektor. The amulet lay against the bronzed skin of his toned chest, and I lowered my eyes.

"I know you're pissed off, but you don't need to get in a shitload of trouble because an overzealous tracker-in-training tattles on you to the wrong person," he said, his voice low and serious.

Technically, speaking any ill of the King was a punishable offense. My saying that he was ridiculous wouldn't exactly get me executed, but I could end up stuck cleaning toilets in the palace, or demoted, even. The changelings were assigned to us based on our rank, and in terms of trackers, I was third from the top.

"You're right." I sighed. "I'm sorry."

"Don't apologize to me. Just don't act stupid because you're mad."

"I'm more valuable out in the field." I stared up into Ridley's dark eyes, imploring him to understand. "And I feel so useless here. I'm not doing anything to help anyone."

"That's not true. You're helping Linus. You know how lost and bumbling changelings are at first."

"He needs someone, yeah, but it doesn't have to be *me*," I countered. "I'm not actually needed here."

"I need you," Ridley said, with a sincerity in his tone that startled me. In the depths of his eyes I saw a flicker of that heat I'd seen before, but just as I'd registered it, he looked away and cleared his throat. "I mean, there's a lot going on right now. Royalty from all over are on their way right now. You're a big asset here. I wouldn't be able to handle everything without your help."

"Anyone can do what I'm doing," I said, deciding to ignore the heat I'd seen in his eyes. "I think that's why Astrid got to me. I already feel like I'm being useless, and she always does such a great job of reminding me how much better than me she is."

He shook his head. "You know that's not true."

I opened my mouth to argue that, but the door to the office opened and interrupted me. I looked back over my shoulder to see Simon Bohlin. Out of habit, I sat up straighter in my chair and tried to look as nonchalant as possible. I still wasn't completely sure how to act around him.

We'd broken up a few months ago after going out for nearly a year. I'd gone against my own rule about not dating other trackers because Simon was funny and cute and didn't seem all that intimidated by the fact that I could kick his ass.

But I don't know why it still felt so awkward. We hadn't even been that serious. Well, I thought we hadn't been serious. Then Simon dropped the *l*-word, and I realized that we wanted two vastly different things out of the relationship.

Simon had been walking into the office, whistling an old tracker work song under his breath, but he stopped short when he saw me.

"Sorry," Simon said. From underneath his black bangs, his

eyes shifted from me to Ridley. "Am I interrupting something?"

"No." Ridley stood up and stepped away from me. "Not at all."

"I just came in to get my orders for the new changeling," Simon said.

"Right. Of course." Ridley walked around to the other side of his desk, shifting around stacks of paper in search of the file for Simon.

"You're leaving?" I asked, flashing Simon the friendliest smile I could manage.

He nodded. "Yeah."

"When?"

"Um, I think later today," Simon said.

Ridley found the file and held it up. "That is the plan."

"So you're not staying for the party?" I asked.

Simon shook his head, looking disappointed. "Not unless it's in the next couple hours."

Then it hit me. Simon was a good tracker, but he'd always enjoyed the parties and balls here more than I had.

I stood up. "We could trade."

"Trade what?" Simon asked cautiously.

Ridley sighed. "Bryn. No."

"I'm supposed to stay here and shadow Linus Berling, but you were always so great with the changelings." I walked over to Simon, getting so excited by the idea that I forgot to feel strange around him. "You could get him all settled and act as his bodyguard, and I could go out into the field."

"I . . ." Simon hesitated. "I mean, I don't know if that's okay."

"But would you?" I asked before Ridley could object. "I mean, if it was okay."

"Why? What's going on?" Simon asked.

"Bryn's just going through a case of cabin fever, and it's making her act crazy," Ridley explained as he walked over to us.

"I'm not acting crazy," I insisted and stared hopefully up at Simon. "So, Simon, are you in?"

"Why don't you come back in, like, half an hour, and we'll have this all straightened out?" Ridley asked and started ushering Simon to the door.

Simon glanced back at me, then shrugged noncommittally as he left. Once he'd gone, Ridley closed the door. He turned around and leaned back on it, letting out a long sigh as he looked over at me.

"What I'm saying makes sense. It works," I insisted, already steeling myself for his protests.

"Sit down." He motioned to the chair.

He went over to the two chairs sitting in front of his desk and turned them so they faced each other. After he sat down, he gestured to the other one, so I went over and sat down across from him. He leaned forward, resting his elbows on his legs, and by the gravity in his eyes, I knew this conversation wasn't going the way I'd hoped it would.

"Do you want me to be completely honest with you?" he asked.

"Always."

"What the hell are you thinking?" Ridley asked with such force and incredulity that it surprised me.

"I . . ." I fumbled for words. "What?"

"Okay, truthfully, yes, I probably can pull some strings and make it happen. If you really wanted to get out of here, I could switch your assignment with Simon's."

I waited a beat, and he didn't add the *but*, so I figured I'd have to ask. "But you're not gonna do it?"

"No, I will," Ridley said. "If that's what you really want. And if you really want to blow your chance at ever becoming a Högdragen."

I lowered my eyes, and when I tried to argue against it, my words came out weak. "It won't hurt my chances."

"This is the first time the King ever gave you a direct order, and it's a very simple one. And you can't follow it." Ridley sighed and leaned back in his chair. "You're already fighting an uphill battle to be a guard because you're half Skojare, not to mention there are only a handful of women in the Högdragen."

I gritted my teeth. "I know what I'm up against."

"I know you know that," Ridley said, sounding exasperated. "Do you even still want to be on the Högdragen?"

"Of course I do!"

He shook his head, like he wasn't sure he believed me anymore. "Then explain to me what the hell is going on with you right now."

"What do you mean?" I asked, but I refused to meet his gaze.

"You know this could ruin your shot at the one thing you

want most in the world, and yet you're still fighting against it. Why do you want to get out of here so badly?"

I clenched my jaw and found it hard to speak around the lump growing in my throat. "I let him go," I said, and my words came out barely above a whisper.

"Konstantin Black?" he asked like he already knew the answer.

I looked away, staring at the wall and struggling to keep my anger under control. Tentatively, Ridley reached out and placed a hand on my knee. It was meant to be comforting, and the warmth of his skin through the fabric of my jeans was just enough to distract me.

"You did the right thing," Ridley told me. "You did what you needed to do to protect Linus."

"Maybe I did." I finally turned to look at him, letting my cool gaze meet his. "Or maybe I could've snapped his neck right then, and we'd all be rid of him forever."

If he saw the ice and hatred in my eyes, he didn't let on. His expression was filled only with concern, and he didn't even flinch at my wishful thinking about murder.

"If you really believe that, then why didn't you kill him?" Ridley asked reasonably.

"The truth?" I asked, and suddenly I felt afraid to say it aloud. But with Ridley staring at me, waiting, I knew I had to finally admit it. "I don't think he wanted to kill my father."

"What? What are you talking about?"

"When I walked in on him, standing over my father with his sword bloodied, he apologized and said that he was bound to something higher than the kingdom," I tried to explain.

"So you think he . . . what?" His forehead scrunched, and he shook his head. "I don't understand."

"There was a look in his eyes. Regret." I thought back to Konstantin, and the pain I'd seen in his smoky eyes. "No, it was remorse."

"Remorse?" Ridley sat up a bit straighter. "You think you saw remorse in his eyes? So, what? You just forgave him?"

"No. *No*," I said adamantly. "I'll never forgive him. But I think he regretted what he did, even before he did it. And it doesn't make sense. I need to know why he did it."

"He could just be insane, Bryn," Ridley said, going to the only reason that anybody had ever been able to come up with for Konstantin's behavior. "Your dad had never had a cross word with him, and then one night Konstantin just snapped."

"No. He's too smart, too calculated. And now with this attack on Linus . . ." I chewed the inside of my cheek as I thought. "It's all connected. He's plotting something."

"If he's still working toward some ultimate goal, then he doesn't regret it," Ridley pointed out. "If he felt genuine remorse, he should be looking for absolution, not trying to hurt more people."

"Not if someone else is pulling his strings," I countered. "And if someone is, I need to find out who it is."

"Konstantin might be an innocent pawn in all of this?" Ridley questioned doubtfully.

"No. I don't know what is motivating him, but he drew his sword against my father with his own hand. That fault lies entirely with him."

Konstantin may have come to regret what he'd done. He could even cry about it every night, but it didn't change the fact that he'd done it, and he knew exactly what he was doing. When I went into the Queen's office that night, he was preparing to finish the job as I watched.

Regardless of what guilt he might feel or what reason might drive him, Konstantin had still acted of his own accord.

"You want to leave here so you can find him and hold him responsible," Ridley said.

"Yes." I looked up at him, pleading with him to let me go, to let me finish what Konstantin had started. "He needs to be brought to justice, and so does anyone else he's working with."

"Justice? Does that mean you'll drag them all back here? Or are you gonna kill them all?"

"Whichever one I need to do. But I'm not letting Konstantin get away again," I told him, and I meant it with all my heart. I'd never killed anyone before, but I would do whatever I needed to do.

Ridley seemed to consider this for a moment, then he pulled his hand back from my leg—leaving it feeling cool and naked without his warm touch—and he rubbed the back of his neck. "You can't go after him alone, and you can't go right now."

"Ridley—" I began, but he cut me off.

"I don't care if you think Linus doesn't need you and the King is an idiot. You are needed here right now." Ridley held up his hand, silencing any more protests I might have before I could voice them. "At least for the time being. Once everyone is gone after the party, and Linus is settled in, if you still need to go on your personal vendetta, we can talk about it. We can make it happen."

"*We?*" I shook my head. "You don't have to be a part of this."

"But I am anyway." He lowered his head and exhaled deeply. When he looked up, his dark eyes met mine, and when he spoke, his voice was softer. "Stay."

"Is that an order?" I asked, but by the look in his eyes, I knew it wasn't.

"No. It's not," he admitted. "But stay anyway."

celebration

By the time I'd finished with Linus for the evening, it was nearly eight o'clock. After my meeting with Ridley, I'd wanted to spend as much time as I could prepping Linus. The next few days were going to be filled with overwhelming madness for the new changeling, and I needed to set my personal feelings aside to do my job.

I ran home just long enough to grab Ember's present, and then I made the trek to her place as quickly as I could. The cottage Ember lived in with her parents was over a mile away from the palace, nestled against the wall that surrounded Doldastam, separating us from the Hudson Bay.

The farther I went, the farther apart the houses were. Near the palace, the cottages and even some of the smaller Markis and Marksinna's mansions were practically stacked on top of each other. But at Ember's house, there was room enough for a small pasture with a couple angora goats, and I heard them bleating before I could even see them.

A rabbit hutch was attached to the front of a house, and a fluffy Gotland sat near the edge of the run, nibbling a pint-sized bale of hay. When it saw me, it hopped over, and I reached my fingers through the wire cage and stroked the soft white fur.

The sun was beginning to set, and Ember's party had been under way for an hour. I knew that I couldn't put it off any longer, so I said good-bye to the rabbit, and I knocked on the front door.

"Bryn!" Annali Holmes—Ember's mother—opened the door and greeted me with a broad smile as the warm air from inside wafted over me. "Glad you could make it."

"Sorry I'm late. I was stuck at work."

I peered around to see who was in attendance, and the small cottage was nearly overflowing. Imagine Dragons played out of the radio loud enough that they hadn't heard me yet, and I spotted Ember laughing in the center of the room. She always fared much better with attention than I did.

A toddler with dark brown hair sticking up like a troll doll came darting past, trying to escape out the door before Annali scooped him up.

"This is Liam," she said, and the little boy stared up at me with wide eyes, looking too adorable for his own good, and then in a bout of shyness he buried his face in the blue folds of his grandma's faded dress. "He's my son's youngest."

"So they made it in okay?" I asked.

Ember's older brother, Finn, worked as a guard at the Trylle palace. The King and Queen of the Trylle had come to town for the anniversary party, and Finn came with them as their guard. Since his parents lived in Doldastam, he'd brought his wife and two kids along for a visit.

"Yeah, they arrived early this morning. Why don't you go in and say hello?" Annali stepped back and motioned toward the living room.

All the gifts were stacked on the dining room table, which had been pushed up against a wall to make more room. I snuck behind the people, nearly sliding up against the wall to add my gift to the pile. Mine was wrapped in butcher's paper and tied up with twine, appearing rather plain compared to some of the brightly colored packages.

I'd meant to get Ember something nice in Chicago, but since I had to make an abrupt departure, I'd had to grab something quick in Winnipeg while Linus and I waited for the train. It ended up being a sweater that I hoped she didn't hate, and a ring with a fox on it that I thought she'd actually like.

There had to be over twenty people crammed into the small living room and dining room. Most of them were fellow trackers, but a few were people Ember just knew from town. She was much more sociable than I was.

Tilda was here, of course, along with her boyfriend, Kasper Abbott. He was a few years older than her, with black curly hair and a carefully manicured beard. Last year, he'd been appointed to the Högdragen, and though he was a very low-ranking member, I'd already begun hitting him up for advice.

In the center of the room, Ember laughed brightly, and Finn stood next to his sister. Though this was just a casual family gathering, he was dressed in a tailored vest and slacks, just like every other time I'd seen him. He held a little girl in a frilly dress on his hip, her dark wild curls pulled into two pigtails.

Next to him was his wife, Mia, who appeared to be pregnant again. Her hands were folded neatly, resting on top of her swollen belly hidden underneath her fitted emerald dress.

"Bryn!" Ember squealed in delight when she finally saw me. "You made it!"

She slid past her brother. When she reached me, she looped her arm through mine, knowing that I would hide in the corners of the room unless she made me actually join the party. "A girl only turns seventeen once, you know, and she needs her best friend at the party."

I hadn't noticed until she was up close, but her eye shadow had a bit of a sparkle to it. Her sweater dress even had a few strategically placed sequins, adding an extra shimmer as well. Several braids twisted through her hair, and then it was pulled back in an updo.

"You remember Finn, right?" Ember pointed to him.

"We've met a few times," I reminded her. He managed to get up here a couple times a year for a visit, bringing his family with him as often as he could. I knew that he was a retired Trylle tracker who now worked as a royal guard, and was Ember's inspiration for joining the Kanin's tracker program.

"How are you, Bryn?" Finn asked, smiling at me.

There was something almost strikingly handsome about

him, and I noticed it more when he smiled. But he emoted so rarely, and no matter what happened he seemed to stand at attention. I respected him for his training and obvious skill in working as a guard, but he was so closed off.

After I'd first met him, I'd asked Ember if he was secretly an android, and I'd only been half joking. The scary part was that Ember told me he'd actually loosened up a lot since he'd gotten married. I'd have hated to meet him before, if this was him relaxed.

"I'm doing well, thank you." I smiled politely at him. "How are you?"

"Can't complain."

"When are we eating cake?" the little girl asked.

"Not right now, Hanna," Finn told her, and that was about the only time I ever saw his expression soften. When he was interacting with his kids, he truly let his guard down.

"Here." Mia held out her arms for the little girl. "I'll take her and get her something. It's getting late for the kids." Hanna squealed in delight and practically jumped into her mother's outstretched arms.

"Sorry about that," Finn said, smoothing down his vest after Mia carried Hanna away to the kitchen. "She gets excited."

"Who can blame her? Everyone gets excited about birthday cake," Ember said. "My mom makes the *best* cake. She uses blueberries as the sweetener, and it's to die for."

Kanin, and really trolls in general, had an aversion to sugar, except for fruit. We didn't have much of a stomach for foods that weren't all natural, nor were we big into red meat. Most of our food was produced in Doldastam, thanks to special "green-houses."

We had a few gardeners that worked to keep fresh produce and wine year-round, and to cultivate flowers that could bloom in the snow. They used psychokinetic abilities to work against the harsh winters of the subarctic, and it took half a dozen of them to keep the garden up and running.

Kasper asked how to change a song, and Ember offered me an apologetic glance before dashing off to help. That left me standing awkwardly with her brother.

"So . . . are you going to be at the anniversary thing tomorrow?" Finn asked.

I nodded. "Yeah. I'm helping a new changeling adapt. But I would probably be there anyway, because of the added security. We should all be there tomorrow."

"That makes sense." He lifted his eyes, surveying the room of people chatting with one another. "Are they all Högdragen? That's what you call it, right?"

"No, most of them aren't." I turned and pointed to where Kasper stood next to Ember, going through her iPod. "Only Kasper is."

Tilda saw us pointing at her boyfriend, so she made her way over to where Finn and I were talking, and relief washed over me as Tilda came to rescue me from awkward party conversation as she had a hundred times before. I liked Finn well enough, but I doubted that the two of us could talk comfortably for very long.

"Did you say something about Kasper?" Tilda asked when

she reached us. It felt warm in the house—at least to me, after walking the mile here—but her dress left her well-toned arms bare, and she rubbed at them absently.

"I was just telling Finn that Kasper's on the Högdragen," I explained.

"That's true." Tilda smiled proudly as she looked back at her boyfriend.

"I've always been curious. How does the Högdragen work?" Finn asked "The Trylle don't have that."

I shook my head. "How do you protect the royalty?"

"Most trackers pull double duty as guards, and when they retire from tracking, many of them guard at the palace." He looked down at me. "It's like how you're working at the party tomorrow."

"I have basic training, but trackers aren't in combat that often. And we're not trained to work together, if there were an invading army," I countered. "The Högdragen have all kinds of specialized training."

"How often do you really have an invading army?" Finn asked. "When was the last time anyone's attacked you guys?"

"That's because they know how good we are. We're the only tribe that has a real army to speak of," Tilda added, bristling a bit. She held her head up higher, making her taller than Finn. "Nobody is equipped to go up against us."

"What about the business with someone going after the changelings?" Finn asked, undeterred.

I looked at him sharply. "What do you know about it?"

He pursed his lips and shook his head. "Not much. We've

heard rumblings back in Förening, and Ember mentioned a few things to me."

I glanced over at Tilda, wondering if I should say anything. Her gray eyes were hard, and her lips were pursed together in an irritated pout. If it were her choice, she wouldn't tell Finn anything. Not just because of his comments about the Högdragen—Tilda preferred to keep private business private. Ember was a bit of a gossip, which was why she'd become closer to me than she had with Tilda. I had a higher tolerance for that kind of thing.

"I'm not a gossip at the market," Finn said, sensing our unease. "I'm a guard, working with an allied tribe. Discretion is something I'm well versed in."

He had a point, so I relaxed a bit. Besides, he was Ember's brother, and she trusted him.

"As of right now, there is no business with any changelings," I told him matter-of-factly. "Two men went after one of our high-ranking Markis. That's all we know, and as far as the King and Queen are concerned, it was an isolated attack."

"And who stopped it?" He narrowed his eyes at me. "It was you, wasn't it?"

"I was—" I started to answer him, but I happened to glance past him and saw Ember go over to answer a knock at the door, barely audible over the music and chatter of the party.

When she opened the door, she let in a draft of cold air, along with Juni Sköld and Ridley. Juni came in first, and Ember helped her slip off her long black jacket. Once Ember took their coats to put them away, Ridley put his hand on the small of Juni's back, and as they walked toward the party, he leaned over and whispered something in her ear.

I had seen Ridley with plenty of girls over the past years, but that was because I'd barged into his office without knocking and caught him kissing someone, or I'd gone to his place after work and found a girl slinking out his door. This was the first time I'd seen him on an actual *date*.

"Bryn?" Tilda asked, leaning toward me. "You okay?"

"Yeah." I shook my head, clearing it, and then I looked back at Finn, forcing myself to keep my eyes on him and not wander to Ridley any longer. "As I was saying, I was tracking the changeling and prevented them from kidnapping him, yes."

"That's exactly my point." Finn folded his arms over his chest. "You're not a member of the Högdragen, and yet you were perfectly capable of fighting off two men without any of their training. Are they really necessary, then?"

"If anything, that's a testament to Bryn's work, not a condemnation of the guard," Ridley interjected. I looked over to see both him and Juni sidling up next to Tilda, joining our conversation.

"Ember really just invited everyone to this, didn't she?" I asked as pleasantly as I could and gave them a crooked smile.

He nodded and adjusted his narrow tie. "Apparently so."

"Ridley, this is Ember's brother, Finn," I said, making the introductions between the two of them. "Finn, this is the Rektor, Ridley. And this is . . ." I pointed to Juni, then feigned a memory lapse. "Sorry. I've forgotten your name," I lied, and Tilda gave me a peculiar look.

"Juni. Juni Sköld." She smiled, making a dimple on her smooth skin. "I went to tracker school years ago with Bryn and Tilda, but I flunked out, so it's no surprise that they've forgotten me."

"I'm sure Bryn didn't forget you," Ridley said, casting a look at me that I deftly avoided meeting. "She's just had a busy week."

"Well, it's nice to meet you both," Finn said, breaking the growing tension.

"Likewise," Ridley said. "So what were we talking about when I so rudely interrupted?"

"Finn doesn't understand the point of the Högdragen," Tilda said, filling him in with a hint of bitterness to her words. Her arms were crossed over her chest, and she turned to look at him as Ridley spoke, as if waiting for Ridley to tell him.

Ridley didn't seem that fazed by it, though. "The Trylle use trackers to guard the King and Queen, right?"

Finn nodded. "Correct."

"Wow, you guys don't have a guard?" Juni asked, sounding genuinely shocked. Her caramel eyes widened, and she put her hand to her chest, making her bracelets jingle. "That is so weird and kinda scary."

"How so?" Finn asked.

"The tracker program is hard, and I'm sure you understand that," Juni went on. "That's why I left. It's not for everyone. But the Högdragen is so much more than trackers are. They're the best of the best, trained to protect us from any number of dangers. I can't imagine feeling safe in Doldastam without them."

"You have the biggest tribe, though you are spread out quite a bit more than we are," Ridley said, elaborating on his date's position. "Förening is less than half the size of Doldastam. But you have the most money. You must have jewels and gems up the ass."

Finn scowled at Ridley's crassness. "I don't think I would use those exact words, but our wealth is well known."

"So why aren't you guarding it?" Ridley asked.

"We are," Finn persisted. "We just don't have a fancy name or a special program for it."

"I don't understand what your issue is with the Högdragen," Tilda said, unwilling to let his disdain for the guard go. She knew what the guard meant to both her boyfriend and me, and Tilda was fiercely protective when she felt people she cared about were being slighted. "Ember's talked about you. I know how important your sense of duty is to your people."

"It is," Finn agreed. "I'm not against the work you all do, but it seems to me that the Högdragen is just another form of elitism, just another class in the system that separates everyone."

Ridley's expression hardened. "We may not have fought wars recently, but we've prevented our share of violence. Viktor Dålig led an attack against the King fifteen years ago that resulted in four men dead." His words were solemn, the same way they were every time he mentioned Viktor Dålig's assault. "If it hadn't been for those men—the members of the classist system you don't understand—Viktor would've been successful, and he could've overthrown the entire kingdom."

Juni reached over, putting her hand on Ridley's arm and leaning into him. I bit my lip and looked away from them.

"You think trackers couldn't have stopped them just as well as members of the Högdragen?" Finn asked pointedly.

"I think that you have no idea what you're talking about," Ridley snapped, making Juni flinch next to him. "You've never served on the Högdragen, and you've never seen them in action. You grew up in a world where you were taught to honor and serve and never think for yourself, so you question anything that isn't exactly the same as you or the Trylle."

"That's not what—" Finn began, but Ridley cut him off.

"This conversation is taking a turn, and you seem like a very respectable gentleman. So, before I say something you'll regret, I'm going to go say hello to the birthday girl." He nodded curtly. "Excuse me." Then Ridley turned and walked away.

"It was very nice meeting you." Juni offered him a polite smile, then turned and went after Ridley, her long, dark brown locks bouncing as she hurried over to him.

"What did I say?" Finn asked, baffled by the hard edge in Ridley's voice. "I wasn't trying to be offensive or hurtful."

"Ridley's dad was on the Högdragen. He was one of the four men that Viktor Dålig killed," Tilda explained. "He died saving the kingdom."

unrequited

F inn apologized for saying anything that might've offended anyone, and I stayed and talked with him and Tilda a bit more, though both of them were careful not to bring up the guard anymore. Mostly Finn just talked about his home, since Tilda seemed strangely interested in what it was like raising a family while working as a tracker.

But how Finn managed to juggle taking care of two kids and his workload wasn't all that interesting to me, and I let my attention wander. Usually—and rather unfortunately—I kept finding my gaze landing on where Ridley and Juni seemed to be enjoying themselves.

No matter when I looked over, she always seemed to be laughing at something. She had to be one of the most cheerful people I'd ever met, which was part of the reason she hadn't been suited for the tracker program. It wasn't that she wasn't tough enough, exactly—she'd just been too friendly, too kind for a job that required a lack of emotion.

When Ridley wrapped his arm around her waist, she leaned into him, laughing warmly, her dark lashes lying in a fan on her bronze skin. Her hair fell down her back in long dark waves, and her dress hugged the full curves of her hips and chest beautifully.

She almost seemed to glow with happiness, a Kanin ability and one of the reasons why she'd had to leave the tracker program. Most of the Kanin who had the skin-changing ability would only blend in with their surroundings when they were distressed, but hers made her radiate when she was happy, and it simply darkened when she was upset. Despite her best efforts, she'd never been able to get it under control, and it had become a detriment.

So I understood exactly why Ridley had invited her here as his date. She may not have been suited to be a tracker, but in every other way, Juni was the perfect Kanin girl.

A painful twisting sensation spread through my chest, and I couldn't stand to watch them anymore. I wanted to make my escape, but on my way to the door Ember intercepted me, insisting that I stay for just a bit longer. But then Tilda—sensing my distress—provided a distraction for Ember and whisked her away so they could dance together to an Ellie Goulding remix.

It was Ember's birthday, so I could hardly go against her wishes, but I needed a break. I went upstairs, and at the end of the hall, heavy French doors led out to a small balcony. I'd left my coat downstairs, but that was just fine.

Pulling my sweater sleeves down over my hands, I leaned against the wrought-iron railing that ran around the balcony. I had no reason to be jealous of Juni. It didn't affect me at all that she was perfect. She was a wonderful, beautiful, nice person, and I had no reason to wish her ill.

In fact, I should be happy that she was apparently dating Ridley, since he'd always been good to me. He'd been nothing but kind, loyal, and supportive to me, and he deserved the same in return. Yes, he had done his fair share of philandering, but Juni was just the right girl to get him to settle down. And nothing about that should make me feel even slightly bad.

And yet . . . it did. It hurt so bad, I found it difficult to breathe.

Below me, goats were bleating in the moonlight, their pleas like those of a lovelorn suitor. I watched them nibbling at the blades of grass bravely poking through the snow, and I refused to acknowledge my feelings. They didn't make any sense, so I just pushed them away.

"Romeo, Romeo, wherefore art thou, Romeo?" I said to the goats, as if speaking to them would ease their loneliness.

"It is the east, and Juliet is the sun," Ridley said from behind me, startling me so much I nearly leapt off the balcony.

I'd left the French doors open, and I turned around to see Ridley standing in the doorway, the curtains billowing around him as the icy wind blew past.

"The balcony is actually facing the north," I told him once I'd found my voice.

"So it is. That would make you . . . Polaris?" Ridley surmised. He walked out on the balcony and closed the doors behind him.

"What are you doing up here?" I leaned on the railing again, so I wouldn't have to look at him.

"I came up here to shut the doors, because Ember's mom was complaining of a cold draft coming downstairs."

I grimaced. "Sorry. I meant to close the doors."

"But the real question is, what are you doing up here?" Ridley asked. He rolled down the sleeves of his shirt and folded his arms over his chest, trying to warm himself. "It's freezing out here."

"It's not that bad." I shrugged. "I just needed a breather."

"From what?"

I said nothing, preferring to stare out into the night rather than attempt to explain what I was feeling. He let it go, and we both stood in silence for a few minutes. Even the goats had fallen silent, and the only sound was the wind blowing through the trees and the faint music from the party below us.

"Did you know that I'm the oldest person here?" Ridley asked.

I thought about it, then shook my head. "Ember's parents are older than you."

"Now I feel much better." He gave a dry laugh. "I probably shouldn't have come here."

"Why not?" I looked at him from the corner of my eye.

He shook his head. "I'm older than the guy that has, like, a dozen kids," he said, referring to Finn.

"I think he only has two kids, and another on the way," I corrected Ridley.

"Still. That's *a lot* of kids for someone his age. He's, like, twenty-four, right?" He looked back down at the balcony and absently kicked a clump of snow stuck to the wood. "That's too young to have that many kids." Then Ridley looked up over at me. "I mean, isn't it?"

"Maybe." I shrugged, unsure of where the conversation was going, which only made me feel more flustered than I already did. "But I don't know what that has to do with you not coming to the party."

"I don't know. I'm just feeling old, I guess." He leaned his head back, staring up at the stars, and his breath came out in a plume of white fog. "I'm having a bit of an existential crisis lately."

"What do you mean?"

"Do you think you'll ever settle down?" Ridley asked, and I was grateful that he was still looking at the sky, so he couldn't see the startled—and probably terrified—expression on my face.

"You mean like get married and have kids?" I asked, buying myself some time until I figured out how I wanted to answer. "Or retire?"

"Both."

"No. Never," I said firmly, and at that moment it felt painfully true.

I would never retire, I knew that with every fiber of my being, but it wasn't until just now that I realized that love was off the table for me too. As my brief romance with Simon had proven, I didn't have the time or the inclination for a relationship. My career would always come first—as it should.

And hopefully that would put the final nail in the coffin of whatever I was feeling for Ridley. Because it didn't matter how I felt or whether he was with Juni or not. I would never be with Ridley. I had more important matters to tend to, and getting involved with my boss would only complicate and ruin everything.

"Never is pretty final," Ridley commented rather grimly.

"I know."

"I used to think that way," he admitted. He rested his arms on the railing beside me, leaning against it, and his elbow brushed up against mine. I could've pulled my arm away so I wouldn't be touching him, but I didn't.

"You are retired," I pointed out.

"No, I meant about getting married. I thought I'd never do it." He paused, letting the silence envelop us. "But now I'm reconsidering."

I swallowed hard and scrambled to think of something supportive to say. It took me far too long, but finally I managed, "Well, Juni seems nice."

"Yeah, she is." Then he said it again, as if convincing himself. "She's very nice."

"And beautiful," I added. "Stunning, even."

Ridley laughed softly at that. "Are you crushing on my date?"

"No. I'm just . . ." Just what? Trying to convince myself that I was happy for him? I didn't have anything, so I let it hang in the air.

"Did you really not remember her?" Ridley asked. "I mean, you guys are about the same age and went to school together, and there aren't *that* many people in town."

"No, of course I remembered her. Her name just slipped my mind," I lied.

"You have had a lot to worry about lately." His tone shifted from playful to thoughtful. "Is that what you were doing out here?"

"What?" I glanced over at him.

"Figuring out how you're going to exact your revenge on Konstantin?"

"Something like that," I muttered, feeling angry at myself that that wasn't actually what I'd been doing.

I *should* have been doing that, but instead I was stupidly and childishly trying not to think about how handsome Ridley looked tonight and the way his hair curled more at the end of the day, when the gel couldn't fight it any longer, and how the stubble darkened his jaw in a way that made me want to touch it, to feel it like sandpaper against my cheek if he leaned in for a kiss, and how badly I wished he were slipping his strong arm around my waist and whispering in my ear instead of Juni's.

"You should clue me in on your plans," Ridley said.

I looked at him sharply, terrified for a second that he'd been able to read my thoughts, but then I realized that he was talking about my plans for Konstantin. "Why? So you can talk me out of them?"

"No. I want to help." He turned to face me, putting his hand on the railing so his fingers brushed against mine. The metal felt icy cold, and his fingers felt like delicious fire against mine, radiating all through me. "I meant what I said earlier. I'm part of this too, and I don't mean just because I'm your boss. I know what this guy did to you and what he did to your family. I want to help you catch him."

It was too dark out for me to really see his eyes, but I could feel the heat from them, the new intensity I'd begun noticing when he looked at me sometimes, and it made my heart forget how to beat properly.

I looked away from him, unable to deal with the way he was looking at me, the way he made me feel, or even how close he was to me. His fingers on mine were cooling against the iron railing, but that didn't stop the heat from coursing through my veins.

And suddenly I couldn't stand it. I didn't want to be around him, making me feel a way that I refused to feel.

I stepped back from the railing, pulling my hand away from his. "Thank you. But right now my only plans are helping Linus get ready and surviving the anniversary party tomorrow night." I motioned to the door behind me. "Which means that I probably should be getting home to get some sleep."

"Good call. I should be heading out soon too."

I took a step backward, still facing him like I was afraid he would attack me if I turned away, and I reached behind me, fumbling for the door handle. Ridley moved closer. The balcony wasn't that big, so it only took a step and he was right in front of me, staring down at me. The light was coming through the glass doors, illuminating his face, and he appeared breathtakingly handsome.

The scent of his cologne blended perfectly with the winter air around us, making him smell tantalizingly clean and crisp, and I imagined that it came in a blue bottle with a name like Aspen or Evergreen. His chest nearly touched me, and for a second time I froze completely, terrified that he would kiss me and terrified that he wouldn't.

Then he reached around me, his arm pressing against my side in a way that made me involuntarily tremble.

"Let me get the door for you," Ridley said as he grabbed the door and opened it behind me. A subtle smile spread across his face, lightening it, but his eyes remained serious and fixed on me.

"Thank you," I mumbled, lowering my head so my hair would cover my face in case I was blushing. Then I slid under his arm and darted inside the house.

"If you wait a second, Juni and I could walk you home," he offered, and I couldn't imagine anything that sounded worse than walking home with him and his date after having a far too vivid fantasy about kissing him.

I had already turned away, hurrying down the hall before he could catch up to me. "Thanks, but I think I got it," I told him over my shoulder, and darted down the stairs.

As quickly as possible, I found Ember and, feigning a stomach bug, I made my excuses and escaped into the night. Just as I'd reached the door, struggling to pull on my jacket and thinking I'd made a clean escape, Juni found me.

"I'm sorry to hear you aren't feeling well." Juni looked genuinely sympathetic, which at that moment only succeeded in making me angrier. *Of course* she felt bad for me, when I was only leaving because my feelings for her date had just become all too apparent to me.

"I'll be fine," I insisted, and when she tried to say something more, I just turned and walked out the door. I think she was offering to walk me home when I shut the door in her face.

Instantly, I felt awful for being rude, and it wasn't like I'd wanted to be rude. I just needed space, a moment without Ridley clouding my thoughts and emotions, where I could breathe and focus on what really mattered.

By the time I reached my place, I was nearly jogging. Instead of going up to my loft apartment, I went to the barn below. Many of the Tralla horses neighed their greetings as I walked past them, but I was on a mission and I went down to the final stall, where "my" horse, Bloom, was waiting.

He wasn't really mine, because all of the horses belonged to the King and Queen. But Bloom and I had a special relationship. As soon as he saw me, he stretched his long neck out over the door and let out a delighted snort. He buried his snout in my hair, sniffing at me as I opened the stall door.

"I'm happy to see you too, buddy," I said, running my hands over him. His thick silver fur felt like satin under my fingers. I grabbed his bridle from the wall, and he happily let me slip it on over his head.

Usually I would brush him or pet him more, but I wanted to get out of here. I needed to feel the wind blowing through my hair. I led Bloom out of the stables, and he followed behind me, his massive hooves clomping loudly on the ground.

I didn't bother saddling him, but the reins were necessary. His long mane was far too soft and glossy to properly grip, and Bloom had a bad habit of stopping and starting quickly. That's why they rarely used him in the parades or to pull carriages, despite the fact that he was one of the most beautiful Tralla horses I'd ever seen. His body was an illustrious silver that shimmered in the light like platinum. Long bangs from his mane fell into his blue eyes, and his mane, tail, and the fur covering his hooves were a beautiful snowy white.

Bloom was a happy, friendly horse, but he loved speed. For an animal with his bulk and girth, one would think he'd be slow and clunky. But Bloom was light on his feet and astonishingly fast.

He headed over to the fence, walking in front of me, and he waited patiently until I came up beside him. I had to climb up on the wooden rails of the fence to climb onto Bloom, since he was so tall.

As soon as he felt me settled in, he lunged forward without waiting for a command from me. Fortunately, I knew that was how Bloom worked, so I already had the reins gripped tightly in my hands, and Bloom raced forward. The gate was open, so he ran out to the open road, running toward the wall.

That's where I usually rode him—along the wall that surrounded Doldastam. It gave him a long, clear path to run as fast as his thick legs would take us. And that was just what I needed. The wind stung my skin and made my hair whip back behind me, so I leaned forward, burying my face in Bloom's neck and urging him to go faster.

I closed my eyes, and it was just me and Bloom. Any thoughts about Ridley or Konstantin or anything else at all just fell away.

TWELVE

anniversary

The anniversary party was even worse than I'd feared.

An insane number of stuffy royals filled up the ballroom. The last time I'd seen this many people in the palace, it had been at the celebration after the Trylle had defeated the Vittra, and that hadn't exactly gone well.

At least that time it had been mostly regular Kanin folks, living it up and getting drunk. It actually had been a rather fun affair, until Konstantin Black ruined it. But this party was all Markis and Marksinna and Kings and Queens. Everyone dressed in their best, holding their heads up so they could look down on everyone else.

I was to spend the evening as Linus Berling's shadow, and that was both a curse and a blessing. He wasn't smug or pompous, so that was refreshing, but being stuck at his side meant that I had to spend far too much time listening to other royals issue backhanded compliments and mutter all sorts of derogatory remarks under their breath.

The dinner service began with King Evert and Queen Mina being seated at the main table in the center of the ballroom. All the guests waited in a procession to enter the ballroom, and as they did, the King's personal guard announced who they were and where they were from. Then they would greet the King and Queen and head to their own table.

As King Evert's cousins and closest friends, the Berlings were right at the front of the line—only entering behind King Loki and Queen Wendy of the Trylle; King Mikko, Queen Linnea, and King Mikko's brother Prince Kennet of the Skojare; and Queen Sara of the Vittra. The Omte Queen had declined to attend, but that was fairly standard for the Omte.

While Linus and his parents were seated beside the King, I had to stand behind Linus. I of course couldn't actually eat with them. I was only there to whisper in Linus's ear, telling him the names, titles, and tribes of the royals who were coming to greet us at the table.

Once all the guests were seated and dinner was served, I was allowed to duck away and sneak back to sit with other trackers. Ember, Tilda, Ridley, and Simon were all seated together at a round table in the corner, and Tilda had been nice enough to save a spot for me between her and Ridley. I didn't really want to sit next to him, at least not right now, but I didn't have a lot of options.

Tilda must've known that because she offered me an apologetic smile and a shrug of her shoulders.

For tonight, being a tracker was a much sweeter gig than being on the Högdragen. They all stood at attention in their black velvet uniforms around the edge of the room. Some were near the doors, some stood behind the royalty, and the rest just lined the walls.

We didn't even have to wear our uniforms tonight. I'd chosen a white and black lace dress with cap sleeves, not only because I thought it was beautiful, but because it allowed easy flexibility for kicking and punching. I actually found that short dresses were much less constraining in fights than jeans or tracker uniforms.

The Kanin trackers were only really here as backup, on the off chance one of the visiting tribes decided to start something tonight, while the Trylle and Vittra brought along trackers for the same reason. The Skojare didn't have trackers, but they had their own bodyguards, who were seated one table down from us.

"Is it weird for you?" Ember asked. She leaned on the table, but her eyes were looking over my head at the Skojare guards behind me.

A glass of red wine had been waiting at my place at the table, along with a plate of steamed vegetables, and I took a sip of the wine before answering her. "What do you mean?"

"Not being the only blonde here anymore," Ember said, and though I knew she didn't mean anything by it, I still bristled a little.

"She's not the only one. Her mom is blond too," Tilda reminded her.

"It's kind of nice, actually," I admitted and set my glass back on the table. "Just blending in with everyone else."

I glanced over at the Skojare. They ranged from nearly albino in complexion, with porcelain skin and platinum hair, to pale beige and golden, closer to my and my mother's appearance. But even looking around the room, it was a veritable rainbow of trollkind.

The Kanin actually had the darkest complexions of all the trolls, with the Trylle, the Vittra, and the Omte looking fairer in comparison. I'd never been able to even remotely blend in with the Kanin, but for the first time in a long while I didn't stand out like sore thumb.

"Really?" Ridley cocked his head and looked over at me, while I stared down at my plate of food and stabbed at a bit of broccoli. "I thought you always liked standing out in a crowd."

"Just because I always do doesn't mean that I like it," I told him flatly.

"I know you hate it, but I've always loved your hair." Ember reached across the table, gently touching a lock of hair that hung free from the updo I'd put it in. "It's beautiful, and it suits you."

"Are you petting her?" Tilda wrinkled her nose and pushed Ember's arm down. "She's not a cat, Ember."

As trackers, we were the lowest priority when it came to getting food, so when we had just gotten our second course—a squash stew that was meant to be served hot and thick but had grown cold and had been watered down to stretch it by the time it got to us—the Kings and Queens had already finished their meal.

King Evert stood up, clinking his glass to draw attention to himself. The chatter among the guests died down, replaced by the sound of chairs sliding against the wooden floor as everyone turned to look at him.

Most of the room was lit by candles on the tables and filling the massive iron chandeliers that hung from the ceiling, and while everyone could see, it was somewhat dim. But a bright electric bulb shone above the head table like a spotlight, and when the King stood up, the silver and diamonds on his tall crown glimmered like a disco ball. He wore the white suit he'd gotten married in, and it reminded me of what a Disney prince would wear, only with far more jewels and adornments, making it even more cartoonish than the actual cartoons.

"I want to thank you all for coming out tonight." Evert spoke loudly, so his voice would carry throughout the cavernous ballroom. I could hear it surprisingly well, even tucked away in the corner. "I know some of you have traveled great distances to be here with us, celebrating this special night with my wife and I, and we want to thank you all.

"I've never been much for public speaking, but I know my wife has a few words she'd like to say." He smiled and gestured to Queen Mina, who stood up next to him.

The bodice of her white gown was covered in so many diamonds I wasn't sure how she was able to move in it. Not to mention her jewelry. Her necklace was covered in such massive rocks, I wouldn't be surprised if it weighed ten pounds or more.

"As the King said, we both want to thank you all for joining us," Mina said. Her voice was softer, but she managed to project it well.

I'd heard her speak many times before, and I'd come to notice that when she talked in private, like in the meeting on Thursday, she had a normal Kanin accent. But when she spoke now, in front of larger crowds, she suddenly had a mild British accent, as if that would make her sound more proper somehow.

"Over the past five years, I have had the pleasure of being your Queen and Evert's bride." She smiled broadly when she spoke, and her hands were folded neatly over her abdomen. "And I can honestly say that these past five years have been far happier and far greater than I ever could've imagined.

"Growing up in Iskyla, I could only dream of a life like this," she went on. "For those of you that may be unfamiliar with Iskyla, it's a small Kanin village that's even farther north than Doldastam, so it's even colder and more isolated, if you can believe that."

This was met with a few chuckles, especially from other Kanins who knew of Iskyla. I'd never been there before, but most people hadn't. From what I'd heard about it, it didn't have any modern amenities like electricity or working phones. Plus, it was in the Arctic.

"My parents died when I was very young, but I still dreamed of getting out. I just knew that I was destined for something more," Queen Mina told us all emphatically. "Then, in the cold dead of winter five years ago, I was invited to a ball in this very room, as were so many of you, though I didn't expect much."

The ball Mina referred to had been actually very Cinderella-esque, as was much of her life, apparently. King Evert's predecessor, his cousin Elliot Strinne, had died rather suddenly with no wife or immediate heirs. This had led to a heated exchange among the royalty, with some lobbying for Elliot's young niece to take the throne, before the Chancellor finally decided that the then-twenty-three-year-old Evert would be more suited to rule the kingdom than a child.

After Evert had been King for ten years and still had no bride and no heirs, the leaders had begun to worry. They didn't want to put the kingdom in turmoil, the way it had been after Elliot's death. So they set up a ball where the eligible women were to come to meet the King, and that's how Mina met Evert.

"That night was like a fairy tale." Mina smiled and touched her husband's shoulder. "The instant I laid eyes on him, I was in love. Luckily for me, he felt the same way. Four short months later, we were wed. Every day since then has been the happiest day of my life, and I can only hope that the next five years of marriage will be just as magical as the first."

She beamed down at King Evert, giving him a look so sweet and adoring that it was almost uncomfortable to watch. And then, quietly, almost too quietly for us to hear, she said, "I am so grateful for you, my love."

Since that seemed to be the end of her speech, the crowd applauded warmly for her, and she offered us all a wide smile before sitting back down next to her husband.

"She's lying," Ridley said as he clapped halfheartedly for her. "She doesn't love him."

"Why do you say that?" Ember asked.

He shook his head and went back to spooning the now-freezing-cold stew. "Nobody loves anybody that much."

"And here you were going on and on about true love last night," I said, surprised by the bitter edge of my own words.

"Was I?" He lifted his head, resting his eye on me, and I quickly turned back toward my own stew. "I remember saying something about settling down, but nothing about true love."

"Same thing," I mumbled.

"I don't know. Some people love each other that much," Ember insisted. "I think the Trylle King and Queen are super into each other."

"I'm not saying that people don't fall in love. People fall madly in love with each other all the time. But that right there"—Ridley gestured behind him, toward where King Evert and Queen Mina were seated—"that was all an act."

"I think you're right," Tilda agreed, talking about the royalty in a way that was unusual for her. When I looked at her in surprise, she shrugged one shoulder simply and took a sip of her water. "Well, he is right. She was a small-town girl with big dreams, and marrying into money and royalty was her way to get what she wanted."

"That's all I'm saying." Ridley leaned back in his seat, a self-satisfied grin on his face. Since Tilda so rarely chimed in on matters like this, having her on his side seemed like a boon.

"Good for her, then," I replied glibly.

"Good for her?" Ember laughed. "You think it's good that she tricked the King?"

"She didn't trick him," I corrected her. "He needed a beautiful wife to bear him children, and that's what he got. Well, no kids yet, but she's still young. She wanted to make a better life for herself, and she found a way. Maybe not the way that you or I would've chosen, but it was one way to do it."

"Would you do that?" Ridley asked. "Would you marry someone you didn't love to advance your life or your career?"

"No, of course I wouldn't," I said.

"Would you even marry someone if you did love them?" he asked. I could feel his eyes on me, but I refused to look at him, preferring to finish my wine in big gulps.

Before I could answer, Evert announced that it was time for the dance, and waiters came out to start clearing the tables and moving them out of the way so there would be more room for people to dance.

Then I didn't have time to worry about Ridley's questions or the way his eyes seemed to look straight through me. I had to hurry and help the waiters take our plates away, and then I was on my feet with the other trackers, helping to stack chairs and push tables to the side of the room.

But that was just as well, because I had no idea how I would answer.

impropriety

At the end of the ballroom, a small orchestra played a mix of contemporary human music along with Kanin folk songs. A singer accompanied them, and she had a pristine voice with an operatic range. The songs would segue seamlessly from the Beatles to a Kanin love ballad, sung entirely in its original low Swedish, and then would switch to a beautiful rendition of Adele.

It was still early in the evening, so the dance floor was relatively full. Most couples swayed to the music, but some glided across the floor with the elegant, practiced steps that came from years of training. The royalty, especially those from Doldastam, lived pampered, sheltered lives with much free time on their hands, so many of them took up ballroom dancing to fill the time.

As the newest returning changeling and one of the highest-ranking Markis, Linus attracted a lot of attention, and his dance card was full. While he could be clumsy, and did trip over his own feet a few times, his dance partners didn't seem to mind.

I watched him from the sidelines, ready to swoop in if he needed me, but he seemed to be doing okay on his own. His dance moves might have been lacking, but he made up for it by being nice and rather charming, in an unassuming kind of way.

Tilda and Ember didn't have any charges to watch out for, so they were free to hang out with me, standing along the wall at the edge of the dance floor. Tilda wore a short flapper-esque dress that showed off her long legs, and as she swayed, the silver tassels would swing and bounce along with her. Even though we were supposed to be standing at attention at the side of the ballroom, Tilda couldn't help herself. She loved to dance far too much. With her eyes closed, her head tilted back slightly, letting her long brown hair flow behind her, she moved gracefully in time with the music.

"I wish I could dance," Ember lamented.

Tilda opened her eyes and glanced down at Ember. "Just dance. It's fun even if you're alone."

Ember stared forlornly out at the crowded dance floor. "When I was a kid, all I wanted to do was go to the palace and attend one of these balls. And now that I am, I'm stuck at the side, unable to join in or have fun."

"You've joined in. You got to have a nice meal, you got all dolled up, and you're listening to the music," I pointed out, trying cheer her up. "You're a part of it."

"Maybe," Ember said doubtfully, but then she shook her head. "No, you're right. I guess I just spent too much time daydreaming about dancing with Prince Charming. Or Princess Charming, as it were."

As the song ended, Linus politely extracted himself from the arms of a lovely but clingy Marksinna in her early teens, and he came over to where I was standing with Ember and Tilda. His cheeks were flushed, but he had a goofy, lopsided grin plastered on his face.

"How are you doing?" I asked Linus as he reached us.

"Good. I mean, I think I am." He ran a hand through his dark hair and his smile turned sheepish. "Did I seem to be making any mistakes?"

"No, you look like you're doing really good," I assured him. "Are you having a nice time?"

"Yeah. It's a little weird dancing with so many strangers, especially when I've never been that into dancing, but most of the people are nice." He glanced back toward where his parents were seated at a table. "And my parents seem really proud."

"They are," I said.

Linus turned back to me, his eyes twinkling. "Are you having fun? You look kinda left out here on the sidelines."

"I'm having fun." I smiled to prove it to him.

"Why don't you come dance with me?" Linus suggested. "Cut loose for a minute."

"Thank you for asking, but I don't think I should." I demurred as graciously as I could. "It wouldn't be proper."

"Not even for one song?" His eyebrows lifted as he stared down hopefully at me, making him appear more like an excited puppy than a teenage boy.

I shook my head ruefully. "I'm afraid not."

"I'll dance with you," Ember piped in and stepped closer to him.

"Ember," I admonished her, but Linus had already extended his arm to her.

She waved me off as she looped her arm through his. "It's one song. It'll be fine."

"That's the spirit." Linus grinned and led her out to the dance floor.

I looked to Tilda for support, hoping she would back me up even though Ember had already disappeared into the crowd and it'd be too late to stop her. But Tilda just shrugged, still swaying her hips along to the music.

"Let them have their fun," she said, smiling as she watched them twirl clumsily away from us.

"Ember is such a rebel sometimes." I stood on my tiptoes, craning my neck in an attempt to keep my eyes on Linus and Ember as they weaved in between other couples.

"They're fine," Ridley said. I'd been so busy watching Linus and Ember that I hadn't noticed Ridley come up beside me. "I doubt anyone will even notice her dancing. Everyone's having fun, and most of the royals are getting drunk on wine."

"Linus actually asked Bryn to dance first, but she declined," Tilda told him, ratting on me even though I knew I'd done the right thing.

She had a mischievous glint in her eyes—parties like this always brought it out in her. While she hadn't had anything to drink tonight, Tilda seemed to get drunk on good music and good dancing. Her relaxed elegance made me feel so rigid in comparison.

"You probably should've said yes. He could actually use a lesson in dance moves." Ridley motioned to where Linus stumbled over Ember's foot, but she helped him keep his balance.

"In private I'll give him a few pointers," I said. "But it wouldn't be proper here. He's my charge. I shouldn't do anything that might blur the lines of professionalism."

"I love it when you talk clean to me, quoting training manuals like sonnets," Ridley teased, but I found his usual flirtation off-putting since I didn't know how to respond.

Seeing him with Juni last night forced me to realize that I had some type of feelings for him. That left me unsure of how to act around him, so I'd rather be around him as little as I possibly could. At least until the feelings went away. And they had to eventually, right?

"There's nothing wrong with being professional," I told him coolly with eyes straight ahead, staring at the dance floor.

"There's nothing wrong with dancing either." Ridley moved so he was standing in front of me, forcing me to look at him. "Come on. Why don't you dance with me?"

"We're working," I replied quickly, making him smirk.

"It's a party, and everyone's dancing. And as the Rektor, I am your boss." He held out his hand to me.

"So this is an order?" I asked, eyeing his outstretched hand and hating how tempted I was to take it.

"If I say no, will you still dance with me?" he asked.

Tilda elbowed me gently in the side. "Just go dance, Bryn."

Without thinking, I reached out and took his hand. His hand easily enveloped mine, and it sent flutters through my stomach, which I tried to suppress. His smile widened, and as he led me away, I glanced back over my shoulder at Tilda, who smiled reassuringly at me.

Once we'd lost ourselves in the sea of well-dressed trolls, Ridley stopped and I put my hand on his shoulder. I was careful to keep some distance between us, but when he put his hand on the small of my back, he pulled me closer to him.

"This isn't so bad, right? Nobody's gawking at us or chasing us with pitchforks," Ridley said, smiling down at me as we danced in time with a dramatic cover of "Love Is Blindness."

"Not yet, anyway," I admitted.

I glanced around just to be sure we weren't getting any dirty looks, but nobody really seemed to be paying us any mind. But I supposed that, based on the formal way both Ridley and I were dressed, and the fact that there were so many royals here from other kingdoms who didn't know each other, they didn't realize that we didn't belong here, dancing alongside them.

Ember spotted us through a break in the crowd, and her jaw dropped. Instinctively, I tried to pull away from Ridley, but his hand was unyielding and warm on my back, holding me to him.

"So what's going on with you?" Ridley asked, and when I looked up, his smile had fallen away and his dark eyes were strangely serious.

"Nothing's going on." I tried to brush him off with an uneasy smile.

"I feel like you're mad at me."

I hedged my answer and lowered my eyes. "Why would I be mad?"

"I don't know. But you've been giving me the cold shoulder all night." He paused. "You've barely even looked at me."

"It's not like I spend all my time staring at you," I said, finding it hard to look up at him even now.

"Bryn. You know what I mean," he insisted firmly, and I did.

I hadn't meant to put a wall between us, but I really didn't know how else to deal with things. He was apparently with Juni now, and even if he wasn't, he was still my boss, and a tracker getting romantically involved with a Rektor was definitely a bad move, one that could cost us both our jobs. It opened up too many possibilities for corruption, manipulation, and nepotism.

So there was no way Ridley and I could ever be together, even if he wanted to. Or even if *I* wanted to, and I didn't. Not really.

I finally willed myself to look at him, meeting his mahogany eyes, even though it made me flush with heat when I did. "I'm not mad at you. I promise."

"If I did something to upset you, you can tell me," he said in a low voice, distressed at the thought that he'd done something to hurt me. "That's, like, the foundation of our friendship. We're always honest with each other."

"I am," I lied as convincingly as I could.

"Good," Ridley said, not because he believed me, but because he didn't know how else to push me.

"Is this why you asked me to dance?" I asked, trying to lighten the mood. "So you could interrogate me?"

"No. I asked you to dance because I wanted to dance with you," he said simply. "You're a good dancer."

With that, he extended his arm and I stepped back away from him. Then he pulled me close, twirling me as he did, and I stopped with my back pressed against his chest. His arms were wrapped around me, and his breath felt warm on my neck.

We stayed that way for only a second, our hips swaying slightly, and my heart pounded so loudly I was terrified he could feel it, but I didn't want to pull away from him. I actually wanted to stay that way forever, with the orchestra swelling, and the singer reaching her crescendo as she warned about the blindness of love. Under the dim candlelight of a chandelier in a crowded ballroom, with Ridley's arms strong as they crossed over me, my body bound to his, I closed my eyes, wishing the moment would last forever.

But it was only a split second, and then he had my hand, and he spun me around again. This time, when he pulled me back into his arms, I extended my leg, the way the dance required. He dipped me down so low, my hair brushed against the floor, and my eyes stayed locked on his as he pulled me back up.

I stayed in his arms, my body pressed against his, feeling breathless and dizzy, and I knew it wasn't just from the dancing. I stared up at him, and I'd never wanted to kiss anybody as badly as I wanted to kiss him then.

But instead I found myself blurting out, "It's too bad Juni couldn't be here."

"Yeah." Ridley sounded out of breath himself, and he blinked, clearing his eyes of whatever had been darkening them. "Yeah, it is."

The song ended, so I pulled away from him and smoothed out my dress. I wanted to rush off the dance floor, retreating back in the shadows to stand with Tilda, but Ridley hadn't moved. He stood in front of me with a puzzled expression on his face.

"What?" I asked.

"Nothing." He tried to smile at me but it faltered. "Thanks for dancing with me."

Ridley turned and walked away, leaving me alone in the middle of the dance floor.

mission

Even though I hadn't drunk much at the anniversary party, I awoke the next morning feeling hung over. I would've been happy to spend the entirety of the day snuggled deep within the recesses of my blankets. It was barely after daybreak when Ember came pounding up the stairs to my loft and threw open the door.

"Unless my building is on fire, go away," I told her as I buried my head underneath the pillow.

"Don't be such a grump. I have good news." Ember hopped on the bed with such force, it bounced me up. When I landed, I peered at her skeptically. "I'm leaving."

"Why are you leaving?" I lifted the pillow from my head and rolled onto my back so I could look up at her. "And why is that good news?"

"I got my next assignment." She beamed at me. "I'm heading out to get a new changeling."

"Congratulations," I said, but thanks to my sleepiness it came out a bit weaker than it should've.

Like me, Ember preferred being out on missions to being cooped up here in Doldastam. So even though it would be less enjoyable for me to be stuck here without her, I was genuinely happy for her.

"Thanks. I just came to say good-bye, and then I have to get going."

"You're leaving right *now*?" I pushed myself up so I was sitting, and glanced at the alarm clock on my nightstand. "It's not even seven in the morning. When did you get the assignment?"

"Like, twenty minutes ago. Ridley called me to the Rektor's office and gave it to me," Ember said. "He did not look excited to be up this early. I think he drank too much wine last night."

"Wait." I rubbed my forehead, trying to clear my head. "None of this makes sense."

Usually we got our assignments a few days to a week before we left. It gave us time to go over the changeling's file and get to "know" them before we met them, and we got our travel arrangements in order, like booking hotels and plane tickets, if needed.

On top of that, it had only been a few days ago that the King and Queen had ordered all the trackers to stay in Doldastam until after all the guests had cleared out. Some of the guests were leaving tonight, but the majority of them weren't heading out until tomorrow morning.

So, barring some kind of emergency, I didn't know why they

would send out a tracker before Monday afternoon. It didn't make sense.

"Ridley said that the King had called him early this morning saying that they got a tip, and they needed someone to get this changeling in right away," Ember explained.

"Which changeling?"

Ember pursed her lips and gave me a hard look. "You know I can't tell you that. Our missions are confidential until after we return."

As a matter of privacy and safety, we were never allowed to tell anyone where we were going or who the changelings were. It was to prevent things like what had happened with Linus, as well as the fact that the royals didn't always want it getting around how well-off (or how not-so-well-off) their offspring had been in the human world.

"I know, I know." I waved it off. "But what was the King's tip? What's so important that he roused Ridley in the middle of the night to start organizing your mission?"

Ember opened her mouth like she wanted to say something, but she couldn't seem to find the words. And that's when it hit me. It was so obvious, I couldn't believe I didn't figure it out instantly. I blamed my sleep-deprived brain for it.

"Konstantin Black," I said.

"They don't know for sure." Ember rushed to ease my anxiety.

"This is ridiculous." I threw the covers off me and leapt out of bed, barely noticing how cold the wood floor felt on my bare feet as I stomped over to my wardrobe.

"What are you doing?"

"I'm getting dressed." I threw open my wardrobe doors, hard enough that the wardrobe nearly tipped forward, but I caught it just in time. I grabbed a sweatshirt and pulled it on over the tank top I'd slept in. "I'm gonna go find Ridley and give him a piece of my mind."

"He's probably back in bed," Ember said.

"I don't care." I turned to face her. "I just can't believe he would do this. This should be my mission, not yours. If Konstantin is back, then I should be the one going after him."

Ember had been sitting on the bed, but she stood up now. Her hands were balled into fists at her sides, and she took a fortifying breath before speaking.

"Bryn. Stop." She spoke harshly enough to break through my frantic agitation, but by the tightness in her voice I could tell she was doing her best to keep calm and not yell at me. "First of all, what you're doing is incredibly patronizing. I am strong and smart and capable enough to handle this mission."

"No, I know that, Ember," I hurried to apologize. "You're an excellent tracker. I don't mean it like that."

"I know what your deal with Konstantin is, better than almost anyone," she went on. "So I get it. But I also know what a massive jerk he is and how much of a threat he is. I understand the danger, and I also understand how important it is to bring him back to stand trial for his crimes."

"I know," I said.

"But—and I mean no offense by this—I'm not clouded by my own personal feelings about him."

I wanted to argue with Ember on the last point, but I couldn't. Only a few days ago I'd confessed to Ridley that I wanted to kill Konstantin and that I wouldn't let him get away again. Since I'd seen him last week, I'd been replaying my fight with Konstantin again and again, thinking about how much worse I would hurt him if I saw him again.

My own need for revenge would make it impossible for me to think as rationally and impartially as Ember, so I fell silent and lowered my eyes.

"I understand the severity of the situation, and I've got it under control," Ember said at length. "That's why Ridley chose me and not you."

"I know that you're right and that he made the right choice. I just . . ." I trailed off.

"You still want to be the one going," she finished for me.

I looked up at her and nodded. "Yeah."

"I get it. But it's actually a pretty big *if* that it is even Konstantin. The reports were sketchy. They'd just heard rumors that he might be in the area of another prominent changeling."

"How do they know?"

"After the incident with Linus, they sent out Konstantin and Bent's pictures to all the tribes so their guards could keep a lookout. They're, like, Trolls' Most Wanted now," Ember explained. "A Trylle tracker was getting one of their changelings, and they thought they saw someone that looked like Konstantin, and that happened to be nearby where this changeling I'm going after lives."

"I know you can't tell me *who* or *where*, but can you tell me if you'll be close, at least?" I asked. "In case you need backup."

"I'll be less than a day's drive from Doldastam, if I need you."

"And you will call me if you need me? Or Ridley or Tilda or somebody, right?" I asked, and I was thinking more of Ember's safety than my own vendetta. Ember was a good fighter, but so was Konstantin, and he wasn't working alone.

"Of course I will," she promised me with a smile. "But I shouldn't. I'm sure everything will be fine. The Trylle tracker was probably mistaken, and I'll find a perfectly safe changeling and bring her home."

"How long do you think you'll be gone?" I asked.

"On the off chance that things get dodgy, Ridley wants me to try to make this a quick mission. I'm hoping a week will be good enough, but I also don't want to risk scaring the changeling off."

"Well, I was only in Chicago for five days, and Linus came back okay," I reminded her. "So I'm sure you'll be fine."

"I'm sure I will too."

"I should let you get going, anyway. If you need to get out of here right away."

Before she left, I hugged her tightly. Ember had gone out on missions before, but this was the first time I felt nervous for her. I was reluctant to let go of her, but eventually Ember pulled away. She smiled at me, promising that everything would be okay, before she turned and headed out my door. It took all my willpower to keep from chasing after her and following her.

repast

I'm not thrilled about this either," my mom said in a hushed voice, as if someone might overhear. Her gray jacket went down to her ankles, and she pulled it tighter around herself as we walked toward the palace. The large diamond studs in her ears glimmered when the sun poked through the clouds in the overcast sky.

"Then why are we doing it?" I asked, trudging along beside her.

"Because they're family, even if they aren't close," she explained with a hint of exasperation. "And because it's a nice gesture."

"But you don't even like them that much," I said, as if she needed me to remind her of that fact. "I don't even know them. *You* don't even really know them."

"I know. But they asked me." We'd reached the palace door, so she stopped and turned to me. The wind had left a rose on her cheeks, but that only made her look more beautiful. "And now I'm asking you."

"Your mother doesn't ask much of us, Bryn." Dad put his arm around her waist, showing his solidarity. "We can do this for her."

"Of course we can," I agreed, and smiled as genially as I could.

There was no point in arguing this or being sullen about the whole thing. It did help to know that my mom didn't enjoy it either, so the three of us were a united front, all pretending to be happy and polite for strangers.

Besides, I had to agree with my mom that it was a nice gesture. After my mom had eloped with my dad, she had been banned from visiting the Skojare, and at first that meant no contact at all. Slowly, their freeze-out had begun to thaw, and she had been allowed to return home for her mother's funeral ten years ago, which had opened the dialogue between her family and her again.

So this was a big step on their part. Queen Linnea Biâelse—the young bride of the Skojare King Mikko—was my second cousin, which made her my mom's first cousin once removed or some other ridiculous relation like that.

The King, Queen, and Prince of the Skojare had invited us for brunch since they were in town, and King Evert had been kind enough to allow us to use one of the meeting rooms in the palace to visit with them.

When we went into the palace, a footman greeted us and took our jackets and boots, and then he led us down to where the brunch was being held. My dad knew where everything was, and so did I, actually, but since we were here as guests of royalty, it was proper for the footman to show us in.

As my mom strode down the corridor, her long white dress flowed out behind her, and it made me happier that I'd chosen to wear a dress myself, although mine was much shorter than hers. My mom always looked beautiful, but she had taken the time to really dress for the occasion, looking more like she should appear on a red carpet than in the dark hallways of a frozen palace, so I knew this was important to her.

The footman opened the door for us, and King Mikko, Queen Linnea, and Prince Kennet were already seated at a long table decked out with fruit and pastries of all kinds. As soon as we entered the room, Linnea got to her feet, followed by Kennet, but the King seemed reluctant to stand.

"My apologies if we've kept you waiting," Mom said, curtsying slightly.

"No, of course not. We're early," Linnea assured her with a warm smile, and she gestured to the table. "Please, sit. Join us."

On the Queen's neck, just below her jawline, were two nearly translucent blue semicircles—her gills. They would've been virtually invisible, except they fluttered every time she took a deep breath.

Since her marriage to Mikko ten months ago, the royalty in all the kingdoms had dubbed her the "child bride." At only sixteen, Linnea had married a man twice her age, but that wasn't all that uncommon in societies like ours—where royal marriages were arranged to provide the best offspring and alignment of powerful families.

The Skojare possessed an odd elegance, as if they weren't human or trolls, but porcelain dolls come to life. While Linnea had that look—the pale, smooth features with undertones of blue, and the striking beauty—her face still had the cherubic cheeks of childhood, while her azure eyes had the youthful rebelliousness of a teenager.

Only her crown filled with sapphires, nestled in her platinum-blond corkscrew curls, gave the indication of her title. Her only makeup was bright red lipstick that stood out sharply against her alabaster skin.

Linnea took her seat between her husband and her brother-in-law, and my mom, my dad, and I sat down across from them, separated by the largest assortment of fruit I'd ever seen served at breakfast.

"I know that you're a relation of Linnea's, but I'm not sure that we've been properly introduced," Kennet said, grinning as he popped a grape into his mouth.

Kennet was a few years younger than the King, and they were unmistakably brothers. Both of them had darker complexions than Linnea, but not by much. Their hair was more of a golden blond, and they had blue eyes that were dazzling even by Skojare standards. Mikko had broader shoulders, and his jaw was a bit wider and stronger than Kennet's. Kennet may have been slighter and shorter than his brother, but he was just as handsome.

Like Linnea, both brothers had gills—nearly invisible until they breathed deeply. I had seen them before, but I still always found it hard not to stare.

"Runa is my cousin," Linnea explained brightly to the men, and motioned across the table to her. "This is her family, although I am embarrassed to admit I don't know them that well."

"No need to be embarrassed. We haven't spent much time together, but I am hopeful that we'll begin to know each other better." Mom smiled at her, then touched my dad's hand. "This is my husband, Iver. He is the Chancellor for the Kanin."

"And who is this?" Kennet was across from me, and he nodded toward me.

"Sorry, this is my daughter, Bryn." Mom squeezed my shoulder gently and leaned into me. "I didn't forget her, I swear."

"No, I didn't think you'd forgotten about her. I can't imagine how anyone could." He grinned at me and winked, and I wasn't sure how I was supposed to reply to that, so I started filling a plate up with berries.

Mom eyed Kennet for a moment, then began to fill her plate too. "So how are you enjoying Doldastam?"

"It's a very lovely town. So much bigger than Storvatten," Linnea enthused. "It is rather cold, though." She pulled her silvery fur stole around her shoulders then, as if she suddenly remembered the temperature. "And we're so far from the water. How do you handle that?"

"As soon as it begins to thaw, I swim out in the Hudson Bay, which isn't all that far from here," Mom explained. "The winters are much tougher, though."

Dad reached over, squeezing her hand. Both my parents had sacrificed so much to be together, but by leaving her family, her town, the very water she craved, my mom had arguably given up more.

"How do you get by?" Kennet asked. He folded his arms on the table and leaned forward. "How do you all occupy your time?"

"We all have our careers to keep us busy." Mom motioned between the three of us. "I teach elementary students, and that keeps me on my toes."

"What about you?" His eyes rested on me again as I picked at a strawberry. "Do you have a career?"

I nodded. "I do. I'm a tracker, and I plan to be on the Högdragen someday."

"Tracker?" Kennet raised a surprised eyebrow. "Isn't that a peasant job?"

"*Kennet!*" Linnea hissed, glaring at him.

"I meant no offense by that." He leaned back and held up his hands. "I was merely curious."

"Forgive my little brother." King Mikko looked at me for the first time since I'd entered the room. His voice was so deep, it was like quiet thunder when he spoke. "He has the awful habit of forgetting to think before he speaks."

"No forgiveness needed," I told him, and turned my gaze back to the Prince. "A tracker is a job mostly filled by nonroyalty, this is true. But as my mother and father both lost their titles as Marksinna and Markis when they were married, that makes me a nonroyal. A peasant."

"I am sorry." His shoulders had slacked, and there seemed to be genuine contrition in his aquamarine eyes. "I didn't mean to bring up class distinction. I was just caught off guard to hear that you had such a difficult job. I've gotten far too used to hearing people describe their jobs as simply being rich, or on the very rare occasion they may be a nanny or a tutor. It's exceptional to find someone who wants to work for something."

"It's very important to Bryn that she earns her place in this world, and she works very hard," Mom told him proudly.

"You seem like an intelligent, capable young woman." Kennet's eyes rested heavily on me. "I'm sure you're a wonderful tracker."

After that, conversation turned to general banalities. Linnea and my mom talked a bit about family members and old friends of my mom's. Kennet interjected some about the goings-on in Storvatten, but Mikko added very little.

Finally, when the banter seemed to run out, the room fell into an awkward silence.

"I very much enjoyed this brunch," Linnea said. "I do hope you can visit us soon. It can be so lonely in Storvatten. There are so few of us anymore."

This was an understatement. The Skojare were a dwindling kingdom. By best accounts, there were less than five thousand Skojare in the entire world—that was half of the Kanin population in Doldastam alone. That's why it wasn't quite so surprising that Linnea was related to us. All trolls were related, of course, but none so closely as the Skojare.

In fact, Mikko and Kennet were actually Linnea's second cousins, and if I understood correctly, my mom was related to them as well, though more distantly. But that's what happened in a community that small when you insisted on royals marrying royals, on purebloods with gills marrying other purebloods with gills to ensure the cleanest bloodline possible.

"Yes, we'll definitely visit as soon as we can," Mom said, and while I was sure it was convincing to them, I heard the tightness in her voice. She had no intention of visiting in Storvatten.

After we made our good-byes, the footman escorted us to the door. I waited until we were bundled back up in our jackets and walking away in the frigid morning air before I finally asked my mom why she'd lied.

"If you enjoyed the brunch, and you did seem to really enjoy talking about Storvatten, how come you don't want to go back there?" I asked.

"I never said I enjoyed the brunch," Mom corrected me, and she looped her arm through mine as we walked next to my dad. "I do like to reminisce sometimes, it's true. But there are few things I enjoy less than spending time with stuffy royals. I know you took that peasant comment in stride, but let me assure you, it's much better being raised a peasant than a royal."

"I'm very happy with the way you raised me," I told her. "I think you guys made the right decision giving up your titles."

"I know we did." She leaned over then, kissing me on the temple. "And besides all that, my life is here with you and your dad. There's no reason to revisit the past."

doldastam

While waiting in the entryway of the Berlings' mansion for Linus to get ready, I pulled my phone out of the pocket of my jeans, checking it for the hundredth time that morning. Ember had been gone for over twenty-four hours, and she hadn't texted me yet.

Ordinarily, she wouldn't check in with me when she was on missions. We would occasionally text or call just to chat and see how things were going, so logically it made sense that she wasn't briefing me and giving me updates on her trip.

But I would feel better if she did.

"So what's the game plan for today, teach?" Linus asked as he bounded up the curved stairway toward me.

"I'm not your teacher," I reminded him again, since he'd recently developed a penchant for calling me *teach*. "I'm your tracker. There's a difference."

"You teach me things. It sounds the same to me." He shrugged.

"Anyway." I decided to move on, since it was clearly a losing battle. "It's a nice day out, so I thought I'd give you a tour around town."

"That sounds great." He grinned. "I haven't really seen much outside of the walls of my house or the palace. It'll be good to get out."

While it wasn't exactly balmy outside, it'd warmed up just enough that the snow had begun to melt. When we stepped out of Linus's house, we were both treated to several huge droplets of water coming down from the roof.

It was the warmest day of the year thus far, and the gray skies had parted enough for the sun to shine through, so everyone seemed to have the same idea. On the south side of town, where Linus lived and the palace and all the royal mansions were, it was usually fairly quiet. But even the Markis and Marksinna were out, going for walks and enjoying the weather.

I showed Linus around his neighborhood, pointing out which mansions belonged to what royals. Astrid Eckwell was standing in front of her expansive house, letting her rabbit roam in the carefully manicured lawn, nibbling at newly exposed grass.

She smiled smugly at me as we passed, and while I told Linus that she lived there, I neglected to explain that her house should've belonged to my dad, if he hadn't married my mom and been disinherited. But he had, so everything that should've been his was passed down to the Eckwells.

As we got to the edge of the south side of town, the houses began getting smaller and sitting closer together. In the center of town, they were practically on top of each other.

What little yard the cottages did have usually had a small chicken coop or a couple goats tied up in it. It wasn't unheard-of to see chickens squawking about on the cobblestone roads or the occasional cow roaming free from its pen.

In the town square, I showed Linus all the major shops. The bakery, the general store, the seamstress, and a few other stores I thought he might find useful. He was surprised and some-what appalled to learn that we had a taxidermist, but many Markis liked to stuff their trophies when they went hunting.

"What's that?" Linus pointed to a brick building overgrown with green vines, untouched by the cold. A small orchard sat to the side of it, with apples and pears growing from the trees. A swing set, a slide, and a teeter-totter were practically hidden below the branches.

"That's the elementary school," I said.

"How are the vines still green?" He stopped to admire the building with its vines and white and blue blossoms. "Shouldn't they die in the winter?"

"Some Kanin have an affinity for plants," I explained. "It's a talent that's much more common in the Trylle, but we have a few special tricks in play, like keeping these alive and bright year-round."

The front doors were open, and he stepped forward to see that the greenery continued inside, with the plants twisting up over the walls and on the ceiling. Then he turned back to me. "Can we go inside?"

I shrugged. "If you want."

"This is the most unusual school I've ever seen," he said as he walked through the threshold, and I followed a step behind. "Why are the floors dirt?"

"It's supposed to take us back to our roots and keep our heritage alive. Some trolls even choose to have dirt floors in their homes."

He looked back at me. "You mean because we used to live with nature?"

"Exactly."

Drawings were posted up on the walls outside the classrooms. In child's handwriting, the pictures had "My Family" written across the top, and then stick figures of various moms and dads and brothers and sisters and even the family rabbit.

"All the kids go to the same place?" Linus asked, noticing that some pictures were simply signed *Ella* or *James,* while others had the title of Markis and Marksinna in front of their names. "The royals and the other town kids all go here?"

"Doldastam is really too small to support two elementary schools, especially when so many Markis and Marksinna are changelings," I said. "When we get older, we split up, with the royals going to high school, and the others going to specialized vocational training."

That was in large part why my childhood experiences hadn't been the greatest. Standing inside the school brought back all kinds of unpleasant memories, usually involving one Marksinna or another making fun of me for being different than the other kids. Astrid had been the worst, but she was far from the only one.

If it hadn't been for Tilda, I wasn't sure how I would've made it through. She was the only one I had by my side, through thick and thin.

But I found my thoughts drifting away from school to the King's Games as I looked down the long hall to the courtyard that lay beyond. Every summer we'd have the King's Games, which were sort of like a Kanin Olympic event, held out in the courtyard behind the school. Members of the Högdragen as well as elite trackers and occasionally well-trained townsfolk would compete in games of sport, like swordplay, jousting, and hand-to-hand, which was similar to kick boxing.

I remember once when I was ten or eleven, and I'd gone to see Konstantin in the games. Tilda had helped me climb up onto a fence so I could see, and we'd sat together, watching with equal fervor as Konstantin knocked his opponents to the ground. Konstantin held his sword to each young man's throat until he finally yielded, and the crowd erupted in applause.

"I almost thought that the other guy wouldn't surrender," Tilda had admitted breathlessly as Konstantin held his hands triumphantly above his head.

"Are you kidding me?" I asked her, with my eyes still locked on Konstantin. "Everyone always surrenders to him. He's unstoppable."

When I was a kid, that idea had filled me with wonder and admiration. Now it only filled me with dread.

"Hey, that lady looks an awful lot like you," Linus said, pulling me from my thoughts. I looked over to see my mom standing in the doorway to a classroom, ushering children out for a bathroom break.

"That's because she's my mom," I said, and lowered my head, as if that would make it harder for her to spot her adult blond daughter standing in the middle of the elementary school hallway.

"Really? Let's go say hi," Linus suggested brightly.

"No, we've got a lot to see," I said, and I turned and darted out of the school without waiting for him. I couldn't wait any longer if I didn't want to risk talking to her.

"Are you mad at your mom?" Linus asked, once he caught up with me outside of the school.

"What do you mean?" I asked, and continued our walk toward the north side of town.

"You just seemed to want to avoid her."

I shook my head. "No, it's not that. I just don't like mixing business with family."

"Why not?"

"She isn't supportive of my job, for one thing," I said, but that was only a half-truth.

"And what's the other thing?" Linus pressed.

I glanced over at him, with his earnest eyes and genuine concern, and I decided to tell the truth. "Most Markis and Marksinna don't exactly approve of her."

This seemed to totally baffle him, the way it would most people who saw past Mom's race to her kindness and strength and wit and beauty. But unfortunately, there were very few Kanin who could do that.

"Why not?" Linus asked in disbelief.

"Because she's Skojare, and I'm half Skojare." I stopped

walking and turned to him, since the conversation felt like it required more attention.

He shrugged. "So?"

"So . . . Kanin tend to look down on anybody that isn't Kanin, especially the royalty," I explained.

"That's dumb." He wrinkled his nose.

"Yes, it is," I agreed. "But it's the way things are."

"Why don't you change things?" Linus asked me directly, and for a second I had no idea what to answer.

"I . . . I can't," I stumbled. "But you can. You're part of an influential family. Someday you may even be King. But even if you aren't, you have the power to lead by example."

"You really think I can change things?" Linus asked with wide eyes.

"I do," I told him with a smile. "Now come on. Let's see the rest of town."

"So when you say people don't approve of you, what does that mean?" Linus asked, falling in step beside me. "Are they mean to you?"

I sighed. "I'd rather not get into it, if that's okay."

"All right," he relented, but only for a second. "But you can tell me stuff. We're friends now."

"Thanks, and I appreciate the sentiment, but . . . we can't be friends," I told him gently.

"What are you talking about? We *are* friends," Linus insisted, and this time I didn't have the heart to argue with him.

confrontations

The fire crackled in my wood-burning stove, and I slipped out of my jeans—muddy and wet from the walk around town with Linus. Wearing only my panties, I pulled on an over-sized sweatshirt and went over to my bookshelf. After a long day, the only thing that sounded good to me was curling up in bed with a book.

I'd finally caved and texted Ember a few hours ago, but she hadn't replied. So I needed a good distraction. Most of the books I owned were old and worn, but I tried to pick up a few new ones every time I went out on a mission. I'd hoped to restock my shelves while I was in Chicago, but that trip had been cut too short.

Since I didn't have anything new, I decided to reread one of my favorites—a battered hardcover of *The Count of Monte Cristo* by Alexandre Dumas. It was wedged stubbornly between several other books, and I'd just finally managed to pull it free when I heard the creak of my front door opening.

I whirled around, brandishing the book with the intention of bludgeoning an intruder with it, but it was only Ridley, his black jacket hanging open and his hands held palm-up toward me.

"Easy, Bryn. It's just me."

"Why are you sneaking up on me?" I demanded, refusing to lower my book.

"I'm not *sneaking*. I just step lightly." He stayed in my doorway, letting a cold draft in around him. "Can I come in?"

I was acutely aware of the way I was dressed—no pants, with the hem of the sweatshirt hitting my midthigh, and the stretched-out neck left it hanging at an angle, revealing my left shoulder and bra strap, along with the jagged scar that ran below it. But I didn't want to seem aware of this, tried to act as if it didn't feel like a big deal to be standing half naked in my small apartment alone with Ridley.

So instead of rushing over to put on pants or hiding underneath a blanket, I shrugged and said, "I guess."

"Thanks." He came inside and closed the door behind him.

And then we stayed that way for a moment, neither of us saying anything. The only light in the loft came from the dim fire and my bedside lamp, casting most of the room in shadows. His eyes bounced around the room, never lingering on anything, and he licked his lips but didn't speak.

"Why are you here?" I asked finally, since it appeared he might never say anything. "You never come to my apartment."

"I've been here before," he corrected me. He shoved a hand in the back pocket of his jeans and shifted his weight.

I folded my arms over my chest. "You don't *usually* come here. Why are you here now?"

"Do you wanna sit down?" He motioned to the couch to the side of me, but I didn't move toward it.

"Why would I want to sit down? What's going on?" My blood pressure had been steadily rising since Ridley had opened the door, and my whole body began to tense up. "What happened?"

"It's nothing bad." He exhaled deeply and brushed his dark curls back from his forehead. "I mean, it's not as bad as it sounds."

"Just spit it out, Ridley."

"Ember ran into Konstantin Black on her mission."

For a moment I couldn't breathe, and I barely managed to get out the word, "What?"

"There was a small altercation, and she was hurt, but—"

That was all I heard, and all I needed to hear, and then I was scrambling to get out of there. I tossed my book down on the couch and ran over to my dirty jeans in the hamper.

"Bryn." Ridley walked over to me, but I ignored him.

"I need to get to her, Ridley," I said, nearly shouting by then, in a quavering voice.

"No, listen to me, Bryn." He put his hands on my arms, and I suppressed the urge to push him off and hit him. His grip felt solid and strangely comforting, so I looked up at him and tried to slow my ragged breaths.

"Ember is okay." Ridley spoke slowly, his words clear and calm. "She was injured, but it's nothing critical, and she managed to get out with the changeling. She's on her way home, and she'll be here tomorrow morning. You don't need to go after her."

I breathed deeply, letting his words sink in, and then I nodded. "She's okay?"

"Yes, I talked to her on the phone, and she sounded good." He smiled crookedly, trying to reassure me.

"What about Konstantin?"

Ridley didn't answer immediately, but he didn't look away, so I searched his eyes, looking for a glimmer of hope, but found none. His smile fell away, and I knew the answer.

"He got away," I surmised.

"The important thing is that both Ember and the changeling are safe," Ridley reminded me.

"I know."

I pulled away from him, and at first he tried to hang on, but then he let his hands fall to his sides. I ran a hand through my hair and sat back on the bed behind me. My legs felt weak, and my shoulders ached. The sudden surge of anxiety and adrenaline, followed by the news of Ember's injury and Konstantin's escape, left me feeling sore and out of sorts.

"I should've been there," I said softly.

"No." Ridley shook his head and came over to sit down next to me.

My legs dangled over the edge of the bed as I stared emptily at the wall in front of me, but Ridley sat so he was facing me.

He rested one hand on the bed, supporting himself, and his fingers brushed against the bare skin of my thigh.

"Why did you send her and not me?" I turned to look at him, and he was so close, I could see my own reflection in his eyes.

"I knew she could handle it, and she did," Ridley said.

"But you didn't think I could."

"I didn't say that."

"Then why didn't you send me?" I asked thickly.

He swallowed, but his dark eyes never wavered from mine. "You know why."

"I could've gone with. I could've helped her. If I had been there, maybe she wouldn't have gotten hurt. Konstantin wouldn't have gotten away."

"Or maybe things could've gone much worse," Ridley countered. "You don't know what would've happened, and everything turned out okay."

"No, it didn't. He got away. *Again*."

"That's not your fault."

"It is my fault! Because I should've been there, and not here doing nothing." I looked away from him, staring down at my lap. "I should've killed him when I had the chance."

"Bryn." He reached out, putting his hand gently on my face and making me look at him. "It's not your fault. You did everything you were supposed to do. Konstantin Black isn't your fault."

"Then why does it feel like he is?" I asked in a voice barely above a whisper.

"I don't know." He brushed his thumb along my cheek, and I closed my eyes, leaning into his touch.

His other hand moved, so that his fingers were no longer brushing against my thigh, and he pressed it against the small of my back. I felt the bed shifting, and even though my eyes were closed, I knew he was leaning in toward me.

"You should go," I whispered, too afraid to open my eyes and see his face hovering next to mine.

"You sure?" Ridley asked, but he lowered his hand, and I felt the weight on the bed change as he moved away from me. I finally dared to open my eyes, and he was still sitting next to me, looking at me with an expression filled with concern.

"If Ember's coming back in the morning, I should get some sleep."

"But are you even gonna get any sleep tonight?" Ridley asked me honestly.

I gave a weak laugh. "I don't know."

"I could stay, keep you company until you fell asleep."

I didn't need him. Or at least I didn't want to need him. But I didn't want to push him away. Not tonight.

"Okay." I nodded, giving in to my feelings for him, at least in some small way.

"Good." He smiled, then slipped off his jacket. "When I came in, it looked like you were grabbing a book."

"Yeah, I was just gonna read before I went to bed."

"Perfect." He stood up. "You go ahead, crawl into bed and get comfy."

"Okay?" I was skeptical, but I did as he told me, sliding under the thick covers and lying back in my bed.

"Here's what I'll do," Ridley explained as he grabbed *The Count of Monte Cristo* from where I'd tossed it on the couch. "I'll read, you relax and fall asleep. Sound like a plan?"

I smiled up at him as he walked back toward me. "Sure."

He sat down on the bed beside me, over the covers with his legs stretched out next to mine, and he cracked open the book and began to read. Eventually his gentle baritone lulled me to sleep. I didn't actually remember falling asleep, but when I awoke with the early morning light spilling in through the windows, my head was on his chest and his arm was around me.

threats

I just can't believe she didn't call me," I muttered.

The Land Rover lurched to the side, and I jerked the wheel, correcting it just in time to keep us from slamming into one of the willow hybrids. Yesterday's early thaw had left puddles and melting snow everywhere that turned into ice today, making the road out of Doldastam more treacherous than normal.

Not that that slowed me down. Ember had texted me thirty minutes ago, letting me know that her train was almost to the station. I still wasn't sure how badly she'd been injured, and I didn't know if driving would be difficult or painful for her.

I'd been at Tilda's house—that had been my excuse to escape a rather awkward morning conversation with Ridley, saying that I'd promised to have breakfast with Tilda. I hadn't, but Tilda was who I ran to when I needed to gather my thoughts and get my wits about me. It'd worked out, because then Ember had texted me, and within minutes Tilda and I were racing to meet her at the train station.

"I'm sure she had her reasons." Tilda pressed her hands against the dashboard to keep from sliding all over as the Land Rover bounced down the road.

"She just lectured me about not calling her after my run-in with Konstantin, and then she turns around and does the same thing."

"Maybe Ember was afraid that you would freak out." Tilda let out a small groan when we hit a bump and she bounced into the air. "And I haven't the faintest idea why," she added drolly and shot me a look.

"I'm not freaking out," I protested, but I slowed down a bit. "She still should've called me."

"But she called Ridley, and she's safe, and that's what counts," Tilda reminded me.

We'd gotten far enough from Doldastam that trees were no longer crowding the path, and the road had widened and smoothed some, so she relaxed back in her seat.

"On the subject of Ridley," Tilda began, and I groaned inwardly. In my telling her about Ember's injury over oatmeal this morning, I'd let it slip that Ridley had spent the night, then Ember had texted me and we'd been on our way.

I tried to evade the question. "There is no subject of Ridley."

"But he did spend the night last night," she said carefully, making sure her words had no trace of accusation.

"He did, but nothing happened. It wasn't like that."

"Okay," Tilda relented, but I wasn't completely sure if she believed me. Hell, I wasn't sure if *I* believed me.

We lapsed into silence after that, so I turned up the music. Thanks to my earlier speeding, we managed to arrive at the station just as the train was pulling in. We'd made the trek in record time.

Ember hobbled off the platform, and her coat hung on her at a haphazard angle thanks to the sling around her arm, which appeared to be made from a couple different fashion scarves. A graze on her left cheek was red and puffy, but otherwise she didn't look that much worse for wear.

She stopped on the steps when she saw Tilda and me rushing toward her. "What are you doing here?"

"We came to give you a lift home and to make sure you're all right," I told her. "Are you okay?"

"I'll live." Ember smiled at us, then turned and gestured to a mousy girl standing just behind her, holding a massive Louis Vuitton suitcase. "This is Charlotte. She's my charge."

"Here, let me help you with that." Tilda ran up the steps to take the bag from Charlotte before it tipped her over.

"Thank you," Charlotte mumbled, but she seemed reluctant to let the bag go. Her eyes were wide and terrified, and her frizzy brown hair stuck out from underneath her knit cap.

"These are my friends Tilda and Bryn," Ember explained to her. "You can trust them. They're good guys."

"I'm sure you've both had a long couple of days. Why don't we get going?" I suggested.

I gingerly took Ember's good arm and led her down the

steps. Even with salt and gravel on the ground, the ice still made it slick in a few places, and it would be awful for Ember to take a tumble and hurt herself worse.

"What about my Land Rover?" Ember asked as we walked past the one she'd driven in to where I'd parked mine rather crookedly in my haste.

"We'll get it another day. Come on," I said. "Let's just get home."

On the ride back to Doldastam, it was hard not to ask Ember a million questions about her fight with Konstantin, but I didn't want to freak out Charlotte any more than she already appeared to be. Tilda sat with her in the backseat, speaking in soft comforting tones about the landscape and her family and how wonderful everything would be for her after she arrived.

Since Ember was injured, Tilda offered to take Charlotte to her parents and help her get settled in. Ember could return to her usual tracker duties once she was patched up, but for now, Tilda would work just fine.

"So what happened?" I asked Ember the instant Tilda and Charlotte had gotten out of the SUV.

"I was staking out Charlotte, like I'm supposed to, and then I had this sense of being watched," Ember said, recalling a scene that sounded familiar.

"I wasn't sure if it was just paranoia, but I decided that I'd better do something, just to be on the safe side," she went on, as I drove through town toward Ember's house. "I was on my way to Charlotte's house, trying to figure out what I'd say to her to get her to leave with me, but I was still scoping everything out, watching every car that went by and scanning for any signs of trouble.

"Then out of nowhere—and I mean like *nowhere*—Bent Stum jumped me."

"He jumped you?" I looked over at her, slumped down in the front seat, her eyes closed and her mouth turned down into an annoyed scowl.

"Yeah. That Bent is strong, but he's pretty dumb. He snapped my arm"—Ember grimaced and touched her broken arm gently—"but I managed to slide out of his grasp. He chased after me, but I managed to lose him when I cut through a backyard and down an alley."

"What happened? How'd you get Charlotte?"

"I got to her house, and Konstantin was already there." Ember paused to let out a pained sigh. "I don't know what his plan was, but when he saw me, he apparently decided that he needed to just go for it. He broke into her bedroom window and just snatched her."

"You mean he kidnapped her?" I asked, a little dumbfounded.

With Linus, back in Chicago, they had been staking him out, like they were planning a careful, quiet extraction. But with Charlotte, it sounded like a clumsy snatch-and-grab. Konstantin and Bent were getting more reckless, which meant that they were probably getting more desperate. That was a dangerous combination.

"Yeah, she was kicking and screaming at first, but he put his hand over her mouth to muffle it," Ember explained. "But it was enough to draw attention. Her parents weren't home, but one of her neighbors came outside and yelled that they were calling the cops."

"Wow." My jaw dropped. Discretion was the number one name of the game. I couldn't believe how risky Konstantin's behavior had gotten.

"Dragging Charlotte around really slowed Konstantin down, and I caught up to them easily and kicked out his legs. He got back up like he meant to fight me, but then we heard the sirens of the approaching cops. And he . . ." She glanced over at me for a moment, then shifted in her seat. "He took off."

"How'd you get Charlotte to come back with you?" I asked.

"She was in shock, so I used persuasion on her," Ember said, referring to her ability.

Persuasion was a psychokinetic ability with which she could make people do what she wanted by using her mind. Trackers were trained to use persuasion only when they had absolutely no other choice, since mind control eventually wore off and wouldn't make the changelings trust us more in the long run.

"I told her that she needed to trust me and come with me," Ember explained. "And she did, so I hurried to steal a car before the cops got there."

"You stole a car?" I asked, surprised, though not too much.

In our training to become trackers, we'd been taught how to steal cars, but I'd never actually done it in real life. Breaking human laws was discouraged, but we also knew that at times it was necessary. In order to get the changelings away from their family, we needed to avoid the police as much as possible, so we didn't end up in jail or have humans snooping around our business as trolls.

That's why we tried not to break laws, so we wouldn't attract unwanted attention from authorities. But sometimes, like in Ember's case, the only way to keep the changeling safe was to break the law.

"My options were pretty limited at that point," Ember said. "I had to get Charlotte out of there. I drove for, like, eight hours, then I stopped to get my arm in a sling and clean myself up, and then Charlotte insisted that we buy luggage and new clothes, which I obliged because I did whatever I could to get her here. Then we caught the train two towns over. I don't know if Konstantin followed us, but I doubt it."

"If he didn't go after you on the train, I'd say you got away safe. He has no reason to follow you here, because he knows where Doldastam is and that the Högdragen are waiting for him here," I said, thinking about what I would do to Konstantin if he set foot behind these walls again.

"I hope so." Ember sat in silence for a moment, then she turned to look at me. "I'm sorry I let Konstantin get away."

"No, there's no reason for you to be sorry." I smiled at her. "You got Charlotte out of there safe and sound, and you kept yourself alive. That's what really matters."

As I pulled up in front of Ember's cottage, she smiled wanly back at me. I got out of the Land Rover and then went around to help her. The goats were bleating loudly in the pasture next to the house, and I looked over to see Ember's mother, Annali, coming out of the pen. The bottom of her long dress was dark from melting snow and mud, and a few pieces of straw were stuck to her dark hair.

"Ember?" Annali asked, her words tight with panic, and she rushed over to us. "What happened? Has the medic seen you yet?" She touched her daughter's injured cheek, causing Ember to flinch a little.

The few medics in Doldastam weren't the same as you'd find in human society. They had medical training, so they could set bones, stitch up wounds, and even perform surgeries. But they'd been recruited from the Trylle tribe for a very specific reason—they were healers. Thanks to the Trylle's psycho-kinetic abilities, with a simple touch of their hands they could heal many minor biological ailments.

"I just got back. I haven't called yet," Ember said.

"Come in the house." Annali motioned frantically toward the house. "I'll call the medic."

She tried to help Ember into the house, but in her fear and frustration, she didn't seem to realize how rough she was being, so I told her to call the medic while I helped get Ember inside. As I got Ember settled on the worn sofa, her mother talked on the phone in the other room, speaking in irritated, clipped tones.

"You can head out if you want," Ember told me in a hushed voice after I draped a blanket over her.

"Nah, I can stay." I glanced over toward the kitchen, where Annali was continuing to swear at the poor person on the other end of the line. "I'd feel kinda bad leaving you alone with her."

"She means well, and she'll calm down." Ember moved the pillow behind her head. "I should probably get some rest anyway."

"I understand." I touched her leg. "Take care of yourself, and let me know if you need anything."

Ember nodded.

I went through the kitchen quietly, not wanting Annali to direct any of her anger at me, and I'd almost made it to the door when Ember stopped me. "Wait. Bryn."

"Yeah?" I turned to her, and she motioned for me to come closer. I went back to the couch, and sat down at the end, next to her feet.

"I was debating on telling you this, but . . ." Ember said so softly I could hardly hear her above her mother, "I think I should."

"What are you talking about?" I asked.

"When I was trying to get Charlotte, I knocked Konstantin to the ground. He got up slowly, and then we heard the sirens." Ember licked her lips. "He didn't leave right away, though. He said something to me, and then he took off."

"What did he say?"

She took a fortifying breath. "He said, 'Run along home, and tell that white rabbit to watch out.'"

"White rabbit?" I echoed. My blood was already pounding so hard in my ears I could barely hear my own voice, but I already knew exactly who Konstantin was talking about.

Ember's eyes were so dark and so solemn, they seemed to pull in all the light around them, like tiny black holes. "He means you, Bryn."

partnership

The number of people crammed into such a small space left it feeling stifling and humid, and everyone's voices blended together in one low, uncomfortable grumble. It was the same meeting room I had been in a couple days before, when I'd been having brunch with my distant Skojare relatives, but now all the tables had been pushed out and replaced with rows and rows of chairs.

I'd arrived ten minutes before the meeting was set to start, and it was already at standing room only. Somehow Tilda had managed to get a seat in the second row, and she offered me an apologetic smile when I came in, since she'd been unable to save me a seat.

Kasper Abbott stood at the side of the room, along with several members of the Högdragen. I wasn't sure if he'd gotten here too late to sit with his girlfriend, or if he'd just chosen to stand with the guards instead. But every tracker in Doldastam, including some of the senior class that hadn't graduated yet, was here, along with about a quarter of the Högdragen. Aside from Ember, who was still at home recuperating.

Ridley was already here, standing in the front of the room talking to a few trackers. He glanced up at me as I found a place in the back of the room, and I gave him a small smile, which he returned briefly before going back to his conversation. I hadn't talked to him since I'd kicked him out this morning, but we were both professionals, so I was determined to act normally around him. At least in situations like this.

I leaned against the wall while I waited for the meeting to get under way. It wasn't that much longer before my dad came in the side door. His head was down as he flipped through a huge stack of papers, so he bumped into a few people as he made his way to the front of the room.

"Ahem." Dad cleared his throat, still not looking up from his papers, and everybody kept on whispering and muttering, ignoring him. His normally clean-shaven chin was covered in salt-and-pepper stubble that he rubbed absently when he looked up at the room. "Excuse me."

With my arms folded over my chest, I glanced around the room, but not a single person had stopped talking. I tried to give my dad a look, encouraging him to speak louder, but he wasn't looking at me.

"If I could, uh, have your attention," Dad said, and I could barely even hear him at the back of the room.

"Hey!" Ridley shouted and clapped his hands together. He grabbed a chair, stealing it from a tracker in the front row, and then he climbed up on it. "Everyone. Shut up. The Chancellor needs to speak to you."

The room finally fell silent, and my dad gave him a smile. "Thank you."

Ridley hopped down off the chair, then offered the chair to my dad. "The floor is yours, sir."

"Thank you," Dad repeated, and with some trepidation, he climbed up onto the chair. "I want to thank you all for coming out for this. I know it was short notice." He smiled grimly. "We've got a lot of great trackers here, and even some of the Högdragen. So thank you.

"Let's get right into it, then." Dad held his papers at his waist and surveyed the room. "We have reason to believe that our changelings are under attack. Last week, Konstantin Black and an Omte associate of his, Bent Stum, went after Linus Berling."

Murmurs filled the room, and I could hear Konstantin's name in the air. Dad held up his hand to silence them, and reluctantly they complied.

"As most of you know, Konstantin Black is considered a traitor for crimes against the King and Queen, and, um, the Chancellor, specifically." He lowered his eyes for a moment, but quickly composed himself. "He's been on the run for the past four years, and we're not exactly sure what he wants with the changelings, but this no longer appears to be an isolated incident.

"Yesterday, Konstantin Black and Bent Stum attempted to take another one of our changelings," Dad went on. "He assaulted a tracker, but thankfully, both she and the changeling weren't seriously injured and made it back to Doldastam."

"You think he's going after other changelings?" someone in the audience shouted.

"Yes, that's exactly what we fear," Dad said. "There've been two incidents with Konstantin Black in the past seven days. We don't want a third. Which is why we've called you all here."

"Are we going after Konstantin?" Kasper asked, and I straightened up.

"We don't know where he is, or where he's going to strike next, so that doesn't seem prudent," Dad did his best to explain. "We're going after the changelings."

Everyone erupted in protests, saying how it wasn't possible or how it would ruin our economy. With over five hundred changelings between the ages of four months and twenty years old out in the field, we didn't have the manpower to bring back every changeling, and it would cripple our finances if we did. Not to mention that a lot of the changelings were still just kids, many under the age of ten. The American and Canadian police would have a field day if we kidnapped hundreds of children.

"Calm down!" Ridley shouted. "We have a plan, and before you guys get your panties in a bunch, you should at least listen to what it is, don't you think?"

"Konstantin's attacks haven't been random," Dad elaborated, once the room quieted down again. "The first changeling he went after was Linus Berling, who as you all know is next in line for the throne if the King doesn't produce an heir. The one he targeted yesterday was Charlotte Salin, who is right behind Linus in line for the throne.

"He's going after royalty," Dad concluded.

"But how is he getting this information?" Tilda asked, speaking for the first time since the meeting had started. "It's classified. Almost no one has access to it."

"We're not sure, but we're investigating," Dad assured her.

"As soon as we find the leak, we'll be able to find Konstantin and put a stop to this," Ridley added.

"But until then, we need to keep ourselves protected," Dad said. "That means more protection here in Doldastam, which is where the Högdragen come in. Linus Berling and Charlotte Salin need extra guards on them. The front gate needs to be locked at all times, and we need to instate a patrol to go around the wall. Doldastam must be impenetrable.

"As for the rest of the trackers, you'll be going out to get our more elite changelings that are coming of age. We think that's who Konstantin will target next, and we want you to get to them before he does." Dad pulled out his papers, looking down at them. "I've got all the placements right here. When I call your name, come up and get your file, and then you're to leave as soon as you're able.

"Tilda Moller and Simon Bohlin, you'll be paired together," Dad began.

"Paired together?" Tilda asked as she stood up.

"Oh, yes, after the incidents, we thought it would be best for the trackers to be paired up," Dad explained. "Both for your safety and for the changelings'."

"But what if we don't need to be paired up?" I protested, and Tilda gave me a look as she made her way to the front of the room.

"Everyone is paired up. No exceptions," Dad told me without looking up.

"But we're wasting resources," I insisted. "We only have so many trackers. If we pair up, then you're cutting our number in half. If we went on our own, we could get twice as many changelings."

"Or twice as many of you could end up dead." Dad pursed his lips and finally looked at me. "The King and Queen made the call, and the decision is final."

"I'm just saying—" I began.

"Bryn Aven, why don't you come up here and get your placement?" Dad asked. "That would probably make the rest of this meeting go much faster."

I groaned inwardly, but I went up to the front of the room, carefully maneuvering around trackers and guards. People had begun whispering and talking among themselves again, but they kept their voices low so they'd be able to hear my dad call their names.

"Where's my file?" I asked when I reached my dad.

"I already gave it to your partner." Dad motioned to Ridley, standing beside him, holding a manila file.

"You're retired," I protested.

"I came out of retirement for one last job," Ridley told me. "This is an important mission, and they needed the best."

"And that's me and you?" I asked.

Smiling down at me, he said, "I don't see anybody better here. Do you?"

enemies

The train ride to Calgary was long, and that should've been a good thing, since it gave me more time to go over the changeling's file. As soon as we'd been assigned, Ridley and I had gone to our respective homes, packed up our things, and within twenty minutes we were on the road out of town. I'd glanced over the file long enough to see where we were headed, noting that there would be a lot of downtime as we passed through the Canadian landscape.

That also meant there was plenty of time to have awkward conversations with Ridley. I hadn't spent this much time alone with him in . . . well, in *ever*, actually, since we'd be together for at least a few days on this mission.

This was coming right after we'd spent the night together—platonically, sort of. And right after I'd realized my feelings for him, feelings I was trying to will away or at the very least pretend didn't exist. Which was much harder to do when he was sitting right next to me, his arm brushing up against mine as I leafed through the file.

The cover page had all her basic information on it.

NAME: Emma Lisa Costar (*Jones*)
PARENTS: Markis Guy Costar and Marksinna Elsa
    Costar, née Berling
HOST FAMILY: Benjamin and Margaret Jones
BIRTH DATE: February 26, 1999
HAIR COLOR: Brown
EYE COLOR: Brown
LAST KNOWN ADDRESS: 1117 Royal Lane SW,
    Calgary, AB T2T 0L7

Paper-clipped to the top were two photos—a baby picture taken right after Emma was born, before she was switched at birth, and a composite photo of what Emma might look like now, based on her baby picture and her parents. I always thought the composite photos looked more than a bit creepy, but they had helped me find changelings in the past.

According to her birthday, Emma was just barely fifteen, but in the composite picture of her, she appeared younger. Her cheeks were still chubby, her eyes wide, her dark hair falling in ringlets around her face.

The packet of pages behind that had all kinds of information about her biological family, in hopes that it would shed some light on what she might be like, as well as information about her host family, to make it easier to find her.

I barely glanced through the packet, though, because I already knew a great deal about her family. Her mother—Elsa Costar—was Dylan Berling's sister, making her Linus's aunt and a cousin to the King. If something were to happen to Linus, when Emma returned from Calgary in a few years according to the original schedule, she would be next in line for the throne. Charlotte Salin—the changeling Ember had just rescued—was only next because she had come of age, and Emma Costar hadn't yet returned to Doldastam.

We kept very rough tabs on changelings while they were gone, since in general the Kanin liked to interact with humans as little as possible. That meant that, rarely, changelings would move or go missing, and we couldn't find them. On other tragic occasions, the changelings died while in the care of their host families, usually due to accident or illness.

The horrible truth was that we had no real way of knowing what was happening to changelings when they were with their host families. Most of the time it was nothing notable—their host parents generally loved and raised them like their own. But right now, when Konstantin Black was on the loose and going after changelings, it was a little scary not knowing where exactly Emma Costar was or if she was safe.

"Anything good there?" Ridley asked.

He sat low in the chair next to me, one of his legs crossed over the other, making his knee bump into mine every time he shifted. His head rested back against the seat, and his eyes were barely open, hooded in dark lashes so I wasn't sure if he even saw anything at all. In his hand he had a small lock of Emma's hair, taken from her when she was a baby and tied with a thin pink ribbon.

"Just the usual stuff," I said with a sigh and tried not to stare at Emma's hair as he twirled it between his fingers.

The Costars hadn't taken Emma's hair in a gesture of affection. It was a tool, an aid in helping trackers find her later. By touching something personal, most trackers had the ability to imprint on a changeling. Ridley couldn't read her mind, but he'd be able to feel if she was terrified or in pain—extreme emotions that meant that she was in trouble and needed our help.

This also turned the changeling into kind of a tracking beacon. If Ridley focused on her, we'd be able to find her. I wasn't sure exactly how it worked, but Ember had explained it as feeling a pull inside of you, like a tug from an invisible electrical current warming you from within and telling you which way to go, and the closer you got to the changeling, the stronger the feeling would get.

Ember had that ability, so did Ridley and Tilda and almost all the other trackers I worked with, as did their parents, and their parents before them. A Kanin's supernatural abilities were passed down through blood, and naturally the trackers were the ones who carried the tracking gift. Since my parents weren't trackers—my mother came from a tribe that didn't even have trackers of any kind—I was born without it.

That was one of the reasons it had been harder for me to become a tracker. I suffered a major handicap compared to everyone else, but I worked twice as hard to compensate for it.

Instinct, intuition, and sheer force of will seemed to make up for my lack of blood-borne talent.

"Are you getting a read on her?" I asked Ridley.

He shook his head. "Not yet, but we're still kinda far away."

"When we get to Calgary, we should go to her house straight off and scope it out." I closed the file and settled back in my seat. Ridley moved his arm so it rested against mine, but I let it. "We can check into the hotel after, but we should get a read on her, at least, make sure she's safe, and then we should come up with the best plan to interact with her.

"Obviously, since I'm younger than you and don't look like a thirty-year-old creeper, I should be the one to make contact," I continued, thinking aloud. "It's going to be a bit trickier, since she's younger than most changelings, but maybe that will work to our advantage. Younger kids tend to be more trusting."

"I have done this before." Ridley looked down at me, a wry smirk on his lips. "Believe it or not, I do know a few things about tracking."

"I know." I met his playful gaze with a knowing one. "I'm just coming up with a course of action." I moved my arm away from his. "I'm not used to working with someone."

"Neither am I, but I think we make a good team. We'll be fine." He reached out, putting his hand on my leg, but only for a second before taking it back.

"I don't know." I looked away, remembering the ominous warning Ember had given me this morning. "Konstantin seems out for blood."

"There's two of us, and we're both strong fighters. Hell, I'm an amazing fighter." Ridley tried to make a joke of it, but I wasn't having any of it, so his smile fell away. "If you could handle him by yourself, there's no reason to think that we can't handle him together."

"Except this time he's escalating," I reminded him. Ember had filled out a report and told Ridley in even greater detail about her fight with Konstantin and Bent, so he knew about Konstantin's blatant disregard for everything when he stole Charlotte from her bedroom.

"But we're prepared for it," Ridley countered.

"I still can't believe you're out in the field for this mission," I said, eager to change the subject from Konstantin and the sense of impending doom he filled me with. "Isn't it, like, illegal to un-retire?"

"No, we just don't often un-retire, as you so eloquently put it, because there's a reason we retired in the first place. For me, it was because my boyish good looks had given way to the ruggedly handsome features of a man, and for some reason teenagers find it creepy when grown men hang around high schools."

"Teenagers can be so unfair," I said with faux-disbelief. "Do you ever miss being in the field?"

He raised one shoulder in a half shrug. "Sometimes, yeah, I do. The one thing that does suck about being the Rektor is being stuck in the same place day in and day out. Don't get me wrong." He turned his head to face me, still resting it against the seat. "I love Doldastam, and I love my job. But it would be nice to see other places, like Hawaii in January."

"Did you ever go to Hawaii?" I asked.

"I didn't. I've tracked changelings to Florida and Texas, and once I went to Japan, which was definitely a trip. Mostly, though, I spent time in Canada," he said, sharing a familiar story. It seemed that only on rare occasions did changelings move someplace far away and exotic after we'd placed them. "What about you? What's the farthest your job has taken you?"

"Alaska. Or New York City." I tried to think. "I'm not sure which is farther away from Doldastam."

"You're young. You've got time. Who knows? Your next mission could be to Australia," Ridley said, attempting to cheer me up.

"Maybe," I said without much conviction. "Other than the lack of travel, you really like your job?"

"Yeah. The paperwork can be a bit much, but it's a good job. Why?" He stared down at me. "You sound skeptical."

"I don't know. Just . . ." I paused, trying to think of how to phrase my question before deciding to just dive right into it. "Why didn't you become a Högdragen?"

He lowered his eyes, staring down at his lap. The corners of his mouth twisted into a bitter smile, and it was several long moments before he finally answered. "You know why."

"No, I don't." I turned in my seat, folding my leg underneath me so I could face him fully. I could let it go, and part of me thought I should, but I didn't really understand why. So I pressed on.

"Because my dad was on the Högdragen, and he got killed for it," he replied wearily, still staring down at his lap.

"But . . ." I exhaled and shook my head. "I mean, I'm sorry for your loss."

Ridley waved it off. "It was fifteen years ago."

"Your dad died a hero," I said, as if that would offer some comfort. "He saved the kingdom. He died an honorable death."

"He did." Ridley lifted his head and nodded. "But he's still dead. My mom's still a widow. I still had to grow up without him. Gone is still gone."

"So what?" I asked. "You're afraid of dying?"

"No. Come on, Bryn." He turned to me, smiling in a way that made my skin flush for a moment. "You know me better than that. I'm no coward."

"No, I never said you were," I said, hurrying to take it back. "I didn't mean it like that."

"I know." He held up his hand, stopping my apologies. Then he let out a deep breath and looked away from me, staring out the window at the trees and lakes that the train raced past. "You know why my dad died?"

"Viktor Dålig killed him trying to overthrow the King," I said.

He laughed darkly. "No, my dad died because Elliot Strinne was a slut."

I shook my head, not understanding. "What are you talking about?"

"Elliot Strinne became King at a young age, and he thought he had all the time in the world to get married and have babies," Ridley explained. "So he decided to sleep with as many eligible young ladies as he could, and that meant when he suddenly fell ill and died of a rare fungal infection at the age of twenty-six, he had no direct heirs. The crown was up for grabs."

Ridley was telling me things I already knew, giving me a refresher of history lessons I'd learned in school. But he was doing it with a decidedly different twist, a bit of snark mixed with sorrow, so I let him.

"Viktor Dålig thought his young daughter should've been Queen, even though she couldn't have been more than ten at the time," he went on. "His wife was Elliot's sister, and she would've been Queen, if she hadn't died years before.

"All these freak accidents fell into place." He stopped for a second, staring off and letting his own words sink in with him. "There should've been a reasonable heir. But there wasn't.

"It was between the child Karmin Dålig, and Elliot's twenty-three-year-old cousin Evert, and the Chancellor had to make a call."

"It made sense," I said when Ridley fell silent for a minute. "It was a logical decision for an adult to be the monarch rather than a child."

"I'm not arguing about whether it was fair or just, because honestly, I don't care." Ridley shrugged. "All that mattered was that Viktor Dålig threw a fit because he felt like his daughter was being passed over."

"Then your dad, and other members of the Högdragen, stood up to him and his friends when they tried to throw a coup," I reminded Ridley.

"Viktor and his friends tried to assassinate a King arbitrarily placed there." Ridley gestured as he spoke, getting more animated the louder his voice got. "The Chancellor could've chosen Karmin Dålig just as easily as he had chosen Evert Strinne. But he didn't. And if Elliot had just gotten married and had a child, the way a King is supposed to, my father wouldn't be dead."

He shook his head, and when he spoke again, his voice was much lower and calmer. "You called his death honorable. He died in the hallway of the palace—a hall I have walked down a hundred times since that day. He died in a pool of his own blood, trying to protect a random stranger in a crown, because another man wanted that crown for his own daughter." He turned to me, his eyes hard and his words heavy. "He died for nothing."

"If you really believe that, how can you do any of the things you do?" I asked. "How can you stay in Doldastam, working for a King and for royals you despise?"

"I don't despise them, and I don't mind working for them. I *like* my job," he insisted. "I just refuse to lay down my life for something that doesn't matter."

"The crown may seem arbitrary to you, and to a point, it is. But for better or worse, our society works because it's a monarchy. Because of the King," I told him emphatically. "And you may think your father died for some jewels wrapped in metal, but he died protecting the kingdom, protecting you and me and everyone in it. And I'm sorry you don't see it that way."

"Yeah. I am too," he admitted.

"Maybe you shouldn't go on this mission," I said softly.

Ridley looked at me sharply. "Why?"

"There's a very good chance that Konstantin Black is going to try to kill Emma, or me, or you, or all of us." I tried to speak without accusation, because I wasn't mad at him and didn't think less of him. I'd just begun to fear that his heart wasn't in this, and that could result in somebody getting hurt. "I wouldn't want you to risk your life for something that you don't care about."

"Emma is an innocent girl. I won't let him hurt her, and there is no way I'd stand by and let you face Konstantin alone." Ridley reached over, taking my hand in his, and the intensity in his eyes made it hard for me to breathe. "I already told you that I'm in this with you."

distance

The house looked like it came straight from a fairy tale. It was a majestic Victorian mansion surrounded by a wrought-iron fence. Trees surrounded the property, all fresh and green thanks to the early warmth of spring, and a few of them had white and pink blossoms. Amid the bustle of a downtown metropolis, this was a slice of another world.

Since we planned on sneaking in, we wouldn't be going in through the front gate, which left us scoping it out near the back. Through the fence and the trees, I could barely see the end of the long, curved driveway, which seemed oddly crowded, with several cars parked in it. I leaned against the fence, trying to get a better look, but Ridley spoke, so I turned back to face him.

"She's not home," Ridley said matter-of-factly.

He stood a few feet behind me, the collar of his thin jacket popped to ward off the icy chill in the air. The wind came up, ruffling his hair. It was so rare to see his thick, wavy hair un-styled, and I realized that it was getting long.

After traveling all night to get here and sleeping on the train, neither of us had had a chance to shower yet, and Ridley hadn't shaved. We'd rented a car, parked it two blocks away from Emma Costar's house, then walked down to stake it out.

"Can you sense her?" I asked.

Ridley stared up at her house with one hand in his pocket, where he kept her lock of hair. His lips were parted just slightly, and his eyes darkened in concentration, then he shook his head once.

"No," he said finally, his voice nearly lost in the wind. "But it's ten in the morning. She should be at school."

"So you're still not getting anything on her?"

"Not yet." He glanced away from me, watching a car that sped by. "I'm probably not close enough. Or maybe it's just harder because I'm out of practice." He turned back to me, try-ing to give me a reassuring grin, but it faltered. "I haven't really done this in four years."

"Well, we should figure out which school she's in," I sug-gested.

"The file had listed two or three private schools in the area they thought she might be in," Ridley said. "Why don't we check into the hotel, then grab something to eat and start mak-ing a plan to get to her?"

"I need to get to a school, so I can get to know her."

"No offense, Bryn, but I don't think enrollment is gonna be

an option this time." Ridley smirked at me. "You can pass for seventeen, sure, but I sincerely doubt that anyone would take you for grade nine, and that's what grade Emma's in. We're gonna have to approach this a different way."

"Do you wanna break into her house?" I suggested. "Check out her room, see if we can find anything on her?"

He seemed to consider this, staring at her house with a furrow in his brow. "No. It just doesn't . . . feel right."

"What do you mean? Is this her house?" I asked.

"I don't know." He sighed. "Maybe. Let's just get out of here and regroup."

Ridley started to walk backward, away from me and away from the house. I stayed behind a few beats, glancing back at the house. He paused, waiting, so reluctantly I went after him. As we walked the few blocks down to our car, a police car sped by with its lights off, and Ridley regarded it warily.

We reached our hotel and checked in quickly, and Ridley spoke little. When I tried to press him about what was going on, he just said that he needed to get something to eat, and then hopefully he could think more clearly.

The diner we stopped at had an expansive organic vegan menu, which was nice and gave Ridley plenty of options to pig out if that would help him. I'd grabbed Emma's file, and I spread it open on the table beside me, leafing through it as I picked absently at a salad. When I glanced over at him, Ridley had his head bowed over his sandwich, his fingers in his thick hair.

"I still think it wouldn't be a bad idea to check out her school," I said.

He sighed. "We just need to find her and get out of here."

"What is going on with you?" I closed the file and rested my elbows on the table, so I could lean in closer to him. "You've been acting strange ever since we got here. Are you just freaking out 'cause you can't sense her? It's not a big deal, and we can still find—"

"It's not that I *can't* sense her," Ridley quietly interrupted me, staring emptily at his plate. "It's that it feels like there's nothing to sense." He looked at me then, the fear in his eyes conveying the gravity of the situation. "She just feels . . . cold."

"What does that mean?" I asked.

"I don't know," he admitted. "I've never felt anything like this before. But it can't be good."

"So . . ." I tried to take in what he was saying. "What do you want to do?"

"I think we should do an Internet search to make sure that's her house. I know her file says that's her last known address, but I'm not completely sure when that was updated," Ridley said. "And then we go to her house, and we wait there until she comes home—*if* she comes home—and as soon as she does, we basically grab her and get out of here."

I glanced around, making sure nobody was nearby, and when I whispered, my words were nearly drowned out by the Laura DiStasi song playing on the diner's stereo. "You want to kidnap her?"

"If we have to, yeah," he said without remorse. "Something bad's going on."

I leaned back in my chair, considering his idea, and then I nodded. "Okay. If it's what you think we should do, then let's do it."

He pulled out his smartphone and took the file from me, double-checking the spelling of the host family's name and the address. I dug into my pocket to pull out my wallet so we could pay for our lunch and then get out of here.

"Shit," Ridley said, and his whole body sagged. Under the dark stubble on his cheeks, his face had gone ashen.

"What?"

Instead of answering, he turned and held his phone out toward me, so I could see the ominous headline that had shown up during his search for Emma's address.

Emma Jones, Teenage Daughter of Software
Mogul Benjamin Jones, Was Found Missing
from Her Bedroom

I scanned the article below, and it went on to say that based on the ransacked state of her room, the authorities suspected foul play, and they were reaching out to the public to see if anyone knew anything about where Emma might be. Worse still, her family said Emma had only been gone since the early morning.

My heart dropped to my stomach. "We missed her by a few hours."

"Then maybe we haven't missed her." Ridley shoved his phone back in his pocket and stood up in a flash.

I threw a couple bills on the table, then pulled on my jacket as I hurried after Ridley. An icy drizzle had begun outside, but Ridley hardly seemed to notice.

"We should split up," I suggested. "We can cover more ground that way."

"Good. That's smart. I'll go back to her house, see if I can get a better sense of where she might be. You should go back to the hotel."

"The hotel? Why?"

"You should get on your laptop, check out her Facebook, Tumblr, et cetera, see if her friends know anything and what people are saying online. You can also figure out what school she's at, and then you can go down and talk to them."

"All right," I agreed reluctantly.

"If I can't find anything at her house, I'll head down to the police station. I might get them to tell me something."

That wouldn't have sounded likely except that Ridley had mild persuasion. He only used it for tracking, and usually on people like host families or school officials. Or in this case he could get a police officer to tell us everything they knew about a missing girl.

I didn't like being stuck on desk duty, but it might give us a clue to what happened to her. If Konstantin Black was trailing her, her friends might have noticed, or Emma might have said something to someone.

She might have even left with Konstantin willingly—before

he'd been on the Högdragen, he'd been a tracker just like Ridley and me, and he was just as capable of talking a changeling into leaving with him as we were. And if he had done that, maybe Emma had told someone about it or where she was going.

That didn't seem likely, especially given how aggressive Konstantin and Bent had gotten with Ember and Charlotte, and given the alleged state of Emma's room. But at this point we couldn't rule anything out, and we had to work as quickly as possible to find Emma.

Ridley and I went our separate ways, and I jogged back to the hotel, holding my jacket up over my head to keep out the rain. By the time I reached the lobby, my jeans were soaked through, and the front of my shirt was damp and sticking to me.

The hotel was cool and modern, with complimentary bottled water and tea in the lobby and hipsters lounging around playing on their tablets in slick chairs and art deco sofas. We'd chosen it because of its proximity to Emma's house, and the clash between our one-bedroom suite and my loft in Doldastam was staggering.

The view of downtown Calgary from the windows was amazing, but the shades were drawn when I came in, leaving the room in relative darkness. I tossed off my soaking jacket, and then I stumbled over an ottoman in the sitting room. Ridley had offered to take the pull-out sofa, so my things were in the bedroom, and I went into it to retrieve my laptop.

If I hadn't been so distracted, hurrying in my worry that something bad had happened to Emma, I would've noticed that things weren't right—that the shades had been open forty minutes ago when we'd dropped off our things but were closed now, and that the ottoman was now out of place, rather strategically placed in front of the bedroom doorway.

I doubt I could've seen him, though—his skin had changed color, blending in with his surroundings perfectly. But if I weren't distracted I definitely would've heard footsteps behind me as I was bent over the bed, digging through my duffel bag. And I'd like to believe that I would've felt the presence of someone standing behind me.

But I didn't. Not until I felt a strong hand covering my mouth, pulling me straight back against him, and a sharp cold blade pressed to my throat.

"Don't make a sound," Konstantin said into my ear, whispering like we were lovers.

TWENTY-TWO

culpability

I stood frozen against him. I could feel the hard contours of his chest pressed against my back, warming me through my wet shirt, and I tried to slow the rapid beating of my heart so he wouldn't feel it. The whiskers from his beard tickled against my cheek and neck, and the skin of his hand felt rough on my lips. He smelled of cold, like ice and snow on the harshest days of winter.

"I know you're devising all kinds of ways that you can kill me," Konstantin murmured in my ear. "But I want to warn you that it won't do you any good."

I went limp in his arms. The blade scraped against my neck, but it didn't slice anything open. He removed his hand from my mouth to wrap around my waist, catching me before I slipped to the floor, and now the knife was aimed at the tender skin under my chin. It would hurt if he sliced across, but it certainly wouldn't lead to death.

In one quick move, I stood back up and thrust my head backward, head-butting him. He groaned, and I grabbed his wrist, twisting it sharply until he released the knife. His arm was still around me, and he squeezed tighter. I leaned forward and, pulling on his arm, I flipped him forward, and he landed on the bed on his back.

The knife was on the floor, so I grabbed it, and then I jumped on top of him. I straddled him and pressed the knife to his throat. His lip was bleeding from when I'd hit him, but he still managed to grin broadly up at me.

"You can't kill me," Konstantin said. "I'm the only one who knows where Emma Costar is."

"How did you find her?" I demanded. "What do you want with her?"

His smile fell away, and his steel eyes looked pained. "I'm afraid that I want nothing with her anymore."

"What do you mean?"

"Did you ever read *Of Mice and Men*?" Konstantin asked. "Bent has always reminded me of Lennie. He even talks about rabbits all the time, but I blame that on his fascination with the Kanin."

"I have a knife to your throat, and I'd like nothing more than to see you dead," I told him, and I pressed the blade harder against his flesh, breaking the skin just slightly. "So you should really answer my questions."

"I will. But maybe you should ask yourself a question first," Konstantin said. "Like, where is my companion? I don't usually work alone."

I lifted my head, taking my eyes off Konstantin only for a moment, and I expected to see Bent lurking in the shadows somewhere. But there was nothing, and that moment of distraction was all Konstantin needed.

He grabbed my shoulders and flipped me over so I was lying on my back on the bed, and he rolled on top of me. He grabbed my wrists, pinning them against the white comforter. My legs were trapped underneath him, and when I fought against his grip, he didn't budge.

"What do you want?" I asked, staring up at him in the dim light of the bedroom. "Why were you here waiting for me? If you have Emma, what's the point?"

"I remember you." Konstantin's eyes were searching mine, and they seemed to soften. "I'm sorry I didn't right away, but I remembered you as soon as you punched me in the stomach in Chicago. You were the plucky tracker, trying to claw your way up to be a guard. Nobody wanted you there, but you didn't care. *You* wanted to be there."

My heart pounded in my chest, and I swallowed back my anger, which was easier since he'd thrown me off my guard by remembering far more about me than I'd thought he'd ever known.

"How did you . . ." I narrowed my eyes at him. "How would you even know that? You didn't know who I was."

"Of course I did. You were that little blond girl, and that alone made you stand out, but you were always fighting twice as hard as anybody else." He paused, grinning down at me. "And I'd always catch you staring at me."

"You were on the guard," I replied coolly. "I was watching the Högdragen."

"No, you were watching *me*. You looked at me like . . . like I could do no wrong." Konstantin sounded wistful.

"I was young and stupid." I looked away.

"I'm sorry," Konstantin said softly. "For what happened with your father."

I snapped my head back to glare up at him. "What happened with my father? You tried to kill him," I snarled, and I tried to fight him off, but he had me pinned.

"Bryn!" Konstantin was calm and firm. "Stop fighting."

"What do you want with me?" I shouted. "If you're gonna kill me, then just kill me."

"I'm not gonna kill you," Konstantin said with an annoyed sigh. "I want you to . . ." He hung his head for a moment.

"Do you even know what you want with me?" I asked.

"I'm trying to protect you!" he yelled in exasperation.

I laughed darkly. "*Protect* me? Why in hell would you do that? I want to kill you, and you want to kill me. You even told Ember you're coming after me."

"What? I never told anyone I was coming after you."

"You told her to 'tell that white rabbit to watch out,' " I said, repeating what Ember had told me.

"That wasn't a threat." He shook his head. "I was warning you. You need to stop this."

"Stop what?" I asked, incredulous.

"Dammit," he muttered.

Konstantin pulled the knife from my grip, then he let go of

me. I stayed where I was, lying on my back on the bed, because I wanted to get a read on what was happening before I made a move. He sat on the edge of the bed, his back to me with the knife in his hand, and he ran a hand through his dark tangles of hair.

"I feel terrible about what happened with your father. And now everything that's happening here." He shook his head. "I made a choice a long time ago, and I'm still trying to make things right." He looked back at me over his shoulder. "But things are in motion, and there's going to be a lot of casualties, and I don't want you to be one of them."

"Why?" I asked in disbelief. I moved so I was sitting on my knees. "Why would you even care what happens to me?"

"Because you saw good in me that wasn't there." He turned away and stood up. "Forget about me. Forget about everything here. Just go back to Doldastam . . . No, don't go there. Just *go*. Forget about the Kanin and everything."

"I'm not forgetting about my family or friends or my people," I told him. "I can't just run off, like you did. And I'm not leaving without Emma Costar."

He rubbed his forehead. "It's better for you if you leave without her."

"Where is she, Konstantin?" I asked.

"Bent just doesn't know his own strength," Konstantin replied, almost sadly.

"What happened to her? If you hurt her, I'll—"

He groaned. "This was going so well. Can we stop with the threats?"

"Not if you won't tell me where she is."

"I don't know where he left her, but it won't do you any good to find her," Konstantin said in a way that made my blood run cold.

"You killed her," I said, my voice trembling with barely contained rage. "You son of a bitch."

I dove at him and punched him in the face, and I think he let me at first, allowing me to hit him in the face and chest a few times before he tried to grab my wrists. Then I kicked him in the stomach, and he grabbed me and twisted my arm behind my back. I tried to buck him off, but he pushed me forward, slamming me against the wall.

"Let me go," I growled, but I was trapped between him and the wall.

"Stop, Bryn. I can't undo what's already been done."

"I'm going to kill you," I warned him.

"I'm trying to make things right. I know you don't believe me, but I'm trying." His words were low and filled with regret, and his beard brushed against my cheek. He let go of my arm, and I pressed my palms against the wall, but I didn't turn around. I didn't fight him. "I know you have no reason to trust me, but please, trust me on this."

I closed my eyes, wishing I didn't trust him, but I did. I didn't know why. Maybe it was the sincerity in his voice, or the fact that he could kill me but didn't, or maybe it was just the memory of the good I thought I'd seen in him when I was younger.

His breath felt warm and ragged on my cheek, and his hand was on my arm. He didn't have me pinned, exactly, but his body was pressed against me, holding me in place. I could push him off, but I didn't.

"I can't let you go," I told him.

"I can't let you follow me," he said softly.

I looked back at him over my shoulder. The curtain had been pulled back a bit in our struggle, and the light landed on his face, so I could clearly see the hurt and regret in his stormy gray eyes.

"I'm sorry, Bryn," he said simply, and before I could ask him why, I felt a sharp pain in the back of my head as he hit me with the butt of the knife, and then everything went black.

TWENTY-THREE

commiserate

When I closed my eyes, I still saw her body. On a river-bank, where ice and snow still clung to the earth, even as a cold spring rain fell around us. Her eyes were open, un-blinking as the drops of water fell into them. She was fifteen, but with her full cheeks and tangles in her curly hair, she looked younger.

Her face stared upward, but her body had been turned at an unnatural angle—her neck had been snapped. The pajamas—pink shorts and a long-sleeve top with hearts and flowers—had been torn, and her knees were scraped.

Emma Costar had put up a fight, and despite Konstantin's proclamations that he was sorry and he was making things right, this young girl had been killed and left on a cold riverbank.

Ridley had come back to the hotel later in the afternoon and found me unconscious on the bed, where Konstantin had left me. I told him that Konstantin had implied that she was dead, and Ridley had redoubled his efforts to track her. He'd gotten a sweater from her bedroom—using his persuasion to get a detective to hand it off to him. Using something recently worn by her, he'd finally been able to get a stronger sense of her.

She hadn't been dead long, and that was the only reason he'd been able to get a read on her at all. We'd finally found her along the riverbank, and I'd wanted to carry her away or cover her up, but Ridley had made me leave her just as we'd found her. He called and left an anonymous tip to the police, and soon her host family would be able to bury her.

Her real parents would get nothing. As soon as we got back to Doldastam, we went to make the notification. They seemed to know as soon as they saw us, Emma's mother collapsing into sobs as her husband struggled to hold her up. We told them everything we knew, and promised that we would bring Konstantin Black and Bent Stum to justice. I wasn't sure if they believed us, or even if they cared.

They hadn't raised her, but they still loved her. They still dreamed of the day when she would come home and their family would be united again. But now that day would never come, and they were left mourning something they had never had.

"This has been one long, shitty week," Ridley said, speaking for the first time since we'd left the Costars' house.

Our boots crunched heavily on the cobblestone road. The temperature had dropped sharply, leaving the town frigid and the streets empty and quiet. It was just as well. Neither Ridley nor I were in the mood to run into anyone.

"The last few days have been some of the longest of my life," I agreed wearily.

"I don't know about you, but I could really use a drink." Ridley stopped, and I realized that we'd reached his house. I'd been so lost in my thoughts that I hadn't noticed where we were.

He didn't actually live that far from the Costars, but his cottage was much smaller than the royals' mansions that populated his neighborhood. It was a very short and squat little place made of stone, with a thatched roof. Small round windows in the front gave it the appearance of a face, with the windows for eyes and the door for a mouth.

"I'd rather not drink tonight," I told him.

"Come in anyway." His hair cascaded across his forehead, and dark circles had formed under his eyes. He still hadn't shaved, but that somehow made his face more appealing. Though he looked just as exhausted as I felt, there was a sincerity and yearning in his eyes that I didn't have the strength to deny.

Ridley saw my resistance fading, and he smiled before turning around and opening the door. His cottage was built half in the ground, almost like a rabbit burrow, and that's why it had such a squat look. Only a few feet of it actually sat above the ground, and I had to go down several steps when I went in.

Inside, it was cozy, with a living room attached to a nice little kitchen, and the door was open to his bedroom in the back. As soon as we came in, Ridley kicked off his shoes and peeled off his scarf, then went over to throw a few logs in the fireplace to get the place warmed up.

"Sure I can't interest you in a drink?" Ridley asked when he went into the kitchen.

"I'll pass." I took off my jacket and sat back on his couch before sliding off my own boots.

I'd been inside his cottage a couple times before, but usually only for very brief visits to ask him a question about work. This was my first real social call, and I took the opportunity to really take his place in.

The coffee table was handmade from a tree trunk, made into an uneven rectangle with bark still on the edges. The bookshelf on the far wall was overflowing with books, and next to it he had a very cluttered desk. On the mantel, there was a picture of a grade-school-aged Ridley posing with his father, who was all decked out in his Högdragen uniform.

"Have you ever had to make a notification before?" Ridley came back into the living room, carrying a large glass mug filled to the brim with dark red wine.

"This was my first," I said. "It's the only time I ever came back without a changeling."

He bent down in front of the fireplace, poking a few logs to help get it going. "I've done it once before. It's never any fun."

"This time must be worse."

"Why do you say that?" Ridley sat on the arm of the couch at the far end from me and sipped his wine.

"This time it's kind of our fault."

"It's not our fault," he said, but he stared down at his mug, swirling the liquid around. "We left as soon as we got our assignment, but she was dead by the time we even got to Calgary. There was nothing we could've done."

"No, there's nothing more *you* could've done," I corrected myself. "But I should've taken care of Konstantin when I saw him in Chicago."

I said that, but I wasn't sure if I meant it anymore. Even after we'd found Emma dead, I felt more conflicted than ever. I didn't know what Konstantin's role had been in her death, and although I was certain he carried some culpability, I also thought things were far more complicated than either Ridley or I had realized.

"What happened with him, exactly?" Ridley asked carefully, giving me a sidelong glance. "Back in the hotel."

I pulled my legs up underneath me, leaning away from him. "I already told you."

"No, you didn't. Not really." He slid down off the arm of the couch so he could face me. "You told me that he'd been in the room, you'd fought, and that he must've knocked you out. That was about it."

"That's about all there is to tell."

"But what I don't understand is, why was he there?" Ridley paused. "Was he waiting for you?"

"I don't know." I ran my hand through my hair.

"Did he hurt you?" he asked with an edge to his voice.

"We fought, and he knocked me out, so yes." I gave him a look. "But other than that, I'm okay, and I got in a few good punches."

"Why didn't he kill you?" Ridley asked. "Don't get me wrong, I'm glad he didn't. But . . . he's tried to kill your dad, he killed

Emma. He obviously doesn't care if he gets blood on his hands, so why did he leave you alive?"

I lowered my eyes. "I think he does care if he gets blood on his hands. And I think Bent killed Emma, not Konstantin."

"Are you . . ." Ridley's expression hardened, and he narrowed his eyes. "Do you have feelings for him?"

I groaned, but my cheeks flushed. "Don't be gross, Ridley."

"There's clearly something going on between the two of you—"

"Why?" I snapped. "Why is there 'clearly something'?"

"Because he should've killed you, and he didn't. And you should've killed him, and you didn't. So something's going on, and I want to know what it is."

"It's not like that." I shook my head.

"Bryn." He set his mug down on the table and moved closer to me. "I'm just trying to understand." He put his hand on my thigh, and I chewed my lip.

"Konstantin Black is a bad man who has done bad things, who will do bad things again," I told him, willing myself to meet his gaze as I spoke. "I know that. But there's something more going on, something much bigger at play."

"I know that you think he's working for someone else, and you're probably right," Ridley said. "But that doesn't mean he deserves your sympathy."

"I'm not sympathetic." I sighed. "At least I don't want to be. But I'm not ready to completely distrust him. Not yet."

"He's done terrible things. He's not to be trusted," Ridley implored me to understand, his eyes dark with concern.

"I know. I will take care of Konstantin. I promise." I put my hand on his, trying to convey that I meant it. "But please, for now, can you not tell anyone that I saw him in Calgary?"

"You want me to lie to the King and Queen?" Ridley asked with exaggerated shock.

"You've done it before," I said with a hopeful smile.

"No, don't look at me like that." He shook his head, then sighed. "Fine. I'll keep this between us. But Bryn, this is a very dangerous game you're playing."

"I know," I admitted, and squeezed his hand. "Thank you for keeping my secret."

"You can always trust me with your secrets," he said with a crooked smile, and the look in his eyes made my heart ache. "You know, that's the real reason I went on this mission."

"What is?" I asked.

"I was afraid you'd run into Konstantin, and I didn't want you to go up against him alone. And then I wasn't even there when you fought with him," he said, and guilt flashed across his face.

"I was fine. I took care of myself," I insisted.

"No, I know." He lowered his eyes for a second, taking a for-tifying breath, as if he were building up to something. His hand was still in mine, and he ran his thumb across it. Finally, he lifted his head, meeting my eyes willfully. "On the train, you questioned my commitment to the mission."

"Ridley, I didn't mean it. I know you did everything you could in Calgary—"

He held up his other hand, silencing me. "I know, and I'm

sorry that things didn't work out better for Emma and for you in Calgary, and I'm sorry that we didn't arrive sooner. But I'm still glad I went. For you, I would lay down my life any day."

If he'd leaned in to kiss me then, I would've let him. I would've gladly thrown my arms around his neck and pulled him tighter to me as his lips pressed against mine.

But he didn't. He just stared into my eyes for a moment, filling me with a heat that made me feel light-headed and nervous and wonderful all at once.

Then there was a knock at the door, and he pulled his hand away from me, and the moment was shattered, and I could suddenly breathe again.

As Ridley got up to answer the door, I looked up through the small windows near the roof and tried to peer through. I got a glimpse of a girl, and I was hit by the painful realization that I'd stayed here too long. That I shouldn't have come to visit at all.

"Oh, good, you're home!" Juni said in relieved delight when Ridley opened the door, and I was already hurrying to pull on my boots. She threw her arms around him, hugging him tightly, and my cheeks flushed with guilt at the fantasy I'd just been having in which I would hold her boyfriend in much the same way.

"I was so worried about you," she said as she held him.

"I'm okay, I'm fine," he tried to comfort her.

I cleared my throat as I put on my coat, since they were standing in the doorway, blocking my exit.

"Oh, Bryn, I didn't realize you were here." Juni let go of Ridley and gave me a wide smile. "I'm glad to see you made it back safely, too." Her smile gave way to sadness. "I heard about the poor girl in Calgary."

"Thank you, but I should really be going," I said, returning her smile with a lame one of my own.

"You don't need to go." Ridley pulled away from Juni so he could turn to me.

"No, I do. You two need to catch up anyway."

I couldn't force a smile much longer, so I slid past them as politely and quickly as I could. With hurried steps, I walked back to my loft, feeling more conflicted and lost than I ever had before.

oath

D o you wanna talk about it?" Ember stood over me looking down, so her bangs were falling into her eyes. Her arm had a brace on it, but otherwise the medic had almost completely healed her, and she spotted me as I did bench presses.

"Nope," I said through gritted teeth and pushed the bar above my chest before slowly lowering it back down.

"Well, I think you should," Ember persisted. "You and Ridley got back from Calgary yesterday, and you've hardly said anything." She paused, waiting until I finished my rep and racked the bar. "I know you must feel terrible about what happened with that girl."

I sat up, wiping sweat off my brow with the back of my arm. "I know you mean well, but I really don't wanna talk about it."

"Okay," she relented. "But I'm here if you need me."

"Thank you." I smiled up at her, but it fell away when I saw Ridley enter the gym behind her.

I'd been avoiding him since yesterday, and I had planned on avoiding him for as long as I possibly could. But since he was walking toward where Ember and I were working out, it seemed like my time was up. He wore slacks and a suit vest, so he definitely wasn't here for exercise.

Ridley stopped when he was near enough that he wouldn't have to shout, and then he motioned to us. "Bryn, Ember, you're needed in classroom 103."

"What do you mean, we're needed in a classroom?" I asked.

"Yeah, and by who?" Ember added.

"It's an impromptu meeting," he said without elaborating, then turned to walk away.

"A meeting? With who?" Ember asked.

"Just come on!" he called without looking back to see if we followed.

Ember exchanged a look with me, and I just shrugged and took a swig from my water bottle. My tank top was sweaty in a couple places, and my yoga pants were frayed and old. I hoped whoever we were having our meeting with wasn't super-important, because Ridley didn't imply that I had time to change.

We walked down the hall out of the gym, past the classrooms where trackers-in-training were studying proper techniques, social etiquette, and human history. Room 103 was one of the larger classrooms and was located right next to the Rektor's office.

When we reached it, Tilda and Simon Bohlin were already seated at desks, along with half a dozen other top trackers who had already returned with their changelings. Ridley stood near the front of the room, and leaning against the teacher's desk with his arms crossed was King Evert.

He was dressed somewhat casually, in a suit with a black shirt and no tie. He hadn't worn his crown, but he rarely did, except for special occasions. Still, I regretted not hurrying to the locker room to change.

"Are these the last two?" Evert asked as Ember and I slowly took our seats at two empty desks near the front.

"Yes." Ridley went over to shut the door behind us, and then he took his spot next to the King. "This is every tracker that's back."

Evert stared out at the room. The light glinted off his slicked-back raven hair, and one ankle was crossed over the other. I'd rarely seen him without his usual smirk, but the expression he wore now was decidedly grim.

"My wife doesn't want us to go to war," he said finally, his words carrying a weight they usually lacked. He looked as if he felt much more resigned to being a leader than he ever had before. "She wants us to solve things peacefully and quietly, sneaking changelings in during the night. And that's why she doesn't know about this meeting.

"An accused traitor killed one of our children, and if he has his way, I'm sure he'll kill more," King Evert went on.

I lowered my eyes, but I could feel Ridley's gaze on me, almost willing Evert's words to take hold in me.

"I agree with my wife on many things. She tries to be kind and fair." Evert uncrossed his arms and put his hands on the desk behind him. "But when someone is shedding the blood of our people, that's where I draw the line. That's when I say fuck it. Let's go to war."

"We're going to war?" Tilda asked, too surprised to be afraid to speak out to the King. "Against who?"

"Konstantin Black and Bent Stum and anyone they might be working with," Evert explained. "There's no point in going after the changelings, because he's one step ahead of us every time. He's anticipating our moves. So now we're going after him."

"How will we find them?" Ember asked.

"We're coming up with a plan now." Evert motioned between himself and Ridley. "But since Konstantin seems to somehow be intercepting our highest-ranked changelings, we're going to set a trap. We'll send all of you to one place, where one change-ling is supposed to be, and when you see Konstantin and Bent, you'll swarm them."

"When we catch them," I began, choosing my words care-fully and hoping that I didn't look as sick as I felt, "we're sup-posed to bring them in to stand trial, right?"

"I've thought about it, and I don't see the point. Why waste resources and time?" Evert asked. "He's enemy number one. You find him, you kill him. He hasn't shown us any mercy, and we won't show him any."

Ridley met my gaze, and the fear flickering in his eyes made me bite my tongue even harder. I couldn't tell the King about my fight with Konstantin, especially not now, not if I didn't want to end up in jail for aiding the enemy. But I could tell Ridley was afraid that I would risk my own neck to defend Konstantin.

While the idea of killing Konstantin made my heart twist, I

couldn't argue with the King. Konstantin was still the enemy, and he was complicit in the attempted kidnappings and murder of our people. Something had to be done. I may disagree on what that "something" might be, but arguing with the King would get me nowhere.

"We're coming up with the specifics now, but the plan is to send you out early next week," King Evert went on.

"Excuse me, sire?" Tilda raised her hand timidly. "Is there a way that we can opt out of this mission?"

I looked sharply at her. Her long chestnut hair hung in a braid, and her skin had begun to shift color when everyone looked at her, paling to match the beige of the walls and the tan of the desk, so she could blend in and disappear—a side effect of her embarrassment.

"Opt out?" Evert's brow furrowed and he crossed his arms again.

"This mission of going after traitors sounds particularly dangerous, and . . ." She stopped and took a deep breath. "I'm fourteen weeks pregnant."

"You're *what*?" I asked, unable to contain myself, and she lowered her head.

Beneath the desk, I saw her hand pressed against her stomach. Tilda had always been so toned, and while lately there had been a very subtle bump to her normally taut stomach, I had barely even registered it, let alone considered that she might be with child.

"Of course, in your condition, you don't need to be on active duty," King Evert said.

"When this meeting is over, I'll have you come into my office to fill out some paperwork," Ridley added, then gave her a smile. "Congratulations."

"Thank you," Tilda said softly and smiled at him.

The King spoke for a few minutes longer, summarizing what he'd already told us, and saying that we should all be ready to move next week. He ended the meeting by saying that he'd be in contact with Ridley later on, and then reminded us all to keep everything he'd said under wraps.

After King Evert left, Ridley dismissed the rest of us, and while the other trackers left quickly, talking among themselves, Tilda, Ember, and I were slow to get up. Ridley was at the main desk, gathering up some paperwork he'd apparently brought in with him for the meeting. I sat hunched over my desk, trying to absorb the newfound revelations.

"You're pregnant?" Ember asked Tilda, echoing my own disbelief. She'd gotten up from her desk to walk over to where Tilda still sat at her desk. "You're one of my best friends. How could you not have told me this?"

"I wanted to tell you," Tilda said emphatically, and she looked over at me. "Both of you. I was just waiting for the right time."

"How could you have let this happen?" I asked. My voice was quiet, but the accusation in my tone was unmistakable, and Tilda sat up straighter, her eyes widening with indignation.

"*Let* this happen?" Tilda asked incredulously.

"You should've been more careful," I went on, unabashed. "Weren't you and Kasper using protection?"

"My sex life with Kasper is none of your business," Tilda snapped.

"I just can't believe you would do this." I shook my head. "Just throw your career away."

"Bryn!" Ember admonished me, but I ignored her.

"I'm not throwing away anything," Tilda said, growing more defensive. "I just don't want to fight while I'm pregnant. Once I'm done with maternity leave, I'll go right back to work."

"Yeah, that's what they all say, and then they never come back," I muttered.

"Things are getting a little heated," Ridley interjected, attempting to be a voice of reason, but both Tilda and I were staring daggers at each other. "Everyone should calm down, and talk about things later."

"They all who? And who gives a damn what other people do?" Tilda was nearly shouting by now. "I'm talking about me. And this is about *me* and *my* baby. Not you. It's not like I did this to you."

"I just can't believe this." I stood up, pushing the chair back from my desk so hard it tipped over. "I always thought you were better than this."

"Wow, Bryn." Tilda's voice was cold and flat, but hurt flashed in her gray eyes. "I could say the same thing about you."

Ember rushed to defend Tilda, but I barely heard her. I just turned and stormed out of the room, dimly aware that Ridley was calling after me. But I just kept going. The muscles in my arms felt tight and electric, and I nearly punched in the door to the girls' locker room. My breath came in angry, ragged gasps, and it was hard for me to think or focus. I wanted to hit something, and I didn't even know why.

"Bryn!" Ridley shouted, busting into the locker room without knocking. I stood next to my locker, my fists balled up at my sides, and I cast an annoyed glare at him. "What the hell was that about?"

"You're in the girls' locker room," I pointed out lamely and struggled to get hold of my temper.

"No one is here, and it's not like they have anything I haven't seen." He put his hands on his hips and stared down at me. "Everything you said in that classroom was totally uncalled-for. You were being a huge asshole."

"I'm the asshole?" I rolled my eyes and laughed bitterly. "She's the one that was negligent and immature! She's abandoning her job for some stupid boy!"

"No, she's not," Ridley corrected me as reasonably as he could. "She's an adult woman starting a family with someone she loves. That all seems relatively normal and healthy to me."

I slumped back on the bench and took a deep breath to calm myself. "Our priority is to this kingdom and these people. We took an oath when we were sworn as trackers, and now there's something major going on, and she's going to be off playing house."

"We're allowed to have lives, Bryn." His tone softened, like he was sad that he needed to explain this to me, and he sat down on the bench across from me. "We can date and have fun and raise families and fall in love."

Running a hand through my hair, I refused to look at him and muttered, "You would say that."

"What does that even mean?" Ridley sounded taken aback.

"Because you're in love with Juni," I told him pointedly, as if I were accusing him of a crime.

"I never said that. I just started dating her, and that doesn't even matter." He brushed it off. "The point is that you're acting insane right now." I scoffed, so he continued. "Tilda is your friend, and you're scared and pissed off and you're taking it out on her for no good reason."

I bristled. "I am not scared."

"You are," he insisted. "You're scared of losing her, that she won't be able to work with you as much anymore. But what I think is really bothering you right now is that the King wants you to go kill Konstantin, and you're not sure if you can."

"That's . . ." I shifted on the bench and shook my head. "You don't know what you're talking about."

"I know exactly what I'm talking about." He leaned forward, trying to get me to look at him, but I refused. "I know you, Bryn."

My shoulders sagged, and I hung my head low, staring down at the cracked tiles of the locker room floor. I put my head in my hands and let out a long, shaky breath.

"I don't want to kill him. I should, and I know I should, but I don't."

"I know," he said. "I may not understand why, since I'd give anything to kill the man that killed my father, but I know that this is how you feel."

I lifted my head to meet his gaze, so he could see that I meant it. "I just want to make sure the right person pays for the right crime, and . . . I don't think that's Konstantin." I groaned, realizing how foolish it sounded. "What's wrong with me?"

"Nothing," Ridley assured me. "You just have strong convictions, and you want to do the right thing."

"Are you going out on the mission?"

He shook his head. "No. The King wants me to stay back." He studied me for a minute, then asked, "If you were to see him, would you kill Konstantin?"

Without hesitation, I answered, "The King ordered me to do something. I am a tracker, a member of the King's court, and I took an oath that I would follow all the orders he gives me. So yes, I will do what's required of me."

motives

Konstantin's gray eyes stared back at me, unyielding, unforgiving. It was his first official photo when he'd joined the Högdragen, in full color on the top page of his file. He'd been younger then, clean-shaven, skin smooth, but unsmiling. The Högdragen were never supposed to smile, not when they were working.

It was strange because in the picture he looked harder than he did now. The years on the run had taken their toll on him, definitely, but he'd softened somehow.

I wish I could know what had changed between the time that proud young man had been photographed in his crisp uniform, and the night he'd run my father through with his sword.

After Ridley had confronted me in the locker room, I'd changed and gone back to apologize to Tilda, but she was already gone. But that might be for the best. She could probably

Amanda Hocking

use some space before I went to her and owned up to how unfair and cruel I'd been.

Ridley had gone off to take care of some pressing Rektor business with another tracker, so I took the opportunity to sneak in and grab Konstantin Black's file from the cabinet behind his desk. Technically, anybody was allowed to look at Konstantin's file, since he was a wanted man, so I had no need to sneak, but I didn't want to talk to Ridley about it. At least not right now.

I sat cross-legged on my bed with Konstantin's file spread out before me, hoping that it would give some kind of insight that would help me figure out what happened and what was going on.

But so far there wasn't anything that I didn't already know. His father had died when he was very young, and he'd been raised by his mother, who died around the time he joined tracker school. He'd graduated at the top of his tracker class, and he went on to successfully bring in 98 percent of the changelings he was assigned to in the eight years he worked as a tracker.

He joined the Högdragen at the age of twenty-three immediately following his retirement from tracking. He'd transitioned seamlessly into their ranks, rising quickly because of his diligence and charm. Shortly after Mina married the King, she'd appointed Konstantin as her guard, where he'd risen to even greater prominence.

Everything in his file showed him as a loyal, intelligent hard worker, even if he was occasionally noted for his pride. If he was arrogant, it seemed justified. He gave a superior performance at his job, and he was beloved by the people.

In every one of the King's Games Konstantin had competed in, he'd walked away with top honors. He was a hero to the people, and a loyal servant to the King and Queen.

That was it. That was all that was in his file. Just accolades and praise, up until the night he attempted to kill my father. Then there was a report explaining the incident and that Konstantin had disappeared in the night's snow.

But there had to be something more. Something I was missing that would make him change so drastically. From a guard full of swagger and promise to a traitor on the run, humbled and worn.

Ember's footsteps pounding up the stairs to my loft interrupted my thoughts, and I scrambled to put everything back in the file. I'd just shoved it underneath my blankets when Ember threw open the door.

"I know, I know," I said as soon as I saw her glaring down at me. "I acted like a jackass toward Tilda today."

"You certainly did." She trudged over to me, her boots leaving snowy prints on the creaking floorboards. "You really hurt her feelings."

"I'll apologize to her later," I promised Ember. "I just thought I'd give her some space."

"Good." Ember kicked off her boots, then flopped back on the bed beside me. She wore thick leggings under a skirt that flounced around her. "It will suck not having Tilda to train with or work with around Doldastam. But she says she's coming back after the baby's born."

"I know," I said, without much conviction.

"I mean, my mom didn't go back to tracking after she had my older brother." Her eyebrows pinched together and her mouth turned down into disappointment. "And that other tracker Sybilla had her baby two years ago, and she still hasn't come back."

"Maybe Tilda will be different." I tried to cheer Ember up. "And even if she doesn't come back, she'll still be in town, and we can still see her."

"You think she's wrong, though." Ember leaned back on the bed, propping herself up with her elbows and looking at me. "You don't think she should have a personal life, that any of us should."

"I have friends, and I've dated, and I thought it was great when Tilda and Kasper started dating. So it's not that we shouldn't have personal lives," I said, trying to explain my position. "I just think we made an oath to make this job our priority, and having strong attachments can interfere with that."

"Is that why you and Ridley never hooked up?" Ember asked.

"What? I—we—we never . . ." I sputtered, and sat back on the bed, moving farther away from her. "We never did anything because neither of us wanted to. I don't have those feelings for him, and I'm sure he feels the same way. He's my boss, and both of us could lose our jobs, and now he's dating Juni, and besides, we didn't want to. So. I don't know what you're talking about."

Ember raised her eyebrows and smirked at me. "Whatever you say, Bryn."

"Nothing good ever comes from falling in love," I told her

definitively. "You act ridiculous and lose your mind and you forget what really matters to you, and then you end up sidelined and married or heartbroken and destitute, and neither of those are good options, so it's better if you just avoid relationships altogether."

"Gosh, I really hope you don't mean that, because that just sounds sad," Ember said, staring up at me with pity in her dark eyes.

I let out an exasperated sigh. "Just never mind." I stood up, grabbing a sweater off my bedpost, and pulled it on over my tank top.

"What are you doing?" Ember sat up straighter, alarmed.

"I should probably head out. I'm supposed to go over to my parents' for supper." If I left now, I'd actually be a little early, but I'd grown tired of talking about romance and Ridley.

"Oh." Her face fell. "Okay." She slowly pulled on her boots and got to her feet. "Sorry if I said something to offend you."

"No, you're okay." I brushed it off. "You're fine. I just have stuff to do."

Ember left, not seeming totally convinced that I wasn't mad at her, so tomorrow I'd probably have to spend some time making up with both her and Tilda. But for now I had other things on my mind. Once she'd gone, I moved Konstantin's file, preferring to hide it in the bottom of my nightstand drawer, underneath odds and ends.

The dinner with my parents had actually been my idea. After I'd read the incident report, going over what had happened with Konstantin in black-and-white, I realized that I needed to talk to my dad and find out what had actually happened that night before I came into the room.

The sun had nearly set by the time I reached my parents' cottage in the town square. It had been a rare day without a cloud in sight, and the sky was darkening from pink to amethyst as the sun dipped below the horizon.

Before I even opened the front door, I could hear my mother, singing an old Skojare seafaring hymn. I paused, peeking through the kitchen window to see her standing in the kitchen, an apron around her waist and flour everywhere. She always sang when she baked, usually Skojare songs in a mixture of heavily accented English and Swedish, or occasionally Barbra Streisand. My mom had always been a sucker for Streisand.

When I came inside, I closed the door quietly behind me, and she didn't hear me as I took off my boots and hung up my jacket. As a tracker, I'd been trained to tread lightly, to move about without making a sound, and I'd made it all the way into the kitchen before she turned around and saw me.

"Bryn!" Mom gasped and put her hand to her chest. "You scared the daylights out of me!" She smiled and swatted me playfully with an oven mitt. "Don't give your mother a heart attack. It's not very nice."

"Sorry," I said, but couldn't help laughing. "What are you baking?"

"Just a gooseberry pie for dessert."

"I'm sure it'll be delicious." I grinned. "Where's Dad? I wanted to talk to him before dinner."

"He's in his study," Mom said, but she stopped me before I turned to go. "Listen, Bryn, I need to talk to you for a second."

"About what?" I asked, and even though I was an adult living on my own, I still felt like a little kid about to be grounded for staying out too late.

"Well." She took a deep breath and tucked a few errant strands of hair behind her ear, unmindful that she was getting flour in it, and her eyes were grim. "I know that Konstantin Black is the one causing all the trouble."

I took half a step back from her and straightened my shoulders, preparing for a fight, but I waited until she'd said her piece before saying anything.

"I know that you have a job to do, but . . ." She pursed her lips. "He nearly took your father and you away from me already. I don't want you messing around with him."

"Mom, he barely hurt me before," I tried to deflect her concern. "It was little more than a scratch, and I was just a kid then. I can handle him now. You don't need to worry."

"Bryn, you are my daughter, my *only* daughter." She walked closer to me and put her hands on my shoulders. "I know how brave and strong you are, but I need to know that you're safe. And I can't know that if you're chasing around after this madman."

She put her hand to my cheek, forcing me to look up at her, and the aquamarine in her eyes was filled with pleading. "Bryn. Please. Promise you'll stay away from him."

"I'll stay away from him if I can," I told her honestly. "But

I'm going to protect myself and this kingdom. I'll do what I need to do, and that's the best I can give you."

Her shoulders slacked, but her hand lingered on my face. "Be safe. Don't be reckless or brave. If you must go out after him, then come back safe."

"I will," I assured her, and she leaned forward and kissed my forehead.

"Okay." She stepped back and smiled at me, trying to erase her earlier seriousness. "I need to finish with the pie. Go ahead and see your father."

remnants

Dad sat at his desk, his head bowed over paperwork and his reading glasses resting precariously on the end of his nose. The only light came from a small lamp next to him, and it made the silver hair at his temples stand out more against the rest of his black hair.

"Can I talk to you for a second, Dad?" I asked, poking my head in his study.

"Bryn." He smiled when he saw me, and pulled off his glasses. "Yeah, of course. Come in."

I closed the door behind me, and then sat down in the chair across from his desk. The walls of his study were lined with shelves filled with old books and Kanin antiquities. On his desk, he used an old artifact—a rabbit carved out of stone—as a paperweight. I'd always felt that in another life, my dad would've made an excellent history professor.

"Is something wrong?" He leaned forward on the desk, and his brow furrowed in concern.

"Not exactly." I crossed my legs and settled back in the chair. "But I need you to tell me about the day that Konstantin Black tried to kill you."

"I'd be happy to tell you anything you want to know, but I don't know how much there is to tell." Dad shook his head. "I mean, you were there and witnessed most of it. What you didn't witness, we've already talked about."

And we had. Dad had been interviewed by multiple Högdragen and even the King himself, as they tried to get to the bottom of what had happened with Konstantin. Beyond that, Dad and I had talked about it after it had happened. I'd been just as confused as everyone else, if not more so.

"It's been a long time, though. I need a refresher," I said.

"All right." Dad set his glasses aside on the desk and leaned back in his chair. "We were at the celebration that night, and everyone was there. Lots of people were drunk. We were all in good spirits about the Vittra King being killed. Konstantin was working, but I don't even really remember seeing him. You probably had a better view of him than I did."

I had had my eyes on Konstantin most of the night. While my duties were to stand at attention during formalities and help keep inebriated townsfolk from causing a ruckus, most of that really meant standing at the side of the room and watching. So my gaze frequently went to Konstantin, who smiled much more than a member of the Högdragen was supposed to.

That was honestly what I remembered most about him that

night. Him standing proud and confident in his lush uniform, smiling and laughing with anyone who bumped into him as he stood by the King and Queen's side. Konstantin had seemed like a man in good spirits—not like one plotting murder.

"I grew weary of the party, probably fairly early in the evening. At least by your standards. I am an old man, after all." Dad offered a small smile to lighten the story. "I headed back to my office, where I worked on a letter to the Trylle. I fell asleep briefly at my desk, I believe, and I kept periodically peeking out so I could catch you before you left."

"You were kind of stalking me that night?" I asked, raising a bemused eyebrow.

"You were only fifteen and it was your first night on the job, and there were far too many drunk idiots dancing around." He shrugged. "I wanted to make sure it went okay for you."

"Thank you." I smiled, warmed by the thought of my dad watching out for me, whether I'd needed it or not.

"You're very welcome," Dad said. "And when you were done, Konstantin found us in the main hall, and that was the first time I'd spoken to him all night."

"When was the last time you'd spoken to him before that?" I asked.

"Um, I'm not completely sure." He scratched his temple. "I think probably the day before. Konstantin had come to get me to ask me something on the Queen's behalf about the celebration. I don't remember exactly what it was, but I think it was just basic palace party stuff. Nothing out of the ordinary, really."

"Had you ever fought with Konstantin?" I pressed.

"No." Dad shook his head. "No, we barely spoke. I saw him around the palace from time to time, but the only times we ever talked was if he was passing along a message from the King or Queen, or vice versa.

"I know he was something of a star to folks around here," he went on. "And I never really bought into the hero worship, but I'd never had a bad word to say about him. He could be cocky, but he was polite and efficient, and he seemed to do his job well, so I never had reason to complain."

"Did he say anything to you?" I asked. "After you left me in the hall, and you and Konstantin walked back to the Queen's office."

"We chatted a bit on the way to the office, talking about the party and how late it was." Dad shrugged. "We were both tired, but it was all basic, nothing giving any indication that he was unhappy with me." He leaned forward, resting his elbows on the desk, and then rubbed the back of his neck. "That's why I never thought it was personal."

"He wasn't mad at you. He was trying to get rid of the Chancellor," I said, surmising what I'd long suspected.

Dad nodded. "Right. I don't know why he went after me and not the King or Queen. Obviously, they have more power than me. But maybe he planned on going after them next. I don't know."

"What did he say to you once you got to the Queen's office?" I asked.

"First he had me looking around for the Queen's document I was supposed to go over, which now I know doesn't exist. I don't know why he was having me search around her desk for something that wasn't real, unless he was stalling for time, but I don't know why he'd do that." He rubbed his chin, contemplating.

"You think he may have been putting off his assassination attempt?" I asked when Dad didn't say anything for a moment.

He shook his head, as if clearing it. "Honestly, I don't know. Maybe. Or maybe he was just waiting for the right moment."

"Did the right moment ever come?"

"Yeah, it must've." He leaned back again, his eyes far away as he was lost in his memory of that night. "When I was bent over, digging through a drawer in the Queen's desk.

"Then Konstantin said, 'Chancellor, I am very sorry.' And I turned around, thinking he was apologizing for misplacing the paper, and I started to tell him it was all right. Then I saw that his sword was drawn.

"I held up my hands, and I said, 'You don't have to do this. We can talk about it.'" Dad fell silent, letting out a heavy breath. "Konstantin shook his head once, and he said, 'I have nothing I can say.' And that was it."

"And then he stabbed you," I supplied quietly.

"I dodged to the side, not enough to miss his blade entirely, but enough so it missed my heart by an inch." He touched his chest, rubbing the spot where his scar was hidden beneath his shirt. "I cried out, and I fell to the ground. And you came running in."

I knew how the rest of the story played out. With Konstantin apologizing to me. Then I charged at him and he stabbed me through the shoulder before escaping into the night.

I leaned forward, looking up at my dad intently. "I need to ask you something, and it's going to sound weird, but I want you to be honest with me."

"I always try to be honest with you," Dad replied.

"Do you think Konstantin wanted to kill you?" I asked him directly.

He ran his hand through his hair, pushing it back from his forehead, and took a minute before speaking. "You know, I thought about that a lot then, and I didn't tell anybody the truth, because it sounded insane. And then after he stabbed me, he'd hurt you, and I couldn't forgive him for that. He had no business going after you. You were just a kid."

"Dad. You didn't answer the question."

"The truth is . . . no." He answered almost sadly. "I don't think Konstantin wanted to kill me. I don't even think he wanted to hurt me. It doesn't make it any better that he did. In fact, it makes it worse. He nearly killed me and hurt you, for no good reason."

"Do you think . . ." I licked my lips, choosing my words very carefully. "Do you think maybe he had a good reason, and we just don't know what it was?"

"He could've killed you, Bryn, and there is no reason in the world that would've been good enough for that," Dad said simply, and I couldn't argue with him.

If Konstantin had killed my dad, I wouldn't even be asking what his reasons were. They wouldn't have mattered. But since he hadn't succeeded, I allowed myself to entertain the idea that something much larger was in place, something that made Konstantin an unwilling agent of evil.

Even though I should only have vengeance in my heart, I found myself struck by something my dad had said. Or, more accurately, something Dad had said that Konstantin had told him right before he stabbed him: *I have nothing I can say.*

Not *there's nothing to say* or *we have nothing to talk about.* No, there was nothing that Konstantin *could* say, as if he hadn't been allowed to.

The more I researched Konstantin, the less I seemed to know. For the past four years, I'd been haunted by the fact that I had no idea why he'd gone after my father, and now his motivations left me even more baffled than ever before.

He hadn't even known my father would be there that late. Konstantin happened to stumble upon us in the hall. If Dad hadn't been waiting for me, Konstantin wouldn't even have had a chance to do anything.

So why that night? Why that moment, when it wasn't something he could've planned for? And why try to kill the Chancellor, and not the King or Queen?

borealis

My mind was still swimming with what my dad had told me as I made the trek home in the darkness. The air was crisp and clean, even if it did leave my face icy, and I shoved my hands deeper in my pockets. The moon had begun to wane, but it was still bright and rather fat, illuminating the clear sky.

It was late enough that the cobblestone roads leading away from my parents' house were empty. Even the chickens and goats that frequently wandered the area had gone home to rest for the night.

I heard another set of footsteps, echoing off the stone, coming toward me from a cross street, but I didn't really register them. I was too lost in my thoughts, trying to figure out what I was missing with Konstantin.

"You don't see enough of me already, so you've resorted to stalking me?" Ridley asked, and I glanced up to see him walking over to me, grinning crookedly.

"What?" I was startled by him, and it took a second for me to realize he was joking. Then I smiled back and motioned toward my parents' place. "No. I was just coming from my parents' cottage."

"Likely story." He'd reached me, and we both stood in the middle of the empty road. "Care if I join you?"

"Sure." I shrugged and started walking north again, and he fell in stride beside me. "We're gonna have to split off soon, though. Your place is west, and mine is east."

"We'll worry about it when we come to it. For now, let's just enjoy the time we have together," he said simply.

We walked for a little while, neither of us saying anything. I wished that silence had felt comfortable and easy between us, like it used to. But now it felt thick and heavy, filled with things that I didn't want to say.

"Aren't you gonna accuse me of being the one stalking you?" Ridley asked finally, and he'd fallen a bit behind, so I slowed to meet his steps.

"No." I stared down at the road, watching pebbles crunch underneath my feet, and I found myself saying something I'd been trying to pretend wasn't true. "I assumed you were coming from Juni's."

"I was," he admitted. "You don't like her very much, do you?"

"No, of course I like her," I said, probably too quickly and too enthusiastically, but that had to be better than confessing how I really felt. "She's fantastic and probably the nicest person that's ever lived. What's not to like?"

"You say that, but you sound annoyed."

"I don't mean to. I'm not." I looked over at him, forcing the brightest smile I could manage. "She's great. I'm happy for you. For both of you."

"Thanks," he said, sounding as halfhearted as I had.

"Just . . ." A lump grew in my throat, thick and suffocating, and yet I continued to talk around it, asking a question that I knew I shouldn't ask. Even as the words fell out of my mouth, twisting my heart painfully, I wished I hadn't said anything at all. "Why her?"

"Why her what?" Ridley asked.

"You dated all these girls for so long, and when I say 'dated,' I'm using the word very liberally." Words kept tumbling out as I struggled to explain away what I really meant. "Because you had a string of girls you saw maybe once or twice, and I get that Juni's perfect." I paused, remembering that she was actually amazing. "I mean, she is *perfect*. But . . ." I trailed off. "I don't know. I don't even know what I'm asking."

He didn't answer right away, which only made me more nervous. My stomach churned, and my heart had begun to beat so rapidly, I'd begun to feel weak. Why had I said anything at all? Why couldn't I just forget that I felt anything for Ridley? Why was it so hard not to want something I knew I could never have?

"Things changed," he said at length. "I'm getting older, and running around doesn't have the same appeal. I realized that I don't wanna do that anymore. That I don't want to be that guy, and I'm sick of living like I'm just a kid without a care in the world. I care about things, I have responsibilities, and I want just *one* girl."

"That all makes sense," I said, even though I wasn't sure if it did or not. I just wanted to end the conversation and move on to something that felt much less terrifying and painful.

"Does it? I hoped it did. Sometimes I just ramble."

"I've long since suspected that." I tried to keep my tone light, to make a joke of things, but I wasn't sure if it worked.

Either way, we didn't say anything more, and we'd finally reached the fork in the road. A small, triangle-shaped sweets shop diverged the road into two paths—one going to the west end, where Ridley lived among the mansions, and one to the east end, where I lived in my loft above the barn.

"Here we are." I stopped and turned to face him, since it seemed rude to just walk away, even though I really wanted to.

Ridley looked around, as if expecting to find something exciting. "Where are we?"

"The point where we should split off." I gestured to the two roads.

"Why here? Why not keep going a block that way?" He stuck his thumb back behind him, at the road that led to his house.

"The road splits here, and that'll take me a block out of my direction."

"Then I'll go that way," he offered and pointed to my road.

I shook my head. "That'll take you a block out of your way."

"Maybe I don't mind going out of my way. Maybe I like the extra detour." He was smiling, but his eyes were serious. "Would it be so bad if I wanted to spend a few more minutes with you?"

"It's not bad. It's just . . ." I stopped when I saw color splashing on his face, and I turned my gaze up at the night sky to the aurora borealis shimmering above us. "Look at that."

Vibrant blue shifting to brilliant violet light illuminated the ether in winding arcs. Stars glimmered like diamonds in the indigo sky as pulsating hues washed across the night sky in luscious waves.

"Oh wow," he whispered.

"It's amazing." I stared up in awe at the dazzling colors dancing across the clear night sky. "No matter how many times I see the northern lights, I'm still stunned by how beautiful they are."

"Yeah, I know exactly what you mean," Ridley said. There was something low and meaningful in his voice that made me turn to him, but he was already looking at me.

"What?" I asked, confused by the somberness in his expression.

"Before when we were talking, were you asking why *her*?" The aurora above us reflected on his face, and his dark eyes were filled with heat. "Or were you asking why *not* you?"

"No. No." I avoided his gaze and ran my hand through my hair. "I would never. No." I swallowed hard. "I know why not me."

"Why not you?" he repeated.

"Because it's wrong." I finally met his eyes and tried to smile at him, trying to play off the growing pain in my chest. "There's a million reasons why not me, and you know them all. And you don't . . . you don't even want to anyway."

He smiled in disbelief at me. "I've wanted to kiss you practically since the day I met you. But I knew you would never let me."

"How would you know that if you never tried?" I asked, and then I was too nervous to even breathe, terrified of what might happen next.

For a second he only stared at me, and I wished I'd never said anything. I wished I'd left my parents' house five minutes sooner so I wouldn't even have seen him at all tonight, and I wouldn't be playing this stupid game where I pretend that we like each other or that we could ever be together. Because I know we can't, and he knows we can't, so it's better if he just walks away. If he just turns around and leaves me here alone, but my heart is thudding painfully in my chest, begging him to kiss me.

And just when I'm certain he won't, and I'm about to turn and hurry away in shame, he's there. His lips are cold, pressing hungrily against mine. His fingers knotting in my hair, pulling me to him. His stubble scrapes against my lips and cheeks, but I don't mind, I like it. I love everything about him that feels so real, touching me, holding me.

I wrap my arms around his neck, and I bury my hands in his hair. It's longer and thicker than I thought it would be, and I feel the curls at the nape of his neck wrapping around my fingertips.

He's strong, stronger than I thought he'd be, and his arm around my waist is crushing me to him so hard that I can barely breathe. But I don't care. I don't want to breathe. I just want to kiss him forever, tasting him on my lips, feeling him against me.

But then he pulls away, gasping for breath, but he keeps his face close to mine.

And then suddenly, as oxygen fills my lungs, my senses take

hold of me, and I realize exactly how wrong that was. I let go of him and step back, even though it kills me a little to do it.

Ridley stands there, his arms falling to his side, as he watches me back away from him.

"I have to go," I say, because I can't think of anything better, and then I turn and I'm running as fast as my legs will carry me, as far away from Ridley as I can get.

TWENTY-EIGHT

contrition

I didn't expect to see you," Tilda said with ice in her voice, but she'd let me into her place, so it couldn't be all bad.

She lived in a small apartment above an electronics store. On the outside, the store appeared to be an ordinary shop, like a haberdashery from a village in a fairy tale. But inside, it was filled with slick gadgets—all of them a model or two behind whatever was most popular with the humans, since we did a horrible job of stocking and ordering things. Besides, there wasn't *that* much of a demand for them in Doldastam.

Still, Tilda's apartment had to be one of the more modern spaces in town. Her furniture reminded me of the hotel I'd visited in Calgary, and she had a stainless steel dishwasher next to her sink—the only one I'd ever seen in Doldastam. A flat-screen TV sat across from her sofa, and while TV wasn't unheard-of here, it wasn't exactly a staple in every home.

"So what is it that I can do for you?" Tilda folded her arms over her chest, and the loose fabric of her tank top shifted, showing the slight swelling of her belly that I should've realized the significance of sooner.

"I just wanted to talk to you." I shoved my hands in my pockets and tried not to visibly recoil under the scrutiny of her glare. "I needed to apologize for the things I said yesterday. I was out of line."

"Damn right you were," Tilda snapped, but she stepped back from me, giving me room to move in from the entryway. She sighed and rolled her eyes before turning to walk into the kitchen. "Do you want anything? I was gonna make some tea."

"Sure. I'll have whatever you're having," I said, following behind her.

"Blackberry and hibiscus it is." Her long chestnut hair was pulled back in a ponytail, and it swayed behind her as she moved around, putting the kettle on the stove to boil, and getting the tea and cups out from the cupboard.

Then she turned back to face me, her arms once again crossed over her chest, her gray eyes staring at me expectantly. "So? Where's the apology?"

"I am really and truly sorry for everything that I said to you at the meeting yesterday," I told her emphatically. "I was upset about things that weren't your fault and really had nothing to do with you, and I shouldn't have yelled at you. You're my friend, and I should've been happy for you."

"That's true." She relaxed a bit. "You have your own bag of issues with love and relationships that I don't even wanna get into, but that is *your* deal, and you had no right to take it out on me."

"No. You're absolutely right," I agreed. "I acted like a jerk for no reason, and I'm sorry. Honestly, I'm very happy for you. If you're happy and this is what you want."

"I am happy, and this is what I want." Her whole face lit up when she put her hand on her stomach. "I love Kasper, and although this baby wasn't exactly planned, I'm happy about it."

"You'll make a great mom," I said, and I meant it.

She smiled gratefully at me. "Thank you."

The kettle whistled, so she turned away and poured the hot water into cups. Carefully, she scooped the fresh tea leaves from the tin, and filled two acorn-shaped infusers with the leaves before dropping them in the cups.

"Now, what's going on with you this morning?" Tilda asked as she handed me a cup.

I leaned back against the counter and sipped my tea before replying. "What do you mean?"

"Bags under your eyes, your hair isn't brushed, and you look like hell," she said bluntly. "Did you get any sleep last night?"

I ran my fingers through my tangles of hair, trying to smooth it out, before giving up. "I got some sleep."

"So what was keeping you up?" she asked.

Last night, I kissed Ridley, and then ran away so fast that by the time I got home I could barely breathe. It was a horrible, terrible mistake that I had no idea how to correct, but it was also wonderful and magical, and part of me—too large of a part, really—kept trying to figure out how to make it happen again.

"That might be too much to get into right now," I said, because it was much easier than explaining anything else, and I bobbed the infuser up and down in my cup.

A key clicked in the lock, and both Tilda and I looked at the front door to her apartment. Her boyfriend Kasper pushed open the door, dressed in his Högdragen uniform. The fabric fit snugly on his broad shoulders, and his black hair was cropped in short, neat curls.

"I didn't expect you home so early," Tilda said. "I thought you were working today."

"I am, but I'm actually here looking for Bryn." He motioned to me, and I straightened up and away from the counter.

"Me? Why? And how did you even know I'd be here?" I asked.

"I stopped by your place, and you weren't there, so I thought maybe Tilda might know where you were," Kasper explained. "There's urgent business at the palace."

I set my cup of tea down. "What do you mean?"

"Is something wrong?" Tilda asked.

"I don't know." He gave her an apologetic look and shook his head. "They just sent me to get Bryn, and said the King and Queen want to see you immediately."

"I'm sure it's fine." Tilda smiled at me, but worry filled her eyes. "And when you're done, just let me know if you need anything, okay?"

I nodded, and then waited as Kasper kissed her briefly on the lips. Tilda walked us to the door, and I followed Kasper down the stairs and out to the street. He took long, deliberate steps, the way all the Högdragen were taught to. I tried to match my pace to his, but he was much taller than me, which made it a bit harder.

"I don't know what it's about, but I don't think you're in trouble." He glanced back at me, making sure I was keeping up.

"Then what is it?" I pressed.

"I really can't say more, Bryn."

He shook his head, and looked ahead again, quickly weaving through the busy marketplace as we made our way toward the palace. People parted for him out of respect for his uniform, and some of the younger kids even stopped to stare.

I had no idea what could possibly be going on, but the King and Queen had a sent a member of the Högdragen to personally retrieve me. That did not bode well.

TWENTY-NINE

departure

The King sat in his high-backed chair beneath the massive portrait of himself as a younger man at his coronation. His wife paced the meeting room, and this was the least formal I'd ever seen the Queen. She wore a simple white dress underneath a long silver satin robe that billowed out around her as she moved, and the length of her hair lay in a braid down her back.

My father stood at the end of the table near the King, with a piece of paper before him. The paper had been rolled, and the ends kept trying to curl back up, so I could see the wax seal at the top. It was blue, imprinted with a fish—the seal of the Skojare.

"Your Majesties, Chancellor." Kasper bowed when he entered the room, and I followed suit before he introduced me. "Bryn Aven has arrived to see you."

"Thank you." King Evert waved at him absently, the heavy rings on his hand catching the light from the chandelier above us.

Kasper left, closing the door behind him, and I stood at the end of the table, opposite the King, and waited to be told why I'd been brought here.

"Thank you for coming here so quickly." Evert spoke to me, but his eyes were elsewhere and he shifted in his seat.

"This is unnecessary," Mina hissed. She'd stopped pacing to glare down at her husband.

"I really do think this is the best course of action," my dad said, looking between the two of them. "Given this letter, and the situation we've been dealing with, it does make sense."

"Sorry for interrupting, Your Highness," I began, and they all turned to look at me, as if they'd forgotten I was there even though I'd just arrived. "But why have you summoned me?"

"Tell her about the letter," the King directed my dad with a heavy sigh.

"This morning we received this letter from Mikko Biâelse, the King of the Skojare." Dad held up the paper. "His wife Linnea, the Queen, has gone missing."

"Missing?" I asked.

"She's only a child. Perhaps she found being married to an old man unbearable and ran away," Mina argued. "I've heard of far stranger things."

It had only been a week ago that I'd met with Linnea, her husband, and her brother-in-law in a neighboring room for brunch. She'd been poised but friendly, and there had been a loneliness about her. And she'd been very young, with an aloof husband, so Mina's claims didn't seem unreasonable.

"In light of the current situation with our own changelings, I think we need to consider kidnapping," Dad reasoned. "Mikko seems convinced that Linnea didn't leave of her own accord and he's asked for help in recovering her."

"Husbands know so little of what their wives are up to," Mina sneered, and Evert gave her a hard look, causing her to roll her eyes. "Oh, you know what I mean."

"I agree with the Chancellor on this one," Evert said, and Mina huffed and began to pace again. "With Konstantin Black out for blood, we need to take all of this seriously."

"It's because of Konstantin Black that we shouldn't get involved!" Mina insisted. "We don't know where he is or when he may strike again."

"Our involvement will be very minimal," Dad said. "Bryn would go to Storvatten, working as liaison for us, and would help if she can. There's a good chance she won't be able to do much more than offer condolences, but that will be enough to secure our position as their friend and ally."

"I'm to be a liaison?" I asked, and though I should've been nervous, my initial reaction was one of pride. I let out an excited breath and tried my best to suppress a smile, but I still held my head up higher.

"Yes. With your Skojare blood, we thought you'd be the best tracker for the job," King Evert informed me.

While I felt a little deflated upon learning I'd been chosen for the job because of who my mom was and not because I was the most qualified, I decided that being Skojare counted as a qualification, and whether the King knew it or not, I was the most capable for the job.

Being the liaison was a very high honor, and one that would

certainly look outstanding on my résumé when I applied to join the Högdragen. But even in the immediate future, this role could lead to other important tasks. It could be the beginning of the career I'd spent my whole life working toward.

Mina shook her head, then looked over at me. "Have you ever even been to Storvatten, tracker?"

"No, my Queen, I have not," I admitted, bristling slightly at being called *tracker* instead of my name, since I knew she knew it. "But my mother grew up there, and she has told me many stories about it and her family."

Dad gave me a look, since I'd exaggerated. Mom very rarely spoke of her hometown, but I would say nearly anything at this point so I wouldn't lose my chance at being liaison.

"See?" Evert gestured widely. "Bryn's perfect for the job. She'll make nice, and everything will be fine."

"She may be the best one for the job." Mina stopped walking and wrung her hands together. "I just think it would be very unwise to send away help when so much is going on here. The Skojare have done nothing for us, and we don't need to risk our kingdom for them."

"They need our aid." Evert held his hand out to her, and reluctantly, she took it, letting him comfort her. "This will go a long way to furthering an alliance with them."

"We don't need an alliance with them," Mina said. "Perhaps this is the beginning of their death rattle, and we shouldn't interfere."

"You say that as if their stockpile of sapphires means nothing to you." The King gave her a knowing look, and Mina's lips pressed into a bee-stung pout. "We are working toward a new era of peace, and they've asked for our help. We can spare one tracker."

"Pardon, Your Highness," my dad interrupted. "But given the state of things, wouldn't it be prudent to send two trackers out on the mission? Just to be safe."

"I've agreed to send this *one* tracker!" Mina pointed at me. "Not anyone else!"

"If I may offer a suggestion, My Queen, Ember Holmes is only on partial duty because of her injury, but she would still be a great asset to me," I said, hoping to ease her anxiety.

"She's suffered a fracture." Dad dismissed the idea with a shake of his head. "It's unfair to ask her to risk further injury by sending her out to work again."

"The Chancellor is right, but so is Mina." Evert still held her hand and offered her a sidelong glance. "I'd rather not spare another good set of hands when we're not sure when Konstantin may strike again."

"What about the Rektor?" Mina asked. "He adds little to our security, doesn't he?"

"Ridley Dresden?" Dad considered this, and my heart dropped. "He's a capable tracker."

"Sire, I don't think that Ridley is well suited for this," I interjected, wanting to put an end to the idea before it got started. I didn't really have any reason other than it sounded like an awkward hell traveling with him after our kiss last night.

Dad raised an eyebrow, surprised by my protest, and he continued on with his support for Ridley. "He's actually more skilled in relations with other tribes than Bryn is, so he'd be a great addition to the mission."

"I had asked him to stay back from the field for a while to focus on paperwork here . . ." Evert shrugged. "But we could spare him for a few days to go on this fact-finding mission with Bryn."

"Your Highness, with all due respect, there are other trackers that may be better," I tried again. "Simon Bohlin is—"

But Mina cut me off. "If they're better, then we need them here, protecting us."

"The Queen has spoken," King Evert decreed. "Now I suggest you pack your things and get on your way as soon as you can. They are expecting you in Storvatten by tomorrow morning."

"Yes, Your Majesty." I bowed before him and the Queen. "Thank you for the opportunity."

shamed

I'd offered to drive, but Ridley had insisted he could do it. That was the last time we'd spoken to each other, and that had been over ten hours ago. We'd stopped for gas, bathroom breaks, and cheap gas station food, and we had managed to do it all without exchanging a word.

Our conversation before we left had been quick and to the point. My dad had been there—either fortunately or unfortunately, I wasn't sure which—and he'd relayed the parameters of the mission to Ridley, so there had been little need for us to speak.

Ridley occasionally hummed along to whatever song was playing on the stereo, but that was it. I stared out the passenger window, watching the barren landscape change from snow-covered plains and lakes to green tree-covered forests the farther south we went.

"It's getting dark," I said finally and turned to look at him.

Ridley's hand tightened on the steering wheel, and he kept his eyes locked on the empty stretch of highway before us. "So it is."

"We can switch. I can drive through the night," I offered.

"No need." He tilted his head, cracking his neck. "You haven't slept this whole time, so it doesn't matter if I drive or not. We'll be in the same boat."

"Do you want to stop for the night?" I asked, even though I thought I already knew the answer.

"We're expected in the morning. We don't have time to stop."

I sighed, and then gave up on talking. I slumped lower in my seat and pulled my knees up, resting my bare feet against the dashboard. But now the silence somehow felt even more unbearable, so I looked over at him.

"I'm sorry."

His jaw tensed, and he waited a beat before asking, "For what?"

"Whatever it is that has you so pissed off at me," I said, because I really didn't know why he was mad. Something to do with us kissing, obviously, but I didn't know what, exactly.

"I'm not mad at you," Ridley said, but he sounded exasperated. "I just . . ." His shoulders sagged, and his hand loosened on the steering wheel. "I don't know what to say to you."

"Things are . . . awkward," I agreed. "But maybe if we talk, it'll be less awkward."

"All right." He rubbed the back of his head and took a deep breath. "That kiss last night was a mistake."

I knew it was. Deep down, I knew it was a mistake. But still, after hearing *him* say it, my heart felt like it had been torn in half. The pain in my chest was so great, I wasn't sure I'd be able to speak. But I did, and I did it while keeping my voice and my expression blank.

"It was," I said, sounding astonishingly normal, and I pushed the heartache down.

He was right, so I had no reason to feel bad about it. And if he hadn't said it was a mistake, I would have. Because we both knew it was. We both knew it was something that could never happen again.

"It happened . . ." He trailed off, like he didn't remember what he wanted to say for a second. "I don't know why it happened, I guess, but it did."

"It did," I said, unsure of what else to say. "But it's over now, and it's probably for the best if we just pretend it never happened."

"Right," he said under his breath. "That'll make everything okay again."

"Do you have any better suggestions?" I asked him pointedly.

He pressed his lips together in a line, and his eyes darkened. "Nope. Your plan will work great."

I ran both my hands through my hair, pushing it back from my face, and I wished he wasn't being so difficult. "Did you tell Juni about it?"

"No. I haven't yet."

I rested my head against the seat and watched as the first

stars began to shine in the darkening sky. "Maybe you shouldn't."

"Why not?" Ridley asked.

"I just think maybe it'd be better if nobody knew about it."

"Okay," he said after a pregnant pause. "I mean, if that's what you want."

"With me being the liaison for the King and Queen, and you coming with and being my boss, I just don't think it would look good. Especially now that I'm getting more responsibility."

"Right. Of course," he said, and the edge to his voice was unmistakable.

"How about some music?" I suggested, since the conversation hadn't gone as well as I'd hoped.

Instead of waiting for him to answer, I leaned over and turned up the stereo. It was Bastille's song "Pompeii," one that I normally loved to sing along to, but now I just wanted it to blanket the silence between us, so I could go back to staring out the window and pretending that it didn't kill me to be this close to Ridley.

We drove all night, and with the aid of energy drinks that Ridley really hated the taste of, he managed to stay awake. I slept some in the very early morning hours, with my head resting against the cold glass of the window, but he refused to let me drive, so I didn't feel guilty about it.

The name *Storvatten* when translated roughly meant "great water," which was fitting, since the Skojare capital was located on the northern coast of Lake Superior, not far from where the province of Ontario met Minnesota.

When we were about twenty minutes away, Ridley pulled

over to the side of the road so we could freshen up. It wouldn't be proper for us to meet with the royalty looking all disheveled and unkempt. He stood to the side of the Land Rover, changing from his jeans into a sharp suit, while I crawled into the way-back of the SUV.

I'd debated whether to wear a pantsuit or a dress before finally deciding that a dress would probably be more fitting, and then hurriedly applied makeup and fixed my hair. Ridley had already gotten back in the driver's seat when I climbed into the front, carefully so he wouldn't get a look up my skirt. With dresses, I never wore anything with a hem that went past my knees, so it wouldn't restrict my movement if I needed to fight.

The Skojare palace was supposed to be quite beautiful, and as we approached it, with the rising sun backlighting it with pinks and yellows on the lake, it did not disappoint. The palace was half submerged in water, with the top half sitting on the lake like an island. The entrance was on land, a docklike walkway made of rocks and wood that led to the front door.

Ridley stopped at the end of the dock, where a footman told us he'd alert the King to our arrival, before taking our SUV to park in a nearby garage. As we walked out on the dock—stretching nearly a mile out to the palace—I raised my hand over my eyes, shielding them from the sun, so I could get a better look at the palace.

It was astounding, unlike the palace in Doldastam or the Trylle palace in Förening that I had visited once. Those were beautiful, but they looked like mansions or castles. This was otherworldly, with glass walls shaped into swirls and spirals that pierced the heavens.

When we reached the doors—made of heavy iron—Ridley knocked loudly, and I stared up at the fantastic structure that towered above us. The Skojare must've had a very strong power of persuasion, so they could convince locals around here that they weren't seeing this majestic castle. It was translucent blue, which helped camouflage it with the lake, but the only real way to get humans from interfering was to trick them with psycho-kinesis.

"You look really nice," Ridley said, pulling my attention back to him. His hands were folded neatly in front of him, and he looked straight ahead at the door. "I always thought you looked good in dresses. You've got the gams for them."

"Gams?" I asked in surprise.

He smirked. "It's a cooler word for legs."

I gaped at him, trying to think of a way to respond, but then the palace door swung open, and we stepped inside.

THIRTY-ONE

great water

Inside, the palace reminded me of ice. Many of the walls were made of frosted glass several feet thick. The glass itself appeared bluish, but it had been sandblasted to make it opaque. The other walls were covered in a silvery blue wallpaper that looked like frost.

The glass walls that surrounded the spacious main hall had been shaped to look like waves, making it seem as if we were standing in the center of a whirlpool. The floor was made of several large panes of glass, allowing us to see down into the pool below.

"Look at that," Ridley whispered, and pointed to a girl in a bathing suit as she swam beneath us.

We'd been left here by the footman who greeted us at the door, while he went to retrieve the King. That gave us plenty of time to admire the unusual and lavish décor of the Skojare palace.

"So good of you to make the trip," a woman said, startling us from our admiration.

As she strode across to meet us, a length of her elegant sapphire dress trailed on the floor behind her, and her lips pressed into a thin smile that didn't quite reach the ice-blue of her eyes. Her porcelain skin had been softly lined by age, and I suspected she was in her early sixties, although she still held all of the beauty she had certainly had in her youth.

"We're very glad to help," Ridley told her.

"And you are . . . ?" She turned to Ridley, her sharp eyes now fixed on him.

"Ridley Dresden. I'm the Rektor for the Kanin."

"Hmm." She considered us both for a moment, then let out a resigned sigh. "I am Marksinna Lisbet Ahlstrom. My granddaughter is the Queen, Linnea."

"We're sorry for your situation, and we will do our best to help you find her," I said.

Her eyes rested on me. "You must be Bryn Aven. You look so much like your mother." She smiled when she said it, but there was something about her voice that made me believe it wasn't a compliment. "Runa was my niece." She corrected herself. "She still is, of course, but since she defected so many years ago, I've gotten in the awful habit of referring to her in the past tense."

"That's understandable," I said evenly.

"Anyway, to the business at hand." Her smile twitched, betraying the sadness underneath, and she absently touched her blond coif. "Linnea is my granddaughter. A tragic car accident left her orphaned eleven years ago, and I've been raising her ever since." Tears formed in Lisbet's eyes, but she blinked them back. "She's all I have."

"Do you have any idea where she might have gone?" Ridley asked. "Was there any indication that she might be unhappy, or that she'd wanted to leave?"

A massive door on the other side of the hall was thrown open, the heavy wood slamming loudly into the wall, and King Mikko burst through, accompanied by his brother Kennet. Like Lisbet, Kennet was dressed formally. He wore a gray suit made of a material that reminded me of shark's skin.

Mikko, on the other hand, looked like an absolute mess as he hurried over to us. One of the tails of his shirt had come untucked, the top few buttons were undone, and his suit jacket didn't match his pants. But beyond that, he was unshaven, his eyes were red-rimmed, and his hair was disheveled.

"You need to find my wife," he insisted, his voice a low rumble. Kennet put his hand on his shoulder, trying to calm his brother.

"They're here to help," Lisbet told him, speaking to him the same way one might speak to a frightened child. "But they've only just arrived."

"She's . . ." Mikko shook his head, then gave me the most demanding, panicked look. "Something bad has happened. She wouldn't just leave. You need to find her before . . ." He choked up, and Lisbet put her arm around him.

"This has been very hard on the King," Lisbet said. "Perhaps it's best if I take him to lie down while the Prince fills you in on the details."

"I want to help," Mikko insisted, but though he was much bigger and invariably stronger than Lisbet, she pulled him away from us without a struggle.

"You need to rest now. That will be a great help to us," Kennet assured his brother.

He watched as Lisbet led Mikko away, and turned back to us once they'd disappeared through the doors that Mikko had burst in through.

"The King seems to be taking it very hard," Ridley commented.

"I'm a little surprised by his display," I said, choosing my words as carefully as I could. "When I met him before, he seemed somewhat . . . aloof."

Kennet gave me a knowing smile. "My brother is a very complicated man."

"What exactly has happened with the Queen?" Ridley asked. "What do you know of her disappearance?"

"The King and Queen retired to their chambers two nights ago," Kennet explained. "Linnea couldn't sleep, so she told the King she was heading down for a swim. He went to sleep, and when he awoke at three in the morning and realized she hadn't returned, he alerted the guards and began a search for her." Kennet gave a helpless shrug. "She hasn't been seen since."

"We would like to speak to the guards who conducted the search, if that's possible," Ridley said.

"Definitely." Kennet nodded. "We'll have a meeting to brief you with the details as soon as the others arrive."

"The others?" I asked.

"Yes. The Trylle have offered to send help as well, and they should be arriving shortly," Kennet said, and though his expression was somber, a light played in his aqua eyes as he looked down at me. "But we very much appreciate you coming. I'm not sure what we would've done if you hadn't."

"We're always happy to help our allies," Ridley said rather brusquely, and Kennet glanced over at him.

"I'm sure you've had a very long drive here." Kennet's expression shifted instantly from grave to megawatt smile. "I'll show you to your rooms, so you can rest and freshen up for a bit. As soon as the Trylle arrive, we'll have the meeting."

"Don't you think it's best if we start the search now?" Ridley asked. "Whether the Queen has left of her own volition or been forced away against her will, the trail to find her will only get colder as time goes on."

"The Trylle are set to arrive within the half hour." Kennet still had a smile plastered across his face, but his tone didn't sound pleased. "The trail won't have frozen over by then. Besides, this was as the King wanted it, and I'm certain you know how to properly follow the King's orders."

Ridley smiled back. "Of course."

"Now." Kennet faced me. "Let's go to your rooms."

He turned and led the way out of the main hall, speaking in slightly bored tones about the history of the palace. The main floor was entirely above the surface of the lake, while the private quarters and the ballroom were located underneath the water. It had been specifically built so from anywhere in the palace, anyone could access the lake within five minutes.

As we went down a spiral staircase to the lower level, I noted that despite the recurring marine theme, the Skojare palace was decorated similarly to other palaces. A sculpture that appeared to be a Bernini sat in the center of the great room at the bottom of the stairs.

"That's Neptune and Triton," Kennet said offhandedly as we walked past it.

The floors were marble tiles, alternating between white and navy, and the walls were covered in the same paper as upstairs—blue with an icy sheen. Crystal chandeliers lit the hallway that led to our rooms.

We reached Ridley's room first, with Kennet opening the door and gesturing inside before quickly walking away. I gave Ridley a small smile, then hurried after Kennet to my room at the other end of the hall.

"And here you are." Kennet held the door open for me, and I slid past him. "I'll let you get settled in a bit. There's a bathroom across the hall. My room is at the other wing of the palace." He pointed toward it. "But if you ask any of the servants, they will tell you where to find me.

"If you need anything," he said, his voice low and deep, "anything at all, don't hesitate to find me."

"Thank you," I said, and he smiled at me in a way that I was sure plenty of girls had swooned over before, but I was not the swooning kind, so I merely smiled politely back.

Once he left, shutting the door behind him, I turned to check out my room, and I realized that an underwater palace sounded much nicer than it actually was. The walls facing outside were rounded glass, making me feel more like I was in an aquarium than a luxury bedroom.

The bed and the furnishings were nice, all silks and velvets in blues and silver, but through the windows the lake looked dark and murky. I pressed my hands against the glass and peered upward through the water at the few rays of sunlight that managed to break through.

A small tuft of dark green mold grew where the window met the frame. That explained the smell. As soon as I'd stepped downstairs, I'd noticed the scent of moisture and mold. It reminded me of a dank old basement.

I noticed a small puddle of water dripping down from a leak somewhere near the ceiling. I looked closer and saw water dripping down the wall, leaving a patch of wallpaper faded and warped.

Once upon a time, I was sure, this palace had been absolutely magnificent, but the Skojare's wealth—and thus their ability to maintain a palace of this caliber—had begun to diminish. Since most of the royalty had gills, the Skojare were often unable to leave their offspring as changelings. Humans might overlook an ill-tempered child with odd habits, but they would definitely notice a set of blue gills on their baby.

If they were to reverse the situation, leaving common gill-less Skojare as changelings, the commoners would inherit the wealth, which the royalty did not approve of. Titles and rankings were determined by abilities, so most of the gilled Skojare were in positions of royalty, leaving the entire system to stagnate.

Those born with gills were trapped in Storvatten, unable to

live or work among the humans, while those born without them were left doing the brunt of the work. Fishing was the main source of income for the Skojare, with the gill-less being forced to do the trading with the humans, and the royalty survived through insane amounts of taxes. The ones who could leave and get jobs with the humans often did, so the population of the Skojare had dwindled.

"Bryn?" Ridley asked, rapping on the door once before pushing it open. "How are you doing?"

"Fine." I turned around to face him. "What do you make of all this?"

"I don't know." He flopped back on my bed and folded his hands behind his head. "It was in poor taste for that Prince to flirt with you while we're supposed to be looking for his missing sister-in-law."

I scowled down at Ridley. "He wasn't flirting."

"You never know when anyone is flirting with you," he muttered.

"I do agree that everyone's behavior feels a little . . . *off.*" I sat down on the edge of the bed. "When I met Mikko last week, he was cold and barely spoke. Now he's falling apart?" I shook my head. "It doesn't quite add up."

THIRTY-TWO

suspicion

The meeting room was even more like a fishbowl. It stuck out from the rest of the palace in a bubble, with one interior wall and one extra wall of glass domed out around us. Half the room was still under the palace, with a white antique tin ceiling and plenty of lighting to keep the darkness of the lake around us at bay.

A very long table sat in the center of the room, but there were only three other people in there when the footman showed Ridley and me in. Papers were spread out over the table, but nobody was looking at them. Prince Kennet stood at the far end of the room, and the other two men had their backs to us.

"Come in!" Kennet waved for us to join them, and then the young men turned to face us as we approached. "These are our allies from the Trylle."

The first had unruly chestnut hair that landed just above his ears, and his tanned skin had an almost greenish hue, subtle but noticeable enough that it meant he had strong abilities for the Trylle. The more powerful a Trylle was, the greener he or she was in coloring. He was dressed the less formally of the two—wearing only jeans and a button-up shirt, while his companion wore a suit.

His companion had short dark brown hair, kept smooth and neat. His features were delicate, almost feminine, with a small nose and smooth skin. It was his eyes that stood out the most to me—they were a bright blue, which meant that although he came with the Trylle, he must have Skojare blood in him, too.

"I'd like you to meet our friends from the Kanin," Kennet told them, motioning to us. "These are two of their finest trackers, Ridley Dresden and Bryn Aven."

"It's nice to meet you," the blue-eyed one said, leaning forward and shaking our hands.

"This is the Trylle Chancellor, Bain Ottesen," Kennet gestured to Blue Eyes. "And this is Markis Tove Kroner, adviser to the Trylle Queen."

"Pleasure to meet you both," I said, bowing slightly to them, since they were both apparently my superiors.

The Trylle were peculiar, and growing more so since their new Queen had begun her reign four years ago. They sent white-collar advisers and Chancellors—high-ranking members of their society—while the Kanin had sent blue-collar trackers. Not only because it made sense for us to go, since Ridley and I knew more about going after missing people than an adviser would, but also because our Markis never would do something like this.

But maybe the Trylle just viewed the situation differently.

They may have sent Bain and Tove more as figureheads to lend support rather than actual aid, while King Evert had sent Ridley and me because there was a real fear that something dangerous might be afoot.

"If we're all here, maybe we should get into it, then?" Tove asked, tucking his hair behind his ears.

"Yes, I was saying before, we have the reports from the guards that night, and I have the layout for the palace, if that will help you." Kennet stepped back and motioned to the papers on the table.

"So will we actually be able to interview the guards that searched for the Queen?" Ridley asked.

Kennet shook his head sadly. "The King thought the reports would be adequate enough."

Tove stepped over to the table and started going through the papers until he found the report. I stood next to him, peering over his shoulder so I could read it. It was handwritten, and I couldn't make out every word. But the general gist seemed to be that the guards had looked everywhere and found no trace of her.

"So the King was the last person to see her?" Tove asked as he reached the end of the report.

"Yes," Kennet said. "They were in their chambers together getting ready for bed when she went for a swim."

"Or at least that's what he told you." Tove looked up from the report, fixing his mossy green eyes sharply on Kennet.

Kennet met his gaze evenly and replied, "Yes. That is what he told me."

"This must be a terrible hardship for the King," Bain said, rushing to soften his companion's veiled accusation. "How is he holding up?"

Tove set down the file and moved on to rummaging through the rest of the papers. I'd turned to face Kennet, wanting to see his reaction about his brother, but I kept half an eye on Tove.

"He's very broken up about it," Kennet said.

"Will we be able to speak with him again?" I asked. "I think it would be a great help to get more details from him directly."

"Perhaps later on this evening." Kennet appeared regretful. "But you saw him this morning. You know he's in no condition to see anyone."

"We understand," I said. "But you will let us know when he's feeling better?"

Kennet smiled easily. "Of course."

"There's at least a hundred rooms in here," Tove announced. He stood hunched over the blueprints for the palace. "Are they all occupied? How many people live here?"

"Storvatten is a very small town, so many of the Markis and Marksinna are invited to live in the palace with us," Kennet explained. "At the present time, there are seventy-eight royal members living here, not including servants."

"There's not enough time to interview them all," Tove mumbled.

"On a related note, *who* exactly can we interview?" Ridley asked, doing his best not to sound harsh. "The King and the guards are off the table, which is disappointing, since they're the closest thing we have to eyewitnesses."

"The guards did interview Mikko that night, and it's all in the report." Kennet pointed to the discarded report on the table, which Bain picked up and began to leaf through. "The guards also interviewed everyone in the palace that night, and came up with nothing."

"But we can't interview them?" Ridley asked.

"The King thinks it would be unnecessary to bother them," Kennet explained.

Ridley sighed and folded his arms over his chest. "I don't mean to speak out of place, but with these limits, the King is greatly hampering our investigation. I'm not completely sure what you're expecting us to do here."

Kennet shrugged his shoulders. "I'm not really sure, either."

"Is this the exit?" Tove tapped the blueprints on the bridge that led from the palace to the dry land. "This is the only way to get out of the palace, right? And it's got guards at the end that we had to speak to before we could enter."

"How could the Queen get by without the guards noticing her?" I asked, drawing the same conclusion as Tove.

"That is the only direct way," Kennet allowed. "But there are doors all over that lead right out to the lake. If she walked out, or anyone walked out with her, the guards would've spotted her, and they made no mention of it in the reports."

"But she could have swum away?" Bain asked.

Abruptly, Tove straightened up. "Can I have a moment alone to consult with the others?" he asked Kennet.

"Um, yeah, yes, of course." He fumbled for a moment, then smiled at him. "Take all the time you need."

Kennet took long, fast strides toward the door, his bare feet slapping on the cold marble tiles and echoing through the bubble. None of us said anything until he'd gone, leaving us in a somewhat strained silence.

"What are you thinking?" Bain set aside the file and looked up at Tove with a mixture of affection and concern.

"There seem to be three clear options." Tove leaned back against the table and crossed one foot over the other. "One, someone kidnapped the Queen, somehow bypassing the guards and all the people in the palace. Two, she snuck out that night and decided to run away. Or three, which seems the most likely to me, is that the King killed her and disposed of her body somewhere nearby."

"You can't accuse the King," Bain said quickly, while both Ridley and I stood in silence, processing what Tove had said.

It really wasn't that surprising, and honestly, I'd been thinking of it myself. Based on everything Kennet had told us, it sounded like the King was feigning grief to stonewall our investigation. Combine that with his marriage to a lonely child bride, and contrast his indifference at the meeting with his overt distress at her disappearance, like he was overcompensating, and something didn't add up.

"No, of course not." Tove shook his head. "If the King did kill her, there's nothing we can do about it. If we were to say anything, it would only start a war between our kingdoms. The only ones who could lobby accusations without the risk of treason would be the Prince or maybe Marksinna Lisbet."

"But if King Mikko did kill her, why call us here?" I asked, deciding to play devil's advocate in all of this. "He'd already gotten away with it. Why draw more suspicion on himself?"

"You know why," Ridley said, making me look back at him. "Konstantin Black."

"What would he have to do with this?" I asked.

"The King has to blame his missing wife on someone, and with everything Konstantin has been up to lately, he would make an excellent scapegoat," Ridley said. "And of course, there is the chance that Konstantin *is* actually the one behind the Queen's disappearance."

"Who?" Tove asked.

"The Kanin traitor," Bain reminded him. "He's been kidnapping Kanin changelings."

Tove grimaced. "Right. Sorry. I'm bad with names."

"You really think Konstantin had something to do with this?" I asked Ridley and shook my head. "It doesn't make sense. It's a totally different MO."

"I'm not saying he did it. There's no evidence supporting he has anything to do with this," Ridley said. "But everyone's a bit jumpier with him and Bent Stum running around, especially since we don't really know why they're doing any of this."

"A Queen is a big leap from changeling, though," Tove reasoned. "Especially the Queen of another tribe."

"Bent Stum is Omte and he's been going after Kanin," I argued. "Maybe their plan is to hit all the tribes. The Skojare don't have changelings, so maybe this is his way of attacking them."

Bain and Tove exchanged a look. Bain pursed his lips, then shifted his weight from one foot to the other.

"That traitor guy probably has nothing to with this." Tove put his hand on Bain's arm, and he seemed to relax a bit.

"Tove is right, and number three is the most likely choice," Ridley said. "But if the King did kill her, or even if she ran away, there's probably not a lot we can do. So while we're here, we might as well go on the assumption that someone kidnapped her. It's the only way we can actually help."

"Even if she was kidnapped, what can we do?" I asked. "We've read over the guards' report, and there's nothing there."

"There was something I saw in the file." Bain turned around and grabbed it, flipping through it quickly. "It caught my eye, then Tove asked Kennet to leave, and I forgot for a moment, but . . . yep. Here it is. The Queen had gone down to the pool area to swim, and she'd discarded her robe, which they found at the side of the pool. And in the blue satin of her fabric, they found a solitary black hair."

"Oh, shit," I said under my breath, and my heartbeat sped up.

"Now, I haven't met everyone in the palace, but the Skojare have always been very picky about mixing bloodlines," Bain said, explaining something I already knew. "If you marry out of your tribe, you're gone. So I sincerely doubt that *anybody* in this place has hair darker than blond."

He was very right. There was absolutely no way my father would've been allowed to live here after he married my mother. In fact, he'd never been allowed to even visit. For a black hair to get on Linnea's robe, it had to come from someone outside of the Skojare.

And although I couldn't say for certain who it came from, I did know for sure that Konstantin's hair was charcoal-black.

THIRTY-THREE

pursuit

The rocks stung my bare feet, but I paid them no mind as I walked with Tove Kroner along the shore of Lake Superior. I had changed into jeans and a sweater before heading out, since a dress didn't seem appropriate for scouting the area for signs of Konstantin Black, Bent Stum, or Queen Linnea herself. The weather was warm enough to go without boots, and I always felt better with my feet touching the earth, so I'd forgone footwear.

During our meeting, we'd come to the conclusion that the only way for anyone to make off with Linnea was through the water. The pool in the lower level of the palace was freshwater, with a tunnel that led out into the lake. Someone could've come inside and taken her out that way. Admittedly, it would be harder for someone who didn't have gills and couldn't breathe underwater, but not impossible.

If Linnea had been taken that way, she would've come out

on the nearby shore of the lake. So we'd decided to split up and search the shore. Ridley suggested that we mix the search parties, with him pairing with Bain, and me with Tove.

I couldn't help but think he was looking for a reason to avoid me. We'd been getting along well since we'd gotten to Storvatten, but I was sure it was because there was work to be done.

Ridley and Bain had gone east, starting at the bridge and moving outward, and Tove and I went west. Thick evergreen forests lined the shore, going right down to the rocky banks of the lake.

Storvatten was more of a village, with scattered cabins and cottages hidden in the trees. There were no paved roads—only dirt and gravel paths connecting them. As Tove and I walked along the lake, I'd glance over and only occasionally get a glimpse of a house. Most of them were overgrown with moss, making them nearly invisible among the trees, but they were all within feet of the lake.

"Should we ask them if they've seen anything?" I asked Tove, and motioned to nearby house.

It was built very low to the ground, so I assumed it was more of a burrow, like Ridley's house. Moss covered the thatched roof, and low-hanging branches shaded it. But in the small front window I saw a face staring out at me—the bright blue eyes locked on me and Tove.

Tove considered my suggestion, then shook his head. "If they'd seen something, they would've told the guards. And if Linnea was kidnapped, her captor was smart enough to get in and out of the palace without being seen, so they were probably smart enough to bring her to the shore outside of the Storvatten city limits, past the prying eyes."

"Do you know how much farther that is?" I asked. Before we left, we'd all looked at a map of Storvatten, but it had been hand-drawn and rather vague on detail and distance.

"Not that much farther, I don't think." He climbed on top of a large rock nearby so he could get a better gauge of the distance, and looked back toward the palace. "Storvatten isn't that big. We must be almost out of it by now."

An engine revved, and it was hard to tell the distance with the sound echoing off the trees, but based on the birds taking flight and scattering in the sky, it couldn't be that far.

"The road must be that way." I pointed toward where the birds had fled from, and Tove slid down the rock and followed me.

We went into the woods, ducking under low branches, and the pine needles stung my feet. Through the trees, I could see a highway, and I could still hear the car. When I glimpsed the black sedan through the branches, I picked up my pace, starting to run toward it.

I broke through the trees and ran onto a worn, deserted stretch of highway. Several feet down the road from me, the car sat idling on the side of the road. The car door opened, and in the seconds before the figure stepped out from it, my heart stopped beating.

Then Bent's lopsided head rose above the door. His left eye appeared slightly larger than the right, and his massive hand gripped the door as he scowled at me.

"What the hell are you doing here?" he shouted. "I thought Konstantin took care of you."

"Where's the Queen?" I asked him and ignored his question.

He laughed, a dumb, heavy sound that bounced off the trees and startled the birds that hadn't left yet. He stepped around the door, lumbering, really, and I realized that he was much taller and larger than I'd originally thought.

"You tell me. You're the one with all the answers." Bent grinned as he walked toward me, his steps large so he'd reach me quickly, but I refused to step back. I never backed down from a fight.

The trees rustled behind me, and I glanced back, expecting to see Konstantin, but it was only Tove finally catching up to me. He hadn't started running when I had.

"You better run while you can, little girl," Bent said, and I turned back to face him. He'd nearly reached me, and I squared up, preparing to do whatever I had to do to take him down. "And this fight ain't going like last time."

Just before he reached me, he suddenly went flying back—soaring through the trees, with branches cracking as he hit them. I stood frozen and stunned, and then looked over to see Tove standing with his arm extended and his palm out.

I knew that the Trylle had the power to move objects and people with their minds, but I'd never actually seen it in real life before. But Tove had just picked up Bent and thrown him through the trees, and honestly, it left me breathless for a moment.

"I'll take care of him," Tove said and nodded toward the trees. "You look for the Queen."

"Okay," I said, and as he started jogging into the woods to go after Bent, I added, "Be careful." Though I wasn't sure if he needed that.

I ran over to the sedan and looked in through the open door. I hadn't exactly expected to see Linnea sitting in the backseat, but it was still disappointing to find it empty. Hurriedly and without really knowing what I was looking for, I searched through the glove box and around the seats—but other than empty food wrappers and water bottles and a pair of jeans and a black T-shirt, there wasn't really anything.

I popped the button for the trunk and I lifted it very slowly, steeling myself in case I found a body. But there was nothing.

Out of the corner of my eye I saw movement, but when I looked over, there was nothing. Dark clouds hovered overhead, but there was no wind, so the branches were still.

Then I saw it again, just in my peripheral vision—something was moving. But when I turned to face it, there was nothing.

And then, intrinsically, I knew it. His chameleonlike skin let him blend in with the trees, and I had no idea where he was exactly, but I was certain of it—Konstantin was here, stalking me.

THIRTY-FOUR

relinquish

I stood in the middle of the highway, not moving—just listening. Twigs snapped, but I didn't look toward them. I didn't want him to know that I had heard. I just listened, following the sounds of his movement.

He was coming closer, trying to sneak up behind me. I kept my head forward, but from the corner of my eye I saw him. The briefest shadow of movement and the dark tufts of his hair, and then I knew exactly where he was.

I waited a second more, letting him take a step closer to me, and then I turned and sprang on him. I swung and my hand connected firmly with his face, and it felt a bit strange, like the air had suddenly become solid matter.

His color instantly began to change, hurrying to blend in with the surroundings, but in his panic ended up more of a mottled gray. I grabbed his hair and I whirled him around, slamming him against the car.

I had no interest in repeating our fight in Calgary, and when he tried to move, I just slammed him harder against the car.

"You don't have to be so rough with me." Konstantin groaned, with his face pressed in the glass.

His skin changed back to flesh tone, and I held his arms, twisted them up behind his naked back. He'd taken off his clothes so he could blend more easily into his surroundings— fabric didn't change color—and his well-toned arms and torso felt cold under my touch.

In my back pocket I had a length of leather strapping that I'd brought with in case of just such a situation. Now I tied it around his wrists, binding him tightly.

"What did you do with the Skojare Queen?" I demanded, once I was certain that he was secure.

"Just because you've got me doesn't mean that I'll confess." He looked back at me over his shoulder. "Now I'm assuming you've taken me prisoner, so you might as well take me to my cell. Because I am done talking, white rabbit."

Still catching my breath from the fight, I met his gaze, trying to get a read on him, but his gray eyes were stony and cold, giving up nothing.

"Why did you come here?" I asked breathlessly. "What are you trying to do?"

"I could ask you the same thing," Konstantin replied. He tried to turn around, so I slammed him harder against the side of the car, letting him know that things were going to go much differently than they had last time.

"I'm trying to make sure that you don't kill anyone else," I told him through gritted teeth.

Konstantin smirked at me, but before he could say anything more, Bent came soaring through the trees and landed on the pavement behind the car, skidding roughly on his stomach. He groaned loudly, but he didn't move.

Tove came charging through the woods behind him. He leapt on Bent's back and, using a heavy leather strap like what I'd used, he hurriedly tied up Bent's wrists. We had heavy chains and shackles that we used in jail cells, but for quick handcuffing, the leather straps were easier to carry and use.

"He put up quite a fight." Tove stood up, wiping sweat from his brow with the back of his arm. "But I think he's done now."

THIRTY-FIVE

susceptibility

"Where is she?" King Mikko shouted, and his deep voice boomed through everything like a terrifying thunder. Tove actually covered his ears, and I didn't blame him.

He stood at the end of the table, and Lisbet was beside him, rubbing his back and trying to calm him. Prince Kennet sat near him, his hands folded in front of his face. The gills underneath his jawline flared violently with each breath he took.

Ridley, Tove, Bain, and I sat farther down the table, all of us cowering slightly under the King's visible rage. His hands were balled into fists, and his jaw clenched tightly as he glared at us with icy blue eyes.

"They won't say," I said quietly, since it appeared that nobody else would speak up. "We've put them in the dungeon, and right now Konstantin is refusing to say anything without immunity."

"*Immunity?*" Mikko scoffed. "He probably killed her! Why would I give him immunity?"

"My King, Linnea may yet be alive," Lisbet reasoned. "We must do what we need to in order to find her."

"Bent Stum is strong but he's not very bright," Tove said. "I broke him down some so I could subdue him enough to get him here. I don't think he'll hold out for much longer. The Omte aren't known for their willpower or their loyalty."

"You think he'll tell us where my Queen is?" Mikko asked.

Tove sighed, reluctant to promise anything, and he turned to Ridley and me for help.

"The Omte are stubborn," Ridley said, choosing his words with care. "And Bent seems to fit the mold."

"Can you get him to talk or not?" Mikko began to raise his voice, and Tove flinched.

"We'll do our best, but we can't make any guarantees," Ridley said.

"All I want is to find my wife, and to see the men that took her hanged," Mikko growled. "I brought you here to help, and now you're telling me you're not sure if there's anything that can be done?"

"No, no, we're not saying that." Bain held up his hands.

"Find her, so I can punish the men that hurt her, or there will be hell to pay!" Mikko shouted, and he slammed his fist down on the table so hard, the wood cracked.

Lisbet started to say something to him, but he ignored her and stalked out of the room. We all sat quietly for a few moments after his outburst, then Kennet sighed and pushed out his chair.

"I'll go check on my brother," he said, and made his exit.

"The King is just very worried," Lisbet said, making excuses for Mikko's anger. "We all are."

"That's understandable," Bain said.

Lisbet took a deep breath, making the large sapphires on her necklace rise and fall heavily, and she folded her hands neatly over her stomach. Her eyes were fixed on the water behind the glass dome around us. The afternoon sun was bright above us, making the water appear clearer than it had this morning.

A small fish swam close to the glass; then, out of the darkness, a large muskie attacked it. Its razor-sharp teeth sank through the prey, leaving the faintest trace of blood in the water, before it disappeared back into the depths of the lake to eat its meal.

"I know that while you are in our kingdom you are supposed to follow the law of our King," Lisbet said at length. "He has made his wishes very clear—he doesn't want anyone to offer Konstantin or Bent anything that would allow them to go unpunished for their crimes.

"While I share his sentiment, justice is a secondary concern for me," Lisbet continued and turned her gaze upon us. "Linnea's return is my only priority. I want you to do anything and everything you need to do to get them to tell you where she is. Do whatever it takes to bring my granddaughter back to me."

With her direct instructions, Lisbet smiled thinly at us, and then left us alone to discuss our course of action. Bain was reluctant to go against the King's orders, but we all agreed that if we could find Linnea, he'd probably overlook our transgression.

But since Bain was hesitant, Ridley and I offered to talk to Konstantin and Bent first. We could do kind of a good cop/bad cop thing, with Ridley and me both playing the good cop and then Tove taking over as the bad cop, since he'd already taken his toll on Bent.

The King's guards had attempted to interrogate Konstantin and Bent, but their guard wasn't quite the same as that of other tribes. The Skojare were small, isolated, and quiet. They had no changelings or trackers, and they rarely interacted with others. That left them with an underdeveloped and somewhat lazy and inadequate guard, since they had no need for anything better.

Now, with a genuine crisis on their hands, the guard had rather wisely turned the investigation over to Ridley, Tove, Bain, and me, since we had far more experience handling criminals than they did.

Despite their low level of crime, the Skojare had a superior dungeon. It was actually buried beneath the bottom of the lake, so escape would require breaking through concrete, then digging through ten feet of earth before swimming up through the lake. A rusted spiral staircase led down to a small, dank tunnel that connected the palace to the dungeon.

Water dripped down through cracks in the tunnel, and most of the stones were slick with water and mold. The path was lit with dim lanterns, just like the dungeon itself. It was a rather small place, with only four cells shut with heavy iron bars.

Konstantin sat on the floor with his back against the bars

and his head slumped forward. After I'd captured him, I'd given him the black T-shirt and jeans from the car to put on so he wouldn't have to stay here naked, and the bars left rusty lines on his shirt.

Across from his was Bent's cell. Bent was covered by a sheet, lying on the plank of wood that served as a bed. These were bare cells, with stone walls and metal toilets in each corner.

"Wake up." Ridley kicked the bars behind Konstantin's back, and he lifted his head. "We're here to talk to you."

"Don't bother trying to raise Bent," Konstantin said without looking at us or standing up. "He won't get up."

"What do you mean?" I asked, and turned my attention to Bent's cell. "Bent? Bent! Get up."

He didn't stir, so I walked over to his cell, pressing my face against the bars to get a better look. I shouted his name again, and then I saw the dark stain at the top of his sheets. The lanterns didn't give off much light, but it was enough that I could see that the stain looked red.

"Ridley, get the keys," I said.

"What? Why?" he asked, coming over to have a look.

"Just get them now," I commanded, and he did as he was told, jogging down the hall away from me.

There was a long stick with a hook at the end leaning against the wall in the tunnel, and I assumed it was used for handing prisoners things from a distance or perhaps poking an unruly inmate who didn't want to get out of bed.

I grabbed it, and then carefully I angled the stick so I could hook the edge of Bent's sheet. I was saying his name, telling him he'd better not being playing any games, but he never replied. As I pulled the blanket back, it became obvious why.

His eyes were open wide, staring vacantly at the ceiling above him, and his throat had been torn open, leaving a jagged gaping wound. By the looks of the bent shackle in his hand, I guessed he'd used the rusted sharp point on the end to do the job, but it couldn't have been easy. The blood still looked wet and bright dripping from his throat, so he couldn't have done it long ago, but it didn't matter. Bent Stum was dead.

penitence

Bryn," Konstantin whispered, and I turned away from Bent's bloody corpse to see that Konstantin was standing now, his hands gripping the prison bars in desperation as he looked out at me.

"Did you just stand there, watching him while he killed himself?" I asked coldly. "Or maybe you talked him into it?"

Konstantin laughed darkly. "You can't really believe he killed himself."

"You're saying that you somehow got out of your cage and did it yourself?"

"No, of course not." He shook his head. "Bent was a dumb oaf. I know I shouldn't speak ill of the dead, but he was. He would talk soon, so somebody silenced him."

"Who?" I stared down at him dubiously. "Who would've come down here to do that?"

"I'll tell you, white rabbit, but you have to let me out first,"

Konstantin said with a sly smile. But beneath the steely gray of his eyes, I saw fear flickering.

"Not a chance," I replied immediately.

"I can't stay here locked up, or they'll come for me next."

"Good." I folded my arms over my chest. "You're a murderer. It's about time you get your comeuppance."

"I've never killed anyone!" Konstantin sounded exasperated. "I know I hurt you and your father, and I've hurt plenty of other people. But I haven't killed any of them."

"Tell that to Emma Costar," I said, and the image of her lying dead on the bank of the river flashed in front of my eyes again.

"That was Bent. He's clumsy and stupid, never knowing his own strength." He rested his forehead against the bars. "I shouldn't have left him alone with her. That is my fault, but I never laid a hand on her."

"Where is Linnea?" I asked. "If you tell me where she is, I'll let you go."

Konstantin groaned and threw his head back. "I don't know where she is."

"Someone is trying to kill you, and they have access to your cell. I suggest you start talking if you want to live."

"I swear, I don't know where she is," he insisted fiercely.

"You're lying. I know you're lying. You wouldn't even be here if it wasn't for her."

"We came here for her, that's true," Konstantin admitted. Then he pursed his lips, pausing before going on. "But things are very complicated."

"Why the Skojare?" I asked. "You've been targeting the Kanin for so long, then why suddenly hit the Skojare?"

"It wasn't my idea. *None* of this was my idea." His shoulders sagged and he let go of the bars. "But I'm not sure that makes any of this any better."

"Whose idea was it?" I asked. "I know Bent wasn't the brains of the operation."

He looked up at me, tears resting in his eyes and a sad smile on his face. "Have you ever been in love?"

I tensed. "That's none of your business."

"No, you haven't." His smile widened and he shook his head. "Lucky you."

"What does this have to do with Linnea?" I asked.

"Everything. And nothing." He stepped back from the bars with a resigned expression on his face. "I've done so many things in the name of love. And lately I've begun to wonder, is it still love if it makes one do terrible things?"

"That just sounds like an excuse to be evil," I told him honestly.

"I would agree with you, but I regret a lot of it." He sighed and sat back on the wooden bed behind him. "I regret most of it, really, but still, I can't bring myself to regret falling in love. Even though I died. The real me, the me I'd once been, the me that you admired so much. He died the instant I fell." He stared intently at me. "But for love, I'd gladly kill myself again."

"If you don't tell me what's going on and where Linnea is, you're going to die in that cell," I warned him, trying to reason with him. "Not metaphorically die, but literally die, the way

Bent did, and as unpleasant as that had to be to watch, it's going to be much worse to experience for yourself."

"Then that's the price that I'll have to pay," he said simply. He laid back on his bed and rolled over so his back was to me. "But you can still heed my advice, white rabbit. Get away from all of this before it's too late for you."

justice

Ridley sat on my bed, hunched over with his fingers tangled in his dark hair. I pulled my own wave of hair up in a ponytail, as if tugging my hair back would help me think more clearly.

"I don't know, Bryn," he said finally and lifted his head so he could watch me walk back and forth, pacing along the window that faced the dark water outside. "Trusting Konstantin might be your downfall."

"I don't trust him." I shook my head adamantly. "I could never trust him."

"You're saying that you believe him about some weird conspiracy going on here?"

"It's not a conspiracy," I corrected him.

"You're saying that somebody in this palace killed Bent Stum and made it look like a suicide to cover up something to do with the missing Queen." He gave me a hard look. "That sounds like a conspiracy to me."

I stopped walking to argue my position. "Bent was gonna talk. Tove thought so."

"No, Tove thought he was most *likely* to talk, but you saw him at that meeting. He was resistant to giving any form of a guarantee on that."

"Konstantin *knows* something, though."

Ridley rolled his eyes. "Of course he does. He knows everything! He's behind it all."

"No, I mean . . ." I chewed my lip. "Just bear with me for a moment. Let's say Konstantin was telling the truth and that someone did kill Bent. Who had access to his cell?"

"I ran upstairs and got the keys from one of the guards, but you know how lax their security is around here." Ridley shrugged. "Any one of their guards had access to the keys, but it wouldn't be that hard for any of the *seventy-eight* other people who live in the palace to get the keys. They just have them hanging up in the guards' station at the top of the stairs."

I groaned. "I just feel like we're missing something. There has to be a connection that we're not seeing."

"All of this is based on something a known traitor said while pleading for his freedom." Ridley stared sadly at me. "I hate to say it, Bryn, but I think you're being naïve."

"No, I'm not. This all just doesn't add up!" I shouted, then lowered my voice so I wouldn't disturb anyone.

After we'd called the guards and dealt with Bent's body, it

had been rather late by the time we got back to our rooms. We'd talked briefly with Tove and Bain before they retired to their rooms, and now we were left rehashing the same ideas over and over again in the dim glow from my bedside lamp.

"Bent is out of the picture, we've got Konstantin, Linnea is probably dead," Ridley said. "There's nothing left to deal with. You may not want to admit it, but it's over, Bryn."

"We don't know that Linnea is dead," I reminded him.

"If you believe Konstantin, then all signs point to her death," he reasoned. "Konstantin says that Bent was an uncontrollable idiot that killed Emma, so he probably killed Linnea, and maybe he didn't tell Konstantin where he dumped her."

"What if Konstantin came here to kidnap Linnea, but she was already missing?" I asked. "Or dead?"

"Who killed her, then?"

"Mikko." I kept my voice low, in case someone might be listening. "He had opportunity, since he was alone with her that night, and he stormed out of the meeting, so he had a chance to kill Bent, too."

Ridley brushed off the theory as soon as I proposed it. "That leaves more questions than answers. If he killed her, why did he call us here? And what would his motive for killing Bent be? Not to mention that he doesn't even have a motive for killing his wife in the first place."

"I don't know," I admitted softly.

"And why were Konstantin and Bent even here in the first place? If this is a simple domestic dispute gone bad, then why would they even come here?"

"I don't know!" I shouted, growing frustrated. "Why is Konstantin everywhere we go?"

Ridley's eyes darkened, and he stared grimly at me. "He's not everywhere *we* go, Bryn. He's everywhere *you* go. And that is a very good question."

"You don't think I have something to do with this."

"No, of course I don't." He sighed. "But . . . once is a fluke. Twice is a coincidence. But three times? That's a pattern. There's some connection I don't understand, but I think you need to start taking a hard look at what's happening here."

"I am, Ridley! I'm looking at this constantly. You think I'm not always worrying about this, and thinking about Konstantin? That for even one second I'm not terrified that I'm missing something or screwing this up somehow?"

I knew I was yelling and I should stop, but I couldn't control myself. Everything with Linnea and Konstantin and the missing changelings, it was all making me feel crazy and helpless. Everywhere I went, I was one step behind, and I didn't know how to fix it. I didn't know how to fix anything.

"I'm sorry. I know." Ridley stood up and put his hands on my shoulders. "Hey, calm down." Roughly, he pulled me into his arms, and I let him, resting my head against his chest. "I know you're doing everything you can, and if anyone can figure this mess out, it's you."

"But I can't, Ridley," I whispered.

He put his hand under my chin, lifting it so I would look up at him. "You can do anything."

Ridley leaned down, his mouth brushing against mine, and

I wanted nothing more than to give in to the moment, to give in to the passion of his embrace and the icy taste of his lips, but I couldn't. As desperately as I wanted to feel nothing but him, the nagging inside my heart pulled me away.

"I can't." I lowered my eyes and stepped back from him. "There's too much to lose. You should probably go."

"Right. You're right," he muttered and rubbed his neck before turning away from me. "You're always right."

When he reached the bedroom door, he paused, half looking back at me. "The right guy is behind bars right now, Bryn. No matter what's going on with us or anything else, you should find some comfort in that."

Ridley left me alone then, and I felt many, many things, but comfort wasn't one of them.

THIRTY-EIGHT

entrapped

The staircase had rusted and weakened so much from lack of use that it felt precarious under my feet. But everything felt precarious at that moment. The iron keys were heavy in my hand, and though my stomach twisted painfully, I didn't turn back.

I wasn't sure if this was the right thing. But it was the only thing I could think to do. I had to find out who Konstantin was working for and what had really happened to Linnea. Until I had that information, this would never feel over to me.

Ridley had been right, though, and getting the keys from the guards had been comically easy. The station was completely unmanned, and the keys were sitting on the desk. I grabbed them quickly, then hurried down to the dungeon.

As I walked slowly through the tunnel, I reminded myself that the keys were only a decoy. I would promise Konstantin that I would set him free if he divulged the truth to me. But I would never let him go free again. I couldn't.

As I approached the dungeon, the hair on the back of my neck began to stand up. The door to Konstantin's cell was wide open, and as my heart thudded in my chest, I feared I'd come too late. Somebody had already taken care of him.

Then he emerged from the shadows. He stepped out slowly, deliberately, with his eyes locked on me. But my eyes went down to the sword in his hand, the long blade battle-worn but sharp.

"You shouldn't be here," Konstantin said when he saw me, and he wore the same expression he had when he'd raised his sword on my father.

"I came to set you free." I raised the keys to show him, and he flinched like he'd been punched.

"Run," he whispered. "Run, white rabbit, as fast and far as you can."

"Not until you tell me what's going on." I stood tall despite my fear.

"This has gone on long enough," a voice grumbled behind me, and I whirled around.

He'd been standing in the shadows, along the wall of the tunnel by the mouth of the dungeon. He wore all black, helping him blend in, and his skin had shifted color, completely matching the stones around him. But now as it shifted back, it was like watching a mirage come to life.

Then I realized that not quite everything had changed color. The scar that ran across his face from just above his left eye down to his right cheek, that had stayed a dull red. His black hair was greasy and landed just below his shoulders, and his beard was more unruly than I'd seen in pictures.

But I knew exactly who he was. I saw his face glaring down on me every time I stepped into Ridley's office. It was Viktor Dålig—the most wanted man of all the Kanin.

"Finish her!" Viktor commanded, and that was enough to snap my senses into motion.

With the keys still in my fist, I swung at Viktor. But he was too fast, and he grabbed my arm, bending it back. He grabbed my ponytail, yanking my head back. I kicked him, but he was unfazed, and then Viktor slammed my head into the stone wall.

The first time, I felt it. A blind searing pain that blotted out everything. Somewhere in the background, I thought I heard Konstantin yell out. But the second time Viktor slammed my skull into the stone, the world fell away, and I collapsed into darkness.

retreat

I shoved my clothes roughly into my duffel bag, and Ridley knocked on the open door to my bedroom.

"How are you holding up?" he asked when I didn't reply.

"I've been better."

My right temple had a scabbed-over gash and a dark purple bruise, but the worst of it was under my hair, where I'd needed six stiches. Viktor had meant business, and the medic that had fixed me said I was lucky that he hadn't actually smashed my skull in.

Twelve hours later, I had a killer headache, and the vision in my right eye still didn't seem quite right. Whenever I looked to the left, I could see a blinding white spot out of the corner of my eye.

"If it hurts, they can give you something for the pain." Ridley leaned forward, inspecting my injuries. He reached out tentatively to brush back my hair from the wound, but I pulled away before he could, so he dropped his hand and straightened up.

"I'm okay. I just want to get out of here and get home."

"Well, I'm all packed up. We can head out whenever you're ready."

My jeans were blocking the zipper, so I pushed my clothes down deeper and continued my fight to get my bag zipped. "I'm just about done."

"You know, you shouldn't blame yourself for what happened," Ridley said. "You went down to reason with Konstantin, who was in a cell. You had no reason to think he could break out and attack you. If they had any kind of security here, they could've stopped him. But they think he went through one of the doors out into the lake, and he has to be long gone by now."

In the morning, Ridley had come to my room to see how I was doing, and when I wasn't there he'd gone down to the dungeon, where he'd found me unconscious and bleeding on the floor. When I first awoke, I remembered nothing of the attack. I only knew that Ridley was holding me in his arms, his eyes filled with fear and affection.

But as the morning had gone on, my memories had been slowly coming back. A hazy blur of the dungeon. Konstantin telling me to run. Viktor Dålig emerging from the shadows. Then the blinding pain.

I knew I would tell Ridley about seeing Viktor, but I wanted to wait until I was certain that Viktor was involved. Everything felt too hazy and blurry, and I wasn't even sure I could trust my memories.

Viktor had killed Ridley's father, and he'd been on the run for years. I'd had the chance to stop him, but I'd let him get away, and I couldn't tell Ridley about it unless I was sure it was true.

"If don't blame myself, then who should I blame?" I asked, sounding much harsher than I meant.

"Konstantin," he said simply, and I let out a deep breath that I didn't even realize I'd been holding.

"Ah, good." Lisbet smiled, entering my room without knocking, and Ridley and I stood at attention. "I'm glad to see you're both here. How is your head doing?"

"Better, Marksinna," I told her politely.

"Good." She walked around my bed, the long train of her gown filling up the floor as she went over to the window. Her gills fluttered lightly, and she glanced down at the bed. "What are you doing? Are you packing your things?"

"Yes, Marksinna," Ridley said. "Bent is dead, and Konstantin is gone."

"You weren't invited here to find Bent or Konstantin," Lisbet said. "You're here to find my granddaughter, and I don't see her anywhere."

Ridley exchanged a look with me, but I lowered my eyes. I didn't agree with the conclusion that Ridley and the Trylle had come to, but I had been outvoted. As soon as I'd been well enough this morning, Ridley had informed me that the Trylle were moving on, and so would we, and that had been the end of the discussion.

"We believe . . ." He stopped, clearing his throat. "We believe that the Queen is no longer alive. We think that Bent or Konstantin killed her. I'm very sorry. Please understand that you have the deepest sympathy of the Kanin people, and you will always have our full support. But our mission here is complete and, like our Trylle allies, duty requires us to return home to serve our own kingdom."

"I see." She lowered her eyes and swallowed hard. After a moment, she said softly, "Then there seems to be no reason for either of you to remain here. Send my gratitude to your King for your aid, and I trust that you can see yourselves out."

Ridley opened his mouth as though he meant to say something, but there was nothing he could say. Lisbet left us alone in the room with a heavy silence covering us.

"So that's it then?" I asked. "We just leave?"

Ridley let out an exasperated sigh. "What else would you have us do?"

"Finish our job!" I snapped.

"We have!" he shot back, then lowered his voice. "The Queen is dead, Bent is dead, and Konstantin is gone, leaving without a trace, and he's almost certainly moving on to his next target. We can't help the Skojare any longer. We need to get back and protect our own people."

He softened and stepped closer to me. "As a tracker, you know that you don't get to pick where your job is or when it will begin or end. You just do the work that is given to you, and then you move on." He put his hand on my arm. "This job didn't work out the way either of us had planned, but it's time to go home."

I nodded, hating that Ridley was right. There was nothing left for us in Storvatten. The only thing we could do was head back to Doldastam. I finished gathering my things so Ridley and I could start the long journey home.